LEFT

By Katherine Brendli

First Printing

Copyright © 2014 by Katherine Rose Brendli

Cataloging-in-publishing data for this book available from
The Library of Congress
ISBN: 978-0-9898812-9-6

Katherine Rose Brendli, Author

All rights reserved. No part of this book may be reproduced or transmitted in any form or by any other means, electronically or mechanical, including photocopying, recording, or by any information storage and retrieval system, without the written permission of the author, or publisher.

For information write:
Dementi Milestone Publishing, Inc.
1530 Oak Grove Drive
Manakin-Sabot, VA 23103
dementi@aol.com
www.dementimilestonepublishing.com

Page layout by Dianne Dementi

Cover design by Jayne Hushen

Cover photograph by Andrei and Sergiu Cosma of PhotoCosma, Zalau, Romania. www.PhotoCosma.com

Printed in the USA

DEDICATION

*For the most inspiring and talented writer,
Whose both presence and poetry make moments brighter,
As one of the most caring grandmothers,
I dedicate my book to Mrs. Arlene Carruthers.*

I love you Grandma.

Katherine Brendli

Chapter 1

His grip tightened and I could do nothing but submit to his power. I fell to my knees and begged for mercy, but he refused my plea with devilish, haunting pleasure. I could feel his hot breath against my ear lobe as he whispered unimaginable and terrifying thoughts into my adolescent mind. I did not have time to react nor the strength to escape him. Suddenly, the sound of a snap muffled over his threats and overwhelmed my eardrums. I gazed down to the only part of my body that truly unified me with my people to see the white bones of my distorted wrist poking out from beneath its skin. Floods of colorless tears gushed down my cheeks as I cried out in pain. He let go of my hand finally to let gravity pull my arm down to the hard stone surface. I imagined his unwashed face smiling down on me at that moment, but all I could focus on was the blood that dripped over the tattoo stamped permanently on the inside of my left wrist.

$\mathcal{A}$ black tear dripped down onto the old-fashioned stationary, proving that the life of the depleting instrument was on the brink of its demise. Yet again, another drop splashed onto the ivory colored paper as the pen's ink melted away in Noreen's quivering hand. She placed the pen onto the oak table and flexed her palm to relieve its tension, yet *both* her hands continued to tremble. The pressure of her mother's tiresome commandments pounded a throbbing pain against her temples. 'The precious paper,' her mother would say, 'you mussen' waste the precious paper!' But her mother's insistence could not foresee the death of the single writing utensil their family owned nor the wreckage of their well-preserved stationary.

Thick clumps of ink now shaded in the empty spaces of the page and seeped through the multiple layers, thus ruining the pieces stacked beneath. The destruction of the coexisting materials sent a brief sensation of joy fluttering through her veins until it dissolved just before reaching her fingertips. The intensity of her trembling left hand brought Noreen's attention back to reality. With her dominant hand incapable of controlling its shakes long enough to perform any small movements correctly, it was up to her right to unnaturally take over those fine duties. Noreen never understood why her mother permitted her to sit and waste two hours every afternoon practicing right handed script when they lived in a town comprised solely of Left Handers, but between a broken pen and stained sheets of paper, her reasoning no longer mattered. Noreen had just lost the opportunity to write forever.

The memory of her first mandatory writing practice flooded through her consciousness. It started the day after the town doctor had forced the bones of her left wrist painfully back into her skin and bandaged it with a dirty cloth and long saved antiseptic. It was the morning after Lawrence had attacked her in the back room of the bar for spilling his precious booze onto the lap of a loyal customer. Little did he know that the drunken customer was at fault for the wasted product, but to think that Lawrence would ever care to hear any of Noreen's excuses would be outright senseless. His attraction toward her combined with his intellect of psychologically twisted thoughts created a monstrous creature that blackened his soul. Lawrence abused Noreen out of his own pure pleasure with the unmistakable knowledge that she was trapped working for him; spilling the liquor was in fact the only time he actually used a reason to harm her other than "for her own good."

Noreen shut her eyes hoping that she could liberate the memory from her thoughts if she squeezed them hard enough, but closing them only made his face even clearer from behind her lids. She reopened her eyes and blinked several times with sudden exhaustion overwhelming her. Bowing her chin toward her chest, Noreen let her eyelids droop to a close and allowed her nightmares to return to her as long as she could get the chance to finally rest for however long she had.

"Noreen!" a harsh, feminine voice hummed distantly through Noreen's eardrums, appearing almost surreal to her own consciousness. "Noreen, are you listening to me?" The sharp words barked aggressively at her and interrupted her senseless dreams that were soon consigned to oblivion. As the woman's incessant mutters increased in volume, the clarity in what was her mother's voice became recognizable. "Noreen Satchell! Stop daydreaming and fetch more water for our potatoes this instant!"

Noreen fluttered her eyes open and lifted her head off the wooden table. After removing the black stained stationary from sticking to her forehead, she glanced around the humble cottage in discomfort. It did not take her long before she found her mother standing before the fireplace as the small room provided her with limited other fixations to look at. The thin woman had her back to Noreen, her weight leaning on her right hip as she used her left hand to stir their supper inside the depths of the stockpot. Beads of sweat formulated a large, wet blotch that clinged the fabric of her maroon colored top to the small of her back. Her sleeves were rolled up to her elbows, and her light blonde hair was tied in a low ponytail that somewhat covered the back of her neck.

She wore the same off-white apron as usual. Its lack of washing broadcasted the dirty brown and yellow stains that coated the material almost entirely, but the overused smock did, though, have its benefits. By covering roughly half the length of the long, shapeless skirt, it protected her clothes from the stains she received from her daily work in the kitchen and garden. Without its protection, her mother's smell would inevitably be more uninviting.

After blowing the blond curls from her face, Noreen felt a large mark indented across the side of her forehead and past the corner of her eyebrow. As she rubbed the mark, she felt a thick liquid on her fingertips and realized that the liquid's texture matched the ink that spilled across her mother's stationary. Gazing down to the ruined paper, she noticed a large splotch of ink in the same shape as the side of her forehead. Hurriedly, Noreen rubbed her palms against her forehead to smudge the ink off her skin, almost forgetting to answer her mother in the process. "I'm going now!" she finally responded.

"You were out for a while." Mrs. Satchell's voice became less aggressive once she noticed that Noreen had fully awakened. "I know you work nightshifts, but normally you just sleep away the morning… Was it really busy at The Cove last night?" she questioned her daughter without peering over her shoulder.

"Sure, I mean yeah," Noreen corrected herself. Though her mother believed she had fully awakened, Noreen still felt as though she were in a daze. "How many buckets do you need filled?" She scrunched her brows in attempts to possibly get feeling back into the side of her forehead.

"Just fill the two. I need them back quickly so don't be out there dillydallyin'!" her mother's focus never left the pot of potatoes in front of her.

Noreen nodded and gripped the edge of the table to help herself rise up to a standing position. The deeply inflamed welts and bruises that spread across her skin ached beneath her clothes. She stared at the wood in the fireplace with empathy. Like the wood, she felt as though her entire body sat in flames, with the dry, flaking scratches on her skin crumbling away until becoming ash. She changed her focus to her mother as she stood, unwilling to let the protective woman notice her struggle.

Before straying too far from the table, Noreen grabbed the papers and hid them behind her back. She was careful not to limp or crumble the papers in her hands until she pushed her way through the back door and was clearly out of her mother's line of vision. Once outside, she closed her fists around the papers and tucked them between an opening in the pile of wood behind the cottage.

Keeping her back upright, Noreen stretched out her arm to reach for the two buckets sitting beside the wooden door but lost her balance when her mother's voice abruptly sounded from behind her. Mrs. Satchell's sudden presence caused Noreen to fall straight forward onto the pile of stacked wood beneath the windowsill, but after pausing to catch her breath, she lifted up her head and glanced back toward her mother. "You scared me!" Noreen exclaimed. She masked her pained expression by lifting the corners of her lips into an uncomfortable smile.

"What on earth did you do to your face?" Mrs. Satchell demanded to know about the black smudge across Noreen's forehead. She grabbed her daughter's arm and yanked her out of the pile. Noreen winced initially from the pain her mother's jolt caused her bruises, but she tried to keep her face indifferent. "I just fell into a pile of wood, mom, it's just dirt." She surprised herself by thinking of a lie so quickly.

Mrs. Satchell pursed her lips but chose not to press her daughter further. She changed the subject to what she had originally intended to tell her. "Now, I know I've told you this before, but you need to make sure you don't let any of our neighbors see you at the community well," she hushed her voice to a whisper. "Our family has already made two trips there this morning, and we are only allowed to fetch water from there once a day! I don't want to be pickin' arguments with anyone, especially that Irma Anderson. I don't trust that woman; she asks too many questions. If she finds out we've made multiple trips to the well today, she won't hesitate to report us!"

"The well is far into the back field, mom, I think I'll be alright." Noreen bent down to grab the buckets for a second try.

"Don't you be fresh young lady, you know we can't afford one of them coming after us!" her mother softened her voice once again after she realized it had unintentionally increased in volume. She cocked her head in either direction before she continued, "I know you're tired, but family comes first." Noreen nodded, fully knowing that her mother's demand was far from an exaggeration. "Now, I need to get back to those potatoes before our whole meal is ruined and if that happens, you'll have to explain to..." she glanced around them again sharply, "to you-know-who why our only potatoes were spoiled. We don't have much, remember that!"

"I know mom, I'm sorry. I'm just tired," Noreen apologized. "I have another long night tonight, and I haven't gotten much sleep." Her mother acknowledged her remark by patting her hands on her apron before she stormed back inside. Noreen watched the woman until the broken backdoor slammed behind her. She knew how important it was not to get caught by their neighbors and how much her family depended on every scrap of food they could get their hands on, but it was not only their supply that was limited; the entire town's food supply was scarce. Every bit of food they could find or harvest could therefore not be wasted.

Poverty grew steadily over time as the government's laws expanded greater dominance over her people. Hunting was forbidden, so the only meat and real source of protein they received either came from the fish swimming in the harbor, which was rare since the Government netted most of the fish in the opposite direction of their town, or came once a month off of the two or three military trucks that would race alongside the right most edge of the town's boundaries. The vehicles never stopped or even paused in motion as the militants dumped the limited supply of carcasses off the beds of their trucks while holding pitchforks in their gloved hands. On the nineteenth day of every month at exactly five in the evening, the trucks would burst through the government's gates and cause mass violence throughout their town, the Town of the West.

According to her older brother, Charlie, the militants on the trucks would wear dark green gas masks and body suits as they carried assault rifles and machine guns in their right hands to protect themselves from the people of the west. Their attire 'supposedly' protected them from her people for fear that any one of them could possibly possess the Infection. Had it not been for her older brother's regular participation on Day 19, though, Noreen would never have known the details of the devilish bloodbath.

During those terrifying thirty minutes of the monthly massacre, Noreen would wait for her brother's return with hopes that he carried the main staple of their supper with him, the meat. Usually, though, he returned home empty handed and covered in his own blood or that of their neighbors'. That same night each month, their mother would pour buckets of parboiled water over him in the grass behind their cottage to clean him. Charlie would kneel down in the dirt fully clothed as he would scrub away the blood with the pitiful soap made from plant fat and wood ashes. By the time their mother considered him clean and their younger sister, Louise, had fallen asleep, Charlie would replay the horrifying scene aloud to Noreen as they would sit outside with their backs against the uneven stones of their family's cottage. From what he explained, Day 19 was the only day of the month the entire town would participate in outright mass violence against one another, only to return back to normal the next day with neighbors greeting neighbors as if nothing had ever happened.

    Focusing back to her surroundings, Noreen squeezed her eyes shut in attempts to end her rambling thoughts from eliciting the painful memories back to her consciousness. Counting down from five, she reopened her eyes to face the chipped and blemished shutters of her family's kitchen window. Hypnotically, she placed the pails onto the ground and climbed, as usual, onto the pile of chopped wood. She stepped carefully onto the pile this time intending to balance herself on the lumber.

    As she gazed between the slight crack of the partially opened shutters, she found her mother staring into the kitchen fire, wiping her eyes with her sleeve. Despite that her mother's back was to her, Noreen could hear the woman struggling to calm her short, irregular breaths. Noreen recognized those sounds as her cries and knew, like any other day, that the water her mother wiped onto her sleeve were tears of sadness she would only express in solitude.

    Guilt overwhelmed Noreen as she watched her mother and wished she had not acted so inconsiderate just moments before despite knowing that the poor woman sobbed daily after she and her siblings would leave her. Every day Noreen would glance back through the shutters before retrieving water from the well and each day her mother would weep alone after she had gone. Not once had her mother ever showed weakness in front of her children and, to Noreen, this kept their family stable, but rather than marching back through the broken doorway, she felt it was best to leave her to weep in solitude.

    Turning her attention back to her balance on the lumber, Noreen slid down the pile of wood awkwardly, tearing a small thread of her sleeve in the process. Once on her feet, she grabbed a pail in each hand and headed toward the well without glancing back. As she limped, she bent her

Left

head to the side to wipe her own tears onto her shoulder. Regardless of her mother's urgency, Noreen knew not to return too quickly and disturb her mother's sobs, so she walked slowly while squeezing the earth between her toes to embrace the filth on her skin.

After traveling past the tall fields of grass, Noreen arrived at the community well hidden amongst the trees. She clasped even more dirt between her toes as she laid the empty buckets beside her. Looking down at the blackish water inside the well, Noreen stared at her reflection and evaluated herself. The ringlets of her naturally platinum curls needed a wash, but thankfully, after ten long days, she would finally be receiving her bath later that evening. Though the pale skin beneath her clothes nearly matched her whitish hair, she had a pink glow that reflected off her dimpled cheeks that grew redder each day as spring's unusual heat persisted to worsen. Sweat stains formulated beneath her small breasts and stained the plain peach dress that covered her severely thin torso. Pulling at her neckline, she could easily find the welts that were hidden well beneath her clothes and covered by her long hair, yet to Noreen these undetected lumps screamed for attention.

Rotating her body side to side, she easily found each of the bruises Lawrence had given her. Looking at each individual welt, she recalled the different times he had beaten her. Noreen's hands began to shake more rapidly than before as she glazed her fingers over the different wounds covering her skin. Anxious and unnerved, she quickly became lightheaded and shoved her hands into the well to break the liquid mirror. Her fingers dripped with the blackish water as she pulled them from the well and combed them indifferently through her pale colored hair. Breathing deeply, she slid down to the ground and turned her back against the shaft with her fingers still entangled in her curls. She closed her eyes once again not realizing the amount of time that was passing.

Chapter 2

*L*ost in her own subconscious, Noreen barely heard the heavy footsteps that thudded toward her until a high pitched voice disturbed her slumbering trance. "Ahem," the feminine voice increased its volume causing Noreen's eyes to fly open in an instant. A girl with long braids looked down upon her with her arms folded across her chest. Her face was tense as she strained to keep from smirking. "Mom's been looking for you. She's pretty mad that you've been taking so long."

"What time is it?" Noreen leaned on the edge of the well to help herself to her feet.

The girl released her strain and allowed her lips to curl up into a smirk. "Time for you to get your *ass* back home!"

"Louise!" Noreen glared back at her younger sister, disapproving of the fourteen year old's foul language.

"Oh come on Noreen, stop treating me like I'm a child." Louise picked up the empty pails beside her sister and held them out in front of her. The first time Noreen tried to grab them, though, Louise jerked the pails back before Noreen could take hold. She laughed teasingly.

On her second try, Noreen ripped the buckets out of the girl's hands and glared down upon her younger sister. "I will when you stop acting like one! Now get back inside, I'm working as fast as I can!"

"HA. Obviously," Louise laughed again as she watched Noreen dip one of the buckets into the well.

Noreen heard the sarcasm in her sister's voice and her eyes narrowed. "What are you doing all the way out here anyway? You know you're not allowed out this far."

Louise's smirk caved wider and formed deep lines at the corners of her lips. "Oh shut up, I should be the one walking out here for the water not you. I mean just look at you, you've been sitting out here for over an hour daydreaming. You're too weak and everyone knows it. You may be able to hide those nasty welts from everyone else but not from me!" She stepped past Noreen and smiled as she looked at her own reflection in the well. "If only you didn't have dad's stubbornness, then maybe you'd let Charlie walk you to The Cove for once and maybe then you wouldn't have so many of those ugly bruises."

Noreen glanced around them before grasping her hand tighter over the bucket's handle and using all her strength to whip the bucket out of the well as fast as she could. Water splashed onto Louise's face, as Noreen hoped, causing the girl to leap back in disgust. "Listen to me you little brat," Noreen towered over her sibling. "We both know that I can't do that. Charlie guards father's room at night and, on top of that, he works all damn day. Unlike you, I have no other choice but to work at that Godforsaken place!"

Louise's lips quivered and her smirk turned into a scowl. She shouted defensively back at her sister. "Fine! Rot in those alleys for all I care. I may be only fourteen, Noreen, but at least I have more sense than you do."

Noreen dunked the second bucket into the well and filled it to the rim. "What do you suggest I do then, Louise? Father is not well and if you expect me to quit my job and have him suffer for *my* selfishness, then you are a foolish little girl!"

Louise fell silent and Noreen pushed past her to walk back toward their cottage. She stood as upright as she could, knowing Louise would be watching, and refusing to allow her body to crumble in front of her sister.

By the time Noreen reached the house, supper was ready and her mother was sitting alone in one of the five chairs surrounding the kitchen table. Her hands clasped together on the oak as Noreen made her entrance into the claustrophobic room. At the sight of her daughter, Mrs. Satchell's expression transformed into a scowl, and she folded her arms boldly across her chest.

Noreen stood in the doorway with her eyes interlocked with her mother's. The woman's glare seemed to trap Noreen enough to prevent her from moving forward, despite that her arms felt as though they were ripping through their sockets from the weight of the well water in her palms. She could tell the woman detected her struggle, yet she purposely made Noreen suffer by staring her down from her comfortable position in the chair.

As the two continued to stare at one another in an unspoken battle, Louise capered behind Noreen close enough to 'accidentally' bump into her back and cause splashes of water to spill across the floor. She skipped past nonchalantly and sat herself by the table with a mischievous grin stretching across her face. Noreen wanted desperately to smack the girl but remained frozen in the doorway until Mrs. Satchell stood and nodded toward the stockpot over the fire. At her mother's gesture, Noreen waddled toward the fireplace and poured each bucket, one at a time, into the pot.

Once the buckets were emptied, Noreen turned around to find her mother holding out a dirty rag in her palm. Noreen took the rag and smiled sheepishly before bending down to clean up the mess Louise had created on the floor. Before soaking the towel with the blackish well water, she used the cloth to wipe the ink off her forehead. She scrubbed it harshly until she detected that no more ink could smudge off her skin.

As she lifted the rag, she could feel her sister's smirk almost burning the red mark that endured across her forehead. Not once, though, did she glance over to Louise and provide her with the pleasing sense of victory. She lowered the rag to the ground after a pause and maneuvered her arm in circles across the floor to spread the pool of water between the cracks of the adjacent stones. She heard her mother exit the room but did not lift her eyes to follow the woman's quick strides down the hall. Each time she shifted her weight from her back leg to her forward foot, Noreen was able to trace her mother's exact position somewhere on the short path. *Two, Three, Four…* Noreen counted her mother's steps noiselessly between her lips until the final step landed on the number seven. *The seventh step.* She took a breath and sat back on her heels.

A heavy, clunking noise echoed off the walls and resonated into the kitchen. Without looking, Noreen knew her mother had just yanked the thick rug off the hidden wooden flap aligned between the stone blocks in the floor. Noreen knew what was coming. At any moment, she would hear the haunting jingle of her mother's keys rattling out of her apron pocket and her brittle father would emerge through the narrow, arched doorway and step into the room.

Noreen leaned forward and stole a brief glance down the hall to find her mother dragging the rug back to its place over the small, wooden hideaway. Her father lay on the ground beside her, helplessly waiting for his wife to assist him now that his ability to stand on his own deteriorated months ago. Each day, Noreen witnessed her father grow weaker, yet each evening she would pretend to ignore it.

Despite her mother's opposition, they were forced to accept her father's overbearing demands to be let out of his secret chamber or otherwise listen to his stubborn cries shake the six elongated wooden boards of his locked door throughout the night and into the next morning. Although his appendages functioned in a restricted manner and his flesh appeared to be eroding away into the soil beneath his mattress, his mind had not yet accepted his condition as a dying man. Noreen decided long ago that the moment his consciousness recognized his ill fate, would be a moment she would find whatever reason she could think of to excuse herself from his presence.

Watching her father now, as he was supported by her mother down the hall, was one of the most pitiful sights she had ever seen. Like always, by the time he entered through the doorway and was in plain sight of his daughters, he broke himself free of his wife's hold and casually placed his arm around her waist to disguise his weakness. Regardless of the apparent fakeness in his act, Noreen pretended, like many other things, to ignore it and greet him affectionately.

She walked slowly toward the living corpse and hugged mostly air as she wrapped her arms loosely around the fragile bones of her father's back. He managed to barely curl up the corners of his lips before violently coughing up drops of blood that trickled down his chin and onto Noreen's shoulder. Noreen bit her lip to restrain herself from saying or doing anything that could possibly embarrass her father, and thus allowed his blood to seep into the thin material of her dress.

Seconds later, his coughing silenced, and she could feel the weight of his chin drop heavily onto her shoulder. The bones in his jaw sunk into a large bruise that darkened the skin alongside Noreen's neckline, inflicting an immense pain beneath her dress. Noreen locked eyes with her mother and motioned for her assistance and the woman wrapped her arms around her husband's chest and pulled his frail body off his daughter. The women gravitated to his sides and guided the man to his usual seat at the table.

Noreen peered over to her sister before sitting beside her father. She frowned at the unhelpful girl, but Louise gave the impression that her sister's scorn could never affect her judgment. She sat casually with her blackened feet propped up onto the chair beside her in a disrespectful manner while she chewed her fingernails habitually. She did not stand to greet her father but disregarded his presence entirely. Freeing her hands from the arms of her chair, she tilted back until the front legs of her seat lifted off the ground.

Noreen cleared her throat to gain her sister's attention, but Louise declined to straighten her posture until their mother clutched the skin of her upper arm and pinched her. Louise shrieked initially, but the influence of her mother's authority silenced her and led Louise to sit up in a courteous manner with all four legs of her chair touching the floor.

As her sister readjusted her seating, Noreen watched her father. She waited for him to somehow acknowledge their scuffle, but he barely seemed to notice. His attention never left his empty drinking glass as he allowed his head to droop toward his chest.

In another phony act, Mrs. Satchell began their conversation with a 'humorous' story involving her struggle to pull the roots of some vegetable from their garden. Although her story lacked humor, Noreen and her sister pretended to laugh. The following exchanges of meaningless chatter rambled mostly between Louise and her mother with a few grumbles from her father when a remark from him was requested. Mr. Satchell had not yet consumed any of his desired liquor to speak more than a few words in their conversation, but as Mrs. Satchell began another one of her endless rants, Noreen could feel the icy touch of her father's tap on her forearm.

"Noreen my darlin'," Mr. Satchell's hollow cheeks lifted slightly as he whispered beneath his breath. He stared forward with his head hanging toward his shoulder as though it weighed far more than bearable. Noreen peered down to his palm as it faced up on the arm of her chair between them. He motioned for her by folding his fingers into a closed fist and back out again in a repeated motion. As usual, Noreen knew exactly what he wanted.

From the softness in his voice, she could tell he was making an effort to be subtle, though her mother's vigilant eyes always silently caught their nightly transactions. Confident that her mother would not object, Noreen slipped one of her hands into the large pocket of her dress and retrieved the stolen miniature bottle of scotch out of its hiding place. Gently, she placed the bottle into her father's hand and closed her eyes as she pictured his appreciative grin from beside her. She reopened them to the sight of golden amber pouring into her father's glass. Once the bottle was empty, Noreen, again, felt the icy touch of her father's trembling hand on her. It rested on her cheek for several seconds while he whispered his appreciation to her. "That's my girl." he said in a crackled voice. The hot wind of his breath, along with the chilliness of his icy touch, sent shivers down Noreen's spine.

Each time her father would do this, Noreen would force a smile and again later on when he would whisper his desired liquor for the upcoming evening. Naturally, she would always find a way to obtain the liquor for her father, though the government outlawed alcohol years prior.

Each night a few hours after supper, Noreen would walk to work completely unnoticed by her neighbors after the candles and flashlights in their households had long been extinguished. If getting caught by her neighbors was not dangerous enough, her actual time spent after hours at The Cove fulfilled the requirement. It was that dreading moment when the sun just barely peeked its rim over the horizon and the customers left the illegal bar to stumble inconspicuously back to their cottages. That moment marked the beginning of when her bruises formed and blood spilled from her veins.

Lawrence Colt, the owner of the bar and her employer, was the vile creature to blame, the same creature undeserving to be labeled within the category of man. His violent actions directed only at Noreen, for reasons she did not know or wish to understand. Whether his treatment toward her sparked from the fear of getting caught for owning an illegal tavern or erupted from his own sick and twisted pleasure was a mystery. Mr. Colt, the name Lawrence demanded to be called when surrounded by his customers, was relentless in his efforts to subdue her.

While the alcoholics would drink in Lawrence's saloon, he tormented Noreen in ways deemed inconspicuous to intoxicated eyes. He would yank her pale curls if she dropped a glass or would fist his knuckles into her kidneys if she dared to speak too loudly. After a great deal of time working under his control, Mr. Colt's sexual harassments transformed quickly to serious threats against her life. His threats forced her to practically tiptoe around him and the bar in fear that any wrong move could gain his attention and ignite his wrath. If it were not for her father, she would never work for such a vile creature, but he needed the bitter morphine, and Noreen decided long ago that she would do anything to help ease his pain.

The sound of her mother's voice fading into silence broke Noreen's trance. She looked up at her mother to find the woman staring plainly at her husband's colored glass. She chose not to acknowledge its presence verbally, but her eyes flashed at Noreen with a haunting disapproval that made Noreen cringe. Before her reddening face could turn the shade of purple, her mother glanced away from her, enabling Noreen to exhale her next breath in quiet, staggering huffs. Her mother knew she stole the liquor for her father but never mentioned it.

"Where's my boy Charlie?" Mr. Satchell grunted, his first few sips of liquor taking effect.

"He'll be home soon," Mrs. Satchell responded as she stood to fill each of their bowls with the cloudy, pale colored liquid from the stockpot. "His shift ended an hour ago, so he should be home any minute now."

"Very good," Mr. Satchell nodded in approval. It was an effort for him to physically lift the glass to his lips for a drink. To Noreen's left, her mother carried two bowls at a time to the table until each of them had a bowl of soup in front of them. Noreen lifted her spoon, dipped it into the bowl and brought the liquid to her lips. If it wasn't for the presence of the onions from their garden, it would have tasted like water. Her stomach grumbled as she dipped her spoon again into the bowl, but she kept her pace slow to practice her manners before her father.

Once they were all seated, Mrs. Satchell dominated the meaningless conversations with Noreen hardly paying attention to them. She finished nearly half of her bowl before lifting her head and peering around the table. Almost instantly, Louise caught her gaze. She was glaring into her untouched bowl of soup with disgust as she dangled the clean spoon between her knuckles. Louise glanced up and Noreen motioned her head toward her sister's bowl and mouthed the word 'eat' silently between her lips. Louise stuck her tongue out at her and with a huff, she dropped her spoon noisily onto the table to call the attention from those around her.

"Something wrong, Louise?" Mrs. Satchell lowered her spoon into her bowl and wiped her hands delicately on her apron. Her voice seemed agitated, but Noreen could not tell what she was thinking.

Louise cleared her throat obnoxiously before she spoke. "May I be excused?"

Mrs. Satchell raised an eyebrow. "No, you may not. Your father has been waiting all day to have dinner with us, and since we are a family, we will eat together as one." Noreen glanced over to her father to see his reaction, but the man never looked up from his scotch. "Aren't you hungry?" Her mother's question brought Noreen's attention back to Louise. "You only had a potato and some carrots at breakfast... Are you feeling alright? Do I need to give you another steam bath?"

Noreen could hear the slight panic in her mother's voice as she said the words 'steam bath,' though the process was, in fact, not even a bath at all. Every morning since her father had returned home, shortly after Noreen's tenth birthday, their mother would force her, Louise and Charlie to take these 'steam baths' by leaning over a pot of boiling water that dangled above the fireplace. The burning air supposedly opened up their pores and seeped into their skin. As explained by their mother, any facial blemishes or noticeable pimples on their chins or foreheads could be seen as signs of the Infection in the eyes of the government, though they were merely consequences of pubescent stages of adolescence.

"Does my face look like it needs another steam bath?" Louise spoke with an attitude. "My skin is flawless." She paused to smile. "It's just, I don't think this…" she gestured toward the soup before her, "that this is even edible. I don't taste anything!"

"You are lucky you even get a supper. We are fortunate enough to-"

"To have this shit as our meal?" Louise cut her mother off.

At the girl's remark, Mrs. Satchell stood with enough force to make the chair behind her tip back and smack against the floor. Louise shut her mouth and slugged down into her own seat as her mother walked over and glared straight into her daughter's eyes with a powerful, interlocking stare. She raised her arm and pointed her index finger out of her fist. "I don't want to ever hear that word come out of your ungrateful little mouth again, you hear me?"

Louise narrowed her eyes and used the arms of her chair to sit up straighter. "Yes, mother." An attitude still lingered in her tone, but Mrs. Satchell ignored it and lowered her finger.

She walked back over to her chair, after patting her apron twice, and bent down to pick it up off the floor. As she brought her seat back to its original position, Louise allowed a few words of profanity to slip through her teeth without realizing her mother could hear her. Before she knew it, Mrs. Satchell had whipped around to face her daughter once again. She grabbed her child's bicep tightly between her fingertips and raised Louise to her feet. She stomped out of the room, dragging her daughter behind her. Silence lasted for only a few moments until the sound of a hard slap echoed out of the bedroom and into the kitchen. Noreen flinched at each sound that followed, from her sister's screams to her mother's hushed threats that were inaudible to her father's aging ears.

Clips of her mother's phrases were decipherable, *"I raised you better than-...how dare you be so disrespectful to-...you're lucky you get to eat!"* Another smack resonated and Noreen shuddered. She peered over to her father, hoping for his comfort, but he did not seem to notice Noreen's distress or the tussle in the bedroom. He stared aimlessly into his glass and hiccupped three times before bowing his head toward his chest. Noreen gathered the napkin off her lap and leaned over to catch the saliva that drooled out of the corner of his lip. As she wiped his face clean, the front door creaked open and everything in the house went quiet. Mr. Satchell lifted his head and stared with glassy eyes directly ahead of him and at the undecorated stones. He placed the bottle of scotch onto the table with a shaky hand and he parted his lips. "Is that you, my boy?"

Noreen dropped her napkin and swiftly placed her hand over her father's mouth despite the fact his voice barely held a medium volume. Without a lock on their front door, Noreen knew that anyone could be wandering into their home, and the sight of her father alone could destroy their family altogether. She whispered into her father's ear and told him to slide out of his chair and crawl out the backdoor, but the stubborn man remained seated with her hand covering his mouth. Just as Noreen was about to give him a push, her brother's voice sounded down the hall.

"Yes, father, it's me!" Charlie answered him. Noreen shook her head and removed her hand from over her father's lips. He glowered at her, but Noreen ignored him and turned his chair toward the front walkway. Charlie stepped into the room a second later with an overjoyed expression strewn across his face. He glided toward his father and shook the old man's hand with a firm grip. "I have wonderful news, dad!" He leaned over to Noreen who now stood beside her seated father and he lifted her off the ground.

"What's going on, Charlie?" Noreen could not help but smile genuinely at his uplifting presence.

Charlie lowered his sister down into her chair and jumped back for emphasis. "You'll need to be seated for this!" He winked and Noreen cocked her head to the side, but she remained quiet. "Where are mother and Louise? They must hear my news at once!"

Noreen winced at the memory of her mother and sister's fight from just moments earlier. "They'll be back in a minute," she began her lie, "they were looking for a seat cushion for father!"

Mr. Satchell glanced over to his daughter and nodded as though able to read her thoughts, neither wanting to spoil the sudden uplifting mood. "That's right, you heard the girl; my behind could use a seat cushion on this damn, wooden thing!" Mr. Satchell proclaimed.

Noreen placed her arm around her father's shoulders, loving him even more than she had before. "Then I shall get you that seat cushion, father!" As Charlie leapt up to retrieve his father the pillow, the sound of a door clicked open and Mrs. Satchell entered the kitchen. Noreen noticed the woman using her thumb to soothe her reddening palm, but she thought it best not to call attention to it.

Charlie waltzed back into the room holding his pillow out at arm's length before him as though the cushion were his dance partner. He spun himself and the pillow until finally tossing the object to Noreen and continuing his step touches in solitude. Noticing his mother, he picked up her arms into his own and twirled her in the confined space. His merriment dispelled Mrs. Satchell's agitation enough that she no longer showed any recollection of discomfort from her fight with his sister just moments prior. Noreen's lips twitched, and the confidence of her smile became questionable as she speculated where Louise was hiding.

Deciding to check on her sister, Noreen planted her feet on the ground, but before she could stand, her father began clapping beside her. Immediately, she turned toward him and watched the man use practically all his strength to make the softest sound resonate between his palms. His actions had enough magnitude that even Charlie and his mother stopped their dancing. Charlie's smile grew wider than Noreen thought possible as he bowed respectfully to his mother and rushed to his father's side. He gathered his father's palms between his and ended the claps by kissing the **L** tattoo stamped on the inside of his father's wrist. In the background, Mrs. Satchell placed her hands on her hips and shook her head with a laugh. "What on earth is with you today, Charlie?"

Charlie eyed each of his family members as they waited impatiently for his explanation. "I have great news." He released his father's hands and stood back to shift his feet from side to side in his own wandering dance. Similar to Mr. Satchell, Charlie almost seemed to be in a world of his own. "You cannot imagine how happy I am!" he almost sang.

"You sure about that?" Louise grumbled as she entered the kitchen. She stood by the doorway holding her left wrist while rubbing it habitually with the fingers of her right hand. Noreen watched Louise stroke her wrist and, as Charlie rushed to embrace her, she noticed the sizable area of redness surrounding her **L** tattoo on the inside of her forearm. Instinctively, Noreen slid deeper into her chair and gently pressed two fingers against the matching **L** tattoo stamped to her own left, inner forearm. She exhaled a staggered breath and removed her fingertips from their position at the nudge of her father's elbow in her side. She glanced over to the smiling man just as he was about to hiccup and cough for several breaths. He, resembling Charlie once again, was completely oblivious to the red marks that wrapped around Louise's wrist and extended up to her shoulder.

"Louise! One of my favorite sisters!" Charlie's laugh turned Noreen's attention back to her brother. He held Louise in his arms and carried her effortlessly toward one of the chairs Mrs. Satchell pulled up beside Noreen. Each of them stared at Charlie with curiosity, but he merely stared back at them with a gleaming smile. The first person to break the silence was Mrs. Satchell, whose now serious tone lingered with irritation. "Charles, what is going on?" she used her son's birth name to emphasize her question. She crossed her arms over her chest and leaned with a single shoulder against the wall behind her.

Charlie grabbed hold of his mother's hand and tugged her away from the wall and toward her husband. He kneeled down before his father and gently interlocked the fingers of his free hand with that of his father's. He inhaled a shallow breath in an attempt to calm his nerves before he made his announcement. "Mother, do you remember a few months back when you were so upset with me for trading my shoelaces for some hemp string at the barter's market?"

"Huh?" Mrs. Satchell scowled. "What does that have to do with anything?"

"Just tell me, please," Charlie shook his mother's hand from side to side as though trying to keep her focused, "do you remember?"

"Why of course I do, but-"

"But everything was fine because the leftover hemp I didn't use replaced my shoelaces anyways, right?"

"Charlie, what on earth are you-"

"I used that string to make something very special for my girlfriend, Madeline, because I wanted to stick with tradition even though I did not believe I could afford it. But, you see, I was wrong, I can afford tradition!"

"Charles, you are not making sense!" Mrs. Satchell proclaimed.

"Let me finish mother, please." Charlie was too excited to hear the agitation in his mother's tone. "By tradition, I mean that I did not want to propose to Madeline without presenting her with a ring, so I braided her one out of all the strings of hemp I traded for! I would show it to you all, but I have already presented it to Madeline earlier today, and she happily accepted it!" He kissed both of his parents' hands. "Mother, father, I'm engaged!"

Before Noreen could even open her mouth to speak, her mother and sister had already begun screaming exclamations of happiness. The air in the room had unnaturally transformed and within a blink of an eye the scene before Noreen had become a joyous celebration. Louise practically jumped onto her brother, and he gleefully picked her up and held the girl around her waist. He kissed her forehead before setting her back down to the ground.

Mrs. Satchell rushed toward him with open arms and a smile. After they embraced, she turned him multiple times as though visually sizing him for groom's attire. Neither Noreen nor her father could even get the chance to express any sort of congratulation until Mrs. Satchell abruptly rushed out the backdoor and into the garden, with Louise following close behind. As the broken door slammed behind them, Mrs. Satchell shouted 'tonight, we feast' over her shoulder.

The shouts and celebrations trailed out the backdoor with the two women, allowing Noreen, Charlie, and their father to talk amongst each other softly. Noreen stood and stepped toward her brother who was facing the back doorway. Her movements came to a halt, though, at the sound of a harsh grunt erupting out of her father's throat. Noreen and Charlie exchanged wary glances before turning to their father. "How long have you been datin' this Madeline girl?" Mr. Satchell questioned his son, with a voice barely audible. He grabbed his scotch from its position between his legs where he had placed it for safe keeping during the commotion. The liquor shook uncontrollably between his fingertips, but he was careful not to spill a single drop from his glass.

"Seventeen months, sir," Charlie answered. His voice became grim and his muscles tensed.

"She pregnant?"

Charlie stepped back in shock. "No!" he gasped. His voice elevated to that of a loud whisper. "Of course, not!"

"Mm," Mr. Satchell grunted once again before bringing the glass to his lips. He paused to swallow some of the amber liquid down his throat. "You realize that you're just a twenty year old boy who–"

"I'm not a boy anymore father, I'm a man!" Charlie interrupted him.

"That statement alone makes you a boy!" Mr. Satchell's forceful tone encouraged a burp to disrupt his insult. "No matter how old you get, Charlie, you'll always be my boy, remember that."

"Yes sir," Charlie answered through his teeth.

With a dip of his head toward his shoulder, Mr. Satchell glanced toward his daughter. "Noreen, would you say this Madeline girl is worthy enough for my boy, Charles?"

Noreen eyed Charlie who anxiously waited for her response, though he knew she could not truthfully answer their father's question. Noreen had, in fact, only ever talked to Madeline twice in all of the seventeen months Charlie had dated her, yet he expected her to lie for him like any true sibling would. The pressure coming from both men in her life prompted her hands to shake just like her father's as he held his glass. Unlike her father's, Noreen's were the product of undesired and uncontrolled nerves, as well as an improperly healed left hand. "Yes, sir," she lied to please her brother.

"And I trust you my child." Mr. Satchell reluctantly removed a hand from around his glass to pat Noreen's with a cold and clammy touch. A lump formed deep in Noreen's throat, and she found herself having difficulty swallowing her own saliva. Her father looked away from her before she could choke from all the tension. "Best wishes to you my boy," Mr. Satchell slowly lifted his hand from Noreen's and used it to support his effort to lift his glass and bring it to his lips.

Unexpectedly, two arms wrapped around Noreen's waist with a force strong enough to lift her feet off the ground. Without having to turn, she knew it was Charlie thanking her. Without saying a word to acknowledge him, she knew he heard her unspoken words of congratulation.

Chapter 3

*D*inner that evening was a feast like Mrs. Satchell had promised and much like the ones on Day 19 when Charlie had the chance to bring home any sort of meat dumped off the government's vehicles. Although the dishes on the table were meatless, Noreen's mother and sister had removed five yams and several handfuls of snap beans from the garden as a form of 'dessert' to be cooked and eaten after they finished their bowls of soup.

Mrs. Satchell and Louise had forgotten, or rather let go of their negative incident that occurred moments before Charlie's return home, and to everyone's surprise, Mr. Satchell even gave Charlie a swig of his scotch, something he had never done. The soup, like always, tasted as bland as it looked but, no one, not even Louise, had the audacity to complain about it. It was an evening Noreen wished would never end.

As Charlie spoke of his fiancée Madeline at the dinner table, Noreen could see the happiness in his face brightening even the darkest parts of his deep blue irises. He was only two years older than Noreen and had been courting Madeline for a little over a year and a half, but she could tell he was ready to wed, and he would make a wonderful husband to his future wife. "So when's the big day?" Louise smiled as she looked up to Charlie sitting beside her. His height towered above her, even while sitting, causing him to hunch over as he looked down at his youngest sister.

"I'm not sure, Louise," Charlie answered. He could not seem to keep from smiling, "but Madeline wants a small, simple wedding overlooking the harbor, and I agree with her."

"HA like anyone in this town could afford a big wedding anyways." Louise scoffed. This time it was Mr. Satchell who scowled at her, pressuring Louise to quickly correct herself out of fear of displeasing her father. "But either way, I'm sure it'll be great!" She smiled with closed lips at Charlie, eying her father for his approval. Mr. Satchell ignored her remark, and stared into his nearly empty glass of scotch.

"Of course it will," Noreen's mother responded for her son.

For the next several minutes, silence followed, giving Noreen the chance to picture Charlie and Madeline's wedding within the peace of her own imagination. It would be a cool, fall wedding with the ceremony held at the very edge of the bay, so that it could overlook the rough harbor's waters far below. Madeline would be wearing a long, embroidered veil that her own mother would embroider. The white lace veil would cover her straight black hair and would flow behind her in a beautiful train that would be held on either side by Noreen and her sister. She and Louise would be Madeline's bridesmaids, Noreen could only assume, since Charlie had mentioned at the table that Madeline lived alone with her father. Noreen liked to think of herself as not just any bridesmaid, though, but rather her future older sister's bridesmaid. She smiled at the thought of holding such an honorable position.

Before imagining Charlie's appearance on his special day, Noreen peeked a glance at him from across the table to get a clearer image of her brother before resuming her imagined fantasy. Dissimilar to his current appearance, Charlie would be standing upright and tall as he waited for Madeline to approach him. His dirty, blond hair would be swept back to reveal his deep blue eyes. His angled and strong jawline would be smooth, clean cut, and free of any imperfections, unlike the short, scruffy hairs that presently connected to his sideburns, overtook his chin and reached roughly halfway down his neck.

Her mother, on the other hand, would be crying discreetly behind her handkerchief, sitting on a wooden bench decorated with red and white carnations. Like most of the women who would attend the wedding, she would be wearing the only formal dress she owned, the one with the tainted blue sash that draped across her left shoulder and connected together slightly above her waistline. Though her customary, tan bonnet would have some discolorations like her sash, it would accent her dress perfectly. Her father would…

Noreen paused mid-thought. She looked up from her soup and over to the helpless man seated beside her. His skin was no longer the golden brown her mother once described but rather a ghostly white color with loose flesh that hung off his body like drool off a baby's lips. His colorless lips were dry and cracked and parted at the center as though anticipating more liquor from the now empty glass. Daily, he lost a few patches of his white hair with his weight also continuing to reveal more and more of his frailty.

Noreen knew he would not make it to Charlie's wedding. Even if he were still living by autumn, he would be forbidden to go. No one else knew of his existence or of his hiding place beneath the stones of their main floor. He was the secret she had to lock away in her mind forever, without any sort of key to open it. That thought alone caused a tear to fall down her cheek. Dropping her gaze from her father, Noreen took the napkin from her lap and brought it to her face. She scanned the table to ensure that no surrounding eyes were upon her before she quickly wiped the water from her skin.

Mrs. Satchell restarted more of the meaningless table chatter as Noreen lowered her napkin back to her lap. The woman turned to face her son, and she asked him basically the same questions he had already answered. Their talk lasted through the distribution of the yams and beans until Mr. Satchell cleared his throat and silenced the table. "My boy," he started. His left hand shook as he lifted his cup of parboiled water in a toast, since his glass of liquor was empty. *"From past to present, from pride of a peasant, the Right may slither, but the Left will not wither.* Congratulations, my son."

For the first time that evening, he sipped his water rather than his scotch, and the worry lines on his forehead disappeared. The rest of the family, excluding Louise, raised their glasses in agreement and toasted to Charlie. Louise looked around the table in confusion. "But father, what does that even mean?"

Mr. Satchell remained silent as Noreen leaned over to help him sip more of his water and place the cup back down to the table. His glassy, blue eyes peered over to Louise as he raised his left arm once again; the black **L** tattooed against his nearly transparent skin appeared to illuminate on his wrist. After a moment of silence, he turned his wrist to face him, and he brought the tattoo to his lips. Mr. Satchell kissed the **L** briefly as hard as he could and then lifted it as though thanking the heavens before he let it fall to his side.

Noreen's mother nodded and mimicked her husband's movements. Louise frowned looking at her own **L** tattooed in the same position on the inside her wrist. "I still don't-"

"Louise," Mrs. Satchell cut her off, "do you need to know every little detail? Think about what your father said, and you are to agree with it!"

Charlie leaned over to Louise once their mother's scowl dropped down to her plate of yams, and he whispered into her ear words indecipherable to Noreen from across the table. Louise smiled at her brother in return. "Anyways," Mrs. Satchell began. She brought her napkin to her lips to clean the skin around the rim of her mouth. She aligned her back even straighter than it already was. "I just wanted to say, Charlie, that I think Madeline is a wonderful girl, simply wonderful." Her abrupt cheerfulness gave way to a brighter conversation, though Noreen silently questioned the truth to her mother's statement since she too had only spoken with Madeline on a handful of occasions. "And she comes from such a great family, too, with such a pleasant father, or at least that's what town gossip has told me. You know, I knew this was gonna happen. Mhm, that's right, yes I did. Mother's intuition, it's always right."

She continued her praise of the girl she barely knew for reasons Noreen did not understand but figured it had something to do with the dying man sitting beside her. The last thing he needed was to stress or worry over circumstances he had no power to control, especially for his eldest and only son. As the overload of tributes to Madeline continued, a giggle from Louise ignited a ripple of laughs through the company, all except from Mrs. Satchell who continued to ramble on.

Unexpectedly, the mood in the room changed once again at the sound of Mr. Satchell's soft laugh transforming into a violent cough with enough desperation to silence the room altogether. Charlie rose to his feet, and he rushed over to his father's side. He rested his knees on the stone floor and grabbed hold of his father's palms. All four family members waited in silence with hopes that the man would gather himself. Several seconds ticked by on the imaginary clock that ticked in Noreen's brain, but his cough only worsened. Along with his cough, a shallow wheeze formulated in his throat, prompting Charlie to lift his father from the chair and carry him effortlessly toward the hall. Mr. Satchell tried desperately to resist, but Charlie ignored him and commanded his mother to open the door that led to his father's room in the basement.

Noreen watched in horror as her father scratched at his throat, desperate for air. He pointed to her with his free hand and, between wheezes, he called to her. Charlie ignored his father's plea and tugged him through the doorway and down the steps hidden beneath the floor. Mrs. Satchell slipped through the secret door after them and locked it frantically behind her. The sound of the door slamming shut seemed to echo like cannon fire through Noreen's eardrums and end the constant ticks of the imaginary clock that pounded through her brain.

Chapter 4

$\mathcal{A}$ gust of wind shoved open the two wooden panels of the arched window with enough force to drive the odious stench further up Noreen's nostrils. Almost instantly, her throat tightened as the repugnant smell coming from her mother and sister practically choked the breath out of her lungs. Neither of the women had bathed in nearly twenty-three days and, like most of their neighbors in the town, they would not bathe again for another seven. Noreen bathed three times as often to follow Lawrence's strict set of guidelines that required her to come dressed clean and presentable for his thirsty customers, an order she could not refuse. Any other night, her mother and sister's smells would not be nearly as bothersome, but since Noreen was given her tenth day bath earlier that evening, their stenches were far more potent.

After spending some time contemplating whether to turn on her side, Noreen decided against it. Given such limited space between her mother and sister on the cot, she barely had enough room to even clasp her hands over top of her stomach without having to tuck her elbows in toward her. But Noreen had no choice but sleep between the two foul smelling women since Louise was known for moving about in her sleep and because Noreen received the majority of her rest in the mornings. For that reason, she was pegged as the divider for the sakes of her mother and sister.

Another gust of wind surged through the frame of the open window causing its two wooden panels to smack repeatedly against the wall. Noreen removed her left hand from beneath the blanket and used it to plug her nose in an effort to block the awful stench that filled the room. Her movements tugged the quilt downward and stirred her sister out of her slumber.

Louise grumbled and yanked the quilt back up to her cheek, unaware of her sister's consciousness. "Sorry, Louise," Noreen whispered. By plugging her nose, Noreen's voice became unrecognizable to her sister, causing Louise to jolt up and unknowingly face her in the darkness.

With the moonlight shining in Louise's direction, the young girl's face was illuminated, but she was unable to see. "Noreen?" she asked as she poked her sister's face with her fingertips.

Noreen freed her nostrils and smacked her sister's hands away from her. "Quit poking me!" she whispered, keeping her voice low since their mother slept beside her.

"Oh, it's you," Louise refrained from hushing her voice; the disappointment in her tone was evident to the both of them.

"Shh!" Noreen hushed the girl. She kept her voice under control despite that Louise's attitude infuriated her. "Who else would it be?"

"How should I know?" Louise failed to lower her voice. "It didn't sound like you."

"How many times do I have to tell you to be quiet?" Noreen muttered through her teeth. "Do you honestly want *mom* to be the one to tell you to shut up?"

Louise grumbled as she laid back down on the cot. Noreen waited until she lowered entirely before returning her gaze to the ceiling. She stared in silence at the moonlight that shined through the small window and danced across the gray tiled stones above her. Outside, the clouds that drifted over the moon generated shadows that danced to the beat of nature's soundless symphony.

Noreen closed her eyes after some time but kept the dancing images alive behind her lids. As the performance ended and the encores drifted smoothly to a close, her consciousness followed in the same wandering fashion. Just when the curtains of her imaginary stage were about to close, a soft whisper pulled Noreen out of her whimsical dreamland. "What now, Louise?" Noreen whined.

"Do you think dad is doing alright down there?" she asked. Her tone had changed, and she sounded almost vulnerable.

Noreen took a moment to gather her thoughts and she shifted her body to face her sister. "I'm sure he's fine, it was only a cough after all. Besides, Charlie is with him tonight. He will keep dad safe."

She could see the terrified look on Louise's face and felt relieved when she realized that the light blocked her own expression from her sister's view. "But he has never wheezed that much before," Louise began, her volume matching Noreen's. "Mom and Charlie were in the room with him for hours doing who knows what. And now Charlie is down there all alone with him. Oh, I can't imagine what it would be like to sleep down there…poor Charlie," Louise closed her eyes, her bottom lip trembling. "Thank god I'm not father's son."

"Being his son has nothing to do with it," Noreen disagreed. "The only reason you or I are not down there right now watching over father is not because we are his daughters or because it would be inappropriate for Charlie to share a bed with us. Hell, Charlie would sleep on the mat outside father's door like he always does if he wasn't already in the room with him.

The reason I am not down there is because I have to leave in less than an hour to go to The Cove and father cannot be left unattended overnight. And since mother takes care of him during the day and you are not old enough to go down there and watch over him on your own, Charlie is the one left to watch over him." Noreen paused as the quilt rustled behind her. When her mother became still, she finished, her voice even quieter. "Don't you forget that it is our father who is the one that is sick; he is the one that needs us!"

"I don't think the reason why I'm not allowed down there is because I'm too young, I think it's because these hands just simply aren't meant for changing diapers or cleaning that gross bed pan of his." The arrogance that returned to her tone stung Noreen's heart, and she wanted nothing more than to hit her uncaring sister in the bottom lip that curled so hideously in the moonlight.

She repeated her sister's words in her brain until coming to a realization. "Wait a minute," Noreen started, "how do you know about father's bed pan if you have never been allowed inside his room before?"

Louise's face transformed as her cheeks drooped and her expression almost appeared nauseous. "I…I was in there once…" Noreen raised her eyebrows and Louise continued. "Please don't' get mad. I-"

"You did what?! When?" Noreen gasped. As soon as her words escaped her lips, she covered her mouth with fear that she had spoken too loudly with her mother sleeping so close beside her.

"Please don't tell mother!" her sister begged. The change in her tone, yet again, was almost laughable. "I was curious because I had never been in there before, so I took mother's keys when she was sleeping and you were at work and I unlocked the door and walked down the steps. But when I saw father laying there like-like a corpse, I froze! I couldn't even breathe! Suddenly, out of nowhere, his hand fell over to the table beside his bed, and he rang that stupid, little bell, the one he uses to call you or mother or Charlie and, as fast as I could, I dove to the floor and crawled under his bed!

Mother came in then, and I knew it was her cause I could see her hideous feet from beneath the mattress." Louise talked faster and faster with each of her breaths. "And then after a few minutes, she called for Charlie, and they both had to help dad, help him use the bed pan." Noreen remained silent as she waited for her sister to finish her confession. "The pan where he, you know..." More silence forced her to continue. "Oh Noreen, please don't make me say it! I didn't see anything I swear, but I could hear it and UGH!"

Noreen jerked her arm forward and covered her sister's mouth. She waited for what seemed like an eternity as her mother shifted behind her before she was able to scold her sibling. "This is exactly what mother was talking about," she began, "you have too much curiosity. You just need to accept the things you are told without question. How did mom not realize you were down there if her keys were gone and the door was unlocked, anyways?"

She removed her hand from Louise's mouth and let her talk. "Charlie noticed me under the bed, and he covered for me."

Noreen rolled her eyes. "That was real dumb, you know that? What if father noticed you were in there? You know how embarrassed he would have been? And what if Charlie never saw you, huh? Everyone would have panicked, thinking someone had found father's hideaway. That room is locked for a reason, Louise. If the Government found out that dad is still alive after everything, after everything they put him through..." she paused at the touch of her sister's hand intertwining with her's beneath the blanket. "Dad is sick, and he will die soon. *They* changed him, Louise, not just physically.

God, there are a lot of things you don't know; there are a lot of things that I don't even know. But there are certain things that mom, dad, Charlie, and I have kept from you because these things would be very hard for you to understand. I don't understand them all completely myself but what I do get is that when the Government took father fourteen years ago, they did not expect him to return home alive."

"But mother told me that…"

"Mother lied," Noreen cut her off, squeezing her sister's hand, "I'm sorry, but she was just trying to protect our family. You weren't born until after father was taken. And as you got older, we were all afraid you would tell people what really happened. We both know that the Government thinks dad is dead, that everyone thinks he is dead, and that is how it must remain."

"But Noreen, what did they do to him?" Louise leaned her head forward, and, despite her repulsive odor, Noreen mimicked her sister until their heads touched.

"I don't know, Louise, I really don't know." Noreen knew she had already said too much, but it was too late to take back her words, and there was no way of erasing her sister's memory.

"Why did they take him in the first place?" Louise asked. Her questions became increasingly more difficult for Noreen to answer.

"Because he's a Left Hander," Noreen responded with the simplest response she could think of.

"But we are all Left Handers, Noreen." Her statement was one Noreen had bothered her mother with ever since her father's return. Like Louise, she too was never told the real reason why their father was taken.

"Just get some rest, Louise, I have to leave soon, but I'll be here when you wake." She began to move away from her sister, but Louise tightened their intertwined fingers to bring them closer.

"Goodnight, Noreen," Louise whispered as she readjusted her position so their heads touched like before.

Noreen smiled and waited for her sister to fall asleep before she separated their hands and carefully slipped out of the cot to escape the room.

Once in the hall, Noreen rushed toward one of the front windows and peered outside. She shoved open the wooden flaps harder than she expected and deeply inhaled the salty, refreshing scent of the harbor, just a short walk from her cottage. There were no lanterns or flashlights, no signs of life anywhere. Other than the light shining down from the half moon, the outside was pure darkness. Noreen took a breath. It was time.

Turning her attention to the kitchen behind her, she used the moonlight shining through the windows to guide her as she walked lightly on the cold floor and around the rug that covered her father's hideaway. She walked over to the table and moved her hands over the lantern her mother had left out for her. She opened its valve gently before feeling across the table for a match, also left for Noreen by her mother.

After finding the match, she struck against the side of the table. Quickly, Noreen lowered it into the lantern and ignited the wick of the candle inside. Once she blew out the flaming stick, she raised the lantern and used its light to examine the fireplace.

She ran her fingertips over the stone blocks and counted each block starting with the chipped stone on the far right side of the hearth. Over two and down four, and her fingers discovered the loose block that she was searching for. Placing the lantern on the floor, Noreen curled her knuckles around the edges of the block. She pulled it toward her and uncovered the hiding place of one of the Government's prohibited treasures. The item she retrieved out of the crevice was her father's old cloak, its purpose to camouflage her with the darkness.

It was illegal to wear anything that veiled their faces, as it could cover up symptoms of the Infection. Therefore, her father's old cloak was hidden whenever it was not in Noreen's use. This meant it was also her job to conceal the hole in the fireplace before she left the cottage each night in case the soldiers were to ever come and have a look around. If the cloak was found, the Government would assume Noreen's family was conspiring against a future inhibition of the Infection, the most petrifying disease that tore their entire country apart before Noreen was born.

As explained by her mother, a group of Government sponsored scientists working to create means of biological warfare used a genetic mutation with an infectious, slow-growing bacterium to generate a new form of leprosy that infects genetic material. The bacterium was intended to infect generations of humanity in enemy populations, but when the scientists tested it on a group of death row prisoners at the penitentiary, the disease uncontrollably leaked out to their own population, resulting in over half of their small country to die. Soon after, the scientists who survived the outbreak discovered that the Infection killed humans with either allele for handedness; however of the survivors, only left-handed people were found to be genetic carriers of the disease, ensuring that only Left Handers (and the few unfortunate ambidextrous peoples labeled as Left Handers) could develop the novel form of leprosy. Though passed from Left Handers to their offspring, the Infection was also found in carrier-free Left Handers who came in close contact with the lepers.

After the leak, Right Handers and Left Handers were separated out of fear that the Infection could mutate and infect the right-handed population as well. Families were torn apart and placed in towns divided by the country's national forest, also known as The Forest of Lepers because the infected survivors were taken there and left to die.

As each new infant is born, their totalitarian government takes the child until its second birthday, when signs of handedness are normally first shown. To this day, all children are taken at birth by the Government for evaluation concerning their dominant handedness. They are also taken as a safeguard, so that their parents cannot alter their baby's dominant handedness to become the more desirable form.

Left Handed parents can carry the biological mutation, and the disease can be passed down to their children and infect future generations. Years can go by and a Left Hander may never exhibit the physical characteristics of the Infection, but it can develop at any moment, and there is no way of stopping it. Once handedness is determined, children are sent to the town that matches their dominance, regardless of family affiliations. Stories from Noreen's father made her jealous of those from the Town of East, of the Right Handers whose lives were far better than her's, but she had no desire to join them. Her father needed her, her family needed her, and those reasons sent her to The Cove each night, as well as that no work for young women like herself in their town resided elsewhere.

Noreen wrapped herself in her father's cloak and inhaled the lingering scent of tobacco from her father's days as a pipe smoker. She closed her eyes and smiled at the rather pleasing scent compared to the horrible odor that permeated the single bedroom of their cottage. Several seconds passed, and she reopened her eyes to focus on reality.

With a shaking left palm, she tied the cloak and picked up the lantern on the floor beside her. Noreen tucked her curls behind her ears and lifted the black hood to cover them. She started for the back door, only to stop after realizing she had forgotten something of great importance. She did not know the type of liquor to bring to her father. Usually, he would inform her of the kind he wanted before making his way back down the basement steps after supper, but with such a terrible coughing fit earlier that evening, he never had the chance.

At that moment, Noreen realized why her father had pointed at her and called after her as he was carried out of the room during supper. He simply wanted to tell her the kind of booze he desired for the following evening, and it was her duty to retrieve it for him. Glancing at the back door, she knew taking the time to wake her father and ask him for his preference would make her late for work, but his happiness was far more important to her.

Noreen ran to the black mat with the lantern jostling by her side and removed the square carpet from its usual arrangement. She lifted her hand to knock the familiar beat for Charlie to recognize her and unlock the hatch, but she paused with her fist in the air. A flickering light gleamed through the cracks of the wooden entryway and through the door's brass keyhole.

It was the first time she had ever seen a light glisten through the keyhole during the hours past her father's bedtime and this caused both a combination of curiosity and fear within her. Holding her breath, Noreen laid her palms gently onto the door and lowered her face toward the keyhole. She closed her right eye as her nose grazed the hard surface. She pressed her left brow against the brass. The light initially blinded her and limited her vision, so she leaned back from the keyhole and blinked several times before peering into the aperture for a second try.

There was no movement in the room other than the flicker of light from a candle outside her line of vision. All she could see were the cobbled stones that comprised the uneven floor, yet she could hear light footsteps sticking and peeling off the stones somewhere near her. Out of nowhere, a thick arm wrapped around Noreen's throat and yanked her away from the hatch. Her body hit the floor as a large hand covered her nose and mouth, and dragged her down the hall.

Noreen's left foot barely missed kicking over the lantern as she fought wildly against her attacker. *It's one of them.* Her worst nightmares surfaced, and she felt herself becoming paralyzed with fear. The bottoms of her heels scrapped the stones beneath her enough to begin grinding away her outer flesh. It was too dark to see who was dragging her out of the cottage and away from her father's chamber, but she knew she must act soon before it was too late!

She looked in every direction, barely noticing her father's bed pan lying in the grass beside her. Unsure what else to do, Noreen attempted to bite into the course palm that blocked her airways, but her attacker threw her onto the ground before her teeth could break its skin. With a hard tug, her hood was ripped off and her curls expanded outward, but before she could face her attacker, her brother's voice ignited with fury. It was her brother, Charlie, the entire time. "God dammit, Noreen!" he barked at her. "What the hell were you lookin' in father's room for? I could've killed you!"

Noreen could not respond, a tight knot formed in her chest from the lack of oxygen and she gasped with quick and shallow gasps. Holding her chest, she gazed up to her brother whose height seemed absolutely massive over her. Her breathing slowly returned to normal as she watched him, but Charlie's continued with deep and heavy pants, his arms hanging away from his sides. He reached one of his hands up to push back the filthy hair that draped over his eyelids to see Noreen's expression in the moonlight. After dropping his hand to his side, he allowed his body to crumble beside her in the dirt. "Noreen, I-I'm-m s-so sorry," he stuttered, "p-please for-forgive me."

Noreen took her brother in her arms and stroked his hair in a soothing manner. "It's alright, Charlie, I know you didn't mean to hurt me. It was my fault, I shouldn't have been so curious. I should've warned you- I should've knocked."

Tears fell off of Charlie's cheeks and dripped onto Noreen's shoulder in the same location where her father's dried blood resided. It was the first time she had seen her brother cry. "I was going to kill you," Charlie whispered, this time without stuttering.

"You thought you were protecting father. I would've done the same."

Charlie leaned out of their embrace. He sat on his heels with his hands covering his face to hide his tears. "I wasn't in the room because I was emptying father's bed pan. I thought I could leave the door unlocked for a few minutes while I quickly emptied it... When I saw a dark figure peeking through the hatch, I thought..." Charlie paused and lowered his hands from his face, "I thought it was one of *them*. I could not let the Government have him, not again. I knew, Noreen, that if they took him, it would be all my fault. It would've killed me to have them take him again, so I tried to kill the cloaked figure instead. I tried to kill you!"

"Stop it, Charlie," Noreen silenced him, "stop this talk right now! You go back in there, lock the door behind you and forget this ever happened. Promise me, Charlie."

Charlie dropped his head toward his chest, unwilling to meet his sister's eyes, so she repeated her command and waited. After several seconds, Charlie eventually mouthed his word of promise and helped Noreen to her feet. She wiped the dirt from her hands and knees and walked on the balls of her feet through the doorway.

With the limited light, her brother did not see the trail of blood Noreen's heels left in the grass nor the awkward way she walked on her toes into the kitchen. He followed, oblivious of her struggle, holding the chamber pot tightly in his grasp. He stepped past Noreen once they reached the kitchen and headed straight for the steps leading to the basement. Curling his knuckles around the edge of the hatch, he lifted open the secret door and stepped down.

As her brother closed the door above him, he mouthed a single word to Noreen, a word she had been waiting for: *Vodka*. After she nodded her appreciation, the hatch to her father's hideaway closed and, for a brief moment, Charlie's key blocked all light from radiating out of the hatch. Noreen waited for the flickering candle in her father's room to blow out before she covered the wooden door with the carpet and grabbed the lantern that still remained on the floor beside her.

Gazing to her left, she saw the only pair of shoes she owned stacked beside the front doorway. She crawled over to her shoes, regretting not putting them on sooner, and picked them up before she stood and jogged the few steps back into the adjacent room. Once in the kitchen, Noreen snatched the same washcloth she had used to wipe the floor before supper off the stone countertop and raced out the back door.

She flinched at the sound of the broken hinges slamming to a close behind her but did not look back. Instead, she blew out her lantern's candle and slid into the shadows alongside the stack of firewood. While sitting on the ground, Noreen examined her abrasions. Thankfully, from what she could see by use of the moonlight, the bleeding had stopped, and the cuts on her heels appeared to be merely flesh wounds. The fact that her cuts were minor injuries, though, did not stop her from wrapping them in the worn piece of cloth for extra padding and protection.

Using her teeth, Noreen ripped the fabric into two strands and wrapped the torn pieces around her heels. She managed to tuck the ends into parts of the cloth that were already wrapped around her foot. For further insurance, she removed her socks from her shoes and stretched them over her bandages to keep them in place. She placed her shoes on her feet before she clutched the door knob above her and held it for support to help her stand. For a second time, Noreen pulled the hood of her cloak over her curls. With her entire body now hidden inside, Noreen moved forward, her figure becoming one with the darkness.

She ran on her toes through the high grass behind her home, holding the edge of her hood between her thumb and index finger to keep her face and hair completely covered beneath the moonlight. She tried to find the roots at her feet but was unable to see the ground. By keeping her head down, though, she was able to find the dirt path at the end of the fields, the path that marked the end of her concealment.

It did not take long before Noreen arrived at the open turf, but she knew not to slow her pace. Her figure was now fully illuminated beneath the moonlight, and she could not afford to slow down until she reached the correct row of neighboring cottages, the eighth row down. It felt like an eternity before she reached the shadows of the backstreet between the compacted cottages, but despite their provided darkness, Noreen knew she was not safe from watchful eyes until she reached her destination.

After three left turns, Noreen came to the end of her journey where the final alleyway narrowed to a V. She positioned herself before the touching cottages with the front of her shoes directly up against the corner. She moved from her position, like the horse in the game of Chess, three spaces back and two spaces to the right until she stood over a large, rickety piece of stone. Before stepping off the piece, Noreen glanced behind her to confirm her solitude. Once certain that she was alone, she stepped aside and bent down to the floor.

Similar to the secret door leading to her father's hideaway, the piece of stone had to be lifted upward. Though, the stone in the ground lead to nowhere, it buried the key to The Cove, a silver bottle opener. Not wasting any time, Noreen grabbed the tool and scrambled back toward the alley's corner. She counted from the bottom stone up to the eleventh until finding the anticipated socket between the matching stacked tablets. She shoved the bottle opener inside the cracks of the adjacent walls and turned the device counterclockwise. As expected, a solid crack split down the center of the V-shaped corner, and the two cottage walls parted inward.

A dim light shone out of the hidden passageway and illuminated the alley's corner, giving Noreen the opportunity to use its light to return the key to its original hiding place and arrange the stone back over it, as though fitting the final piece correctly into what seemed like a life-sized puzzle. Noreen looked over her shoulder once more before she slipped between the cottage walls and closed the stones behind her. She moved briskly down the long path of the cylinder-shaped tunnel while untying the strings of her cloak from around her neck. Rather than walking, Noreen sprinted down the curvy path and reached the circular stairs in no time. She skipped down every other step to increase her speed until reaching a round, wooden door at the bottom of the stairwell. With the black cloak now draped over her forearm, she knocked on the entrance to The Cove and waited.

Chapter 5

*T*he eye slit at the very center of the door slid open to reveal the John Doe's narrowing, green eyes. Noreen noticed a great pulling tension in the muscles between his brows, and she knew they were silently scolding her for her tardiness. The John Doe asked for the password, as required, and Noreen answered him. "lloq'e." Her voice was soft and timid.

"You're late," John declared. Noreen could hear him unchaining and unbolting the several locks that secured The Cove's secret entrance, but as she began her apology, the forceful opening of the door silenced her. She stepped into the room and passed him without making a sound.

"Lawrence has been at the beer tap since we opened," John said as he rolled up the sleeves of his checkered flannel. He took the cloak from Noreen's hands and handed her an apron. The thick muscles in his forearms flexed as he held the piece of clothing out to her. "So I don't think he's noticed that you haven't been here."

Noreen half smiled at him, knowing that the John Doe usually worked the beer tap, not Lawrence. This was not the first time he covered for her, but like always, before she could thank him, he walked away without expressing a single emotion. He sat back on his stool and lifted one knee until the sole of his shoe sat comfortably on one of its horizontal supports.

She watched him as she tied the apron around her waist, but he did not seem to notice. The Doe's gaze dropped to his palm as he examined his calluses. He picked at the corns while also thickening the veins in his forearm as he put pressure on his hand. Like the end of the alleyway, his upper body formed a V with his chest being the broadest of his frame. On the stool, his body hunched forward, making it harder for Noreen to evaluate him, but she did not need him to stand to know his impressive stature. He was quite massive, even compared to her own height, as she reached one-fourth shy of two meters. She knew that he often ducked beneath doorways and looked far down upon those he spoke with, but never once, when he stood, did he slouch to make himself seem shorter. He took pride in his height, Noreen could see it, but he never once flaunted it with arrogance.

John continued to look down until the voice of a man sitting by the bar reached above The Cove's normal and required whisper. His head snapped upward at the sound causing his dark bangs to whip to the side and reveal the tension still lingering between his brows. His eyes instantly caught Noreen's, and his brows narrowed further. "Well, what are you waiting for?" he growled through his teeth. He stood and huffed past her. Noreen could tell the drunken man agitated him, so she simply moved out of his way rather than answering him. She continued to stare after the Doe as he approached the drunk.

Using one of his fists, John snatched the shoulder of the loud man's jacket and whispered something in his ear, but the man was far too intoxicated to comprehend. Despite John's aggressive stance, the man grabbed at the hand on his shoulder, but John's grip never left him. Rather than peering down at the drunk, John stared directly behind the bar at Lawrence who simply nodded back to him. At Lawrence's silent command, John lifted the man off the stool and started for the door, dragging the drunk behind him.

Realizing they were heading in her direction, Noreen dodged between the pair of double doors at her side to avoid the potential collision. She made it safely behind the flaps, but once on the other side, her attention refocused. She stood in the opening of the stock room where shelves among shelves of beer and liquor funneled down in what seemed like a never ending path of booze. Each type of alcohol was separated, with the most expensive liquor kept on the left side for good luck and the cheaper booze kept on the right. Since Noreen helped stock the shelves each month when her neighbor Irma Anderson arrived with her homemade liquor, she knew exactly where the different types of alcohol were kept.

    The vodka, Noreen thought to herself, was kept on the top shelf about twenty-three paces forward between the whiskey and rum, but she did not have time to retrieve it now. Instead, Noreen grabbed a stein of dark beer from the bottom shelf on the right side of the room, using the light from the doorway to guide her. She knew Lawrence would expect her to sell the cheapest, most tasteless crap they had to the drunkest customers, pretending it was among the most valuable to make what Mr. Colt called a "smart profit."

    Glancing down at her clean apron, she tilted the handle of the stein toward her and spilled the beer in patches onto herself while also lowering the amount of booze she held in the glass. She needed to appear as though she had already been working among the sloppy drunks. After leaving the backroom, Noreen walked through the double doors and reentered the bar scene. She knew most of the drunken men and women who occupied the room, though most were fathers and husbands wasting their money on the cheap liquor. Despite her familiarity with her neighbors, Noreen was forbidden to ever mention The Cove to them outside of the bar itself; in fact, it was never mentioned by anyone outside the bar at all.

    The discreetness of The Cove was overwhelming, regardless of the number of her neighbors drinking inside. Somehow, John always kept the place under control and quiet, so the Government would not find them. The most noise heard usually came from either the customer's routine whispers or from their slurps of the foam that floated over top of their freshly brewed beers. While her job was to serve the customers, they were always the farthest thought from her mind. Most important to Noreen was to keep a watchful eye on Lawrence.

She looked first toward the bar, and like John had told her, Lawrence was manning the beer tap. The wrinkles around the beast's mouth caved into his skin as he expressed the same fake smile he wore to please his customers. He had a small, pouching stomach that was covered by his dark red vest and black pants, but Noreen could always pinpoint his imperfections. His gray, thin hair was slicked back from the oil and grease that coated his scalp from a long overdue need of washing while his forever partially closed right eye twitched every so often. According to what John had once told her, Lawrence's drooping eye was the result of an unevenly matched fight that Lawrence initiated and lost. It seemed to twitch whenever his impatience got the best of him, a flaw of frequent occurrence.

To Noreen, Lawrence was the worst kind of man; a man who beat her regularly and used a sick and twisted sort of persuasion in attempts at seducing her. Luckily, though, with John usually around after closing, Lawrence had yet to succeed having his way with her. If it was not for the Doe, Noreen would never have been able to continue working at The Cove nor would she have been able to provide for her family and steal the numbing morphine her father desperately requested.

While Noreen did not understand why John always bothered to protect her, she never questioned him and neither did Lawrence. John's strength was his insurance; he was The Cove's best asset after the booze itself. He guarded and protected its privacy by regulating the noise from the inside. Lawrence could not afford to lose him, and neither could she.

The beast finally caught Noreen's stare. She mimicked his phony smile and waved to him from across the room, but rather than appearing excited at her arrival, his slanted eye twitched and his lips formed a scowl. As he continued to watch her, Noreen leaned down to her first customer of the night and began her perfected act. "Good evening Mr. Burns, you havin' a good time tonight?"

"Mighty fine, Noreen, mighty fine," the man whispered back to her, pausing casually to hiccup, "but you know my dear, I told you to call me by my first name, that is unless you have forgotten it?"

Mr. Burns pretended to look sad as he puffed out his lower lip in a teasing manner. Noreen played along as usual, though she was in fact quite disgusted by her neighbor's impropriety. "Now *Eddy*," she emphasized his name each time she spoke it, "you know I could never forget your name. Why you're one of my favorite customers!" Mr. Burns smiled, revealing numerous stained teeth as Noreen continued. "Now, how would you like to have some of this tasty dark beer, *Eddy*?"

The intoxicated man hiccupped again, and he slapped his coins on the table. "Fill me up pretty lady, and you better not stray too far once you do!"

"Don't worry, Mr. Burns," Noreen continued to tease him as she swiped the coins and poured the beer into his glass, "I've got my eye on you!"

He took a swig and smiled again, this time even wider, too drunk to notice the beer's lack of flavor. "Splendid."

Noreen leaned away from Eddy and straightened her back until she was upright once again. She looked back toward the beer tap to find Lawrence, but he was no longer there. His sudden absence terrified her, and she could feel her heart almost pounding out of her chest. Looking around the quiet room, Noreen wished more sound could distract her from her paranoia. She scrambled her eyes through the crowd of soft spoken drunks in search of Lawrence, but he was nowhere to be found. "Noreen!" A voice whispered harshly from behind her. Noreen flinched at the sound of her name but relaxed once she realized that the person calling her was not Lawrence. "What the hell are ya doin' girl'? Sleepin'?"

Noreen softly cleared her throat to calm her nerves before she responded to her friend. "Hey Mags."

Mags smiled and laughed under her breath, her bubbly, happy nature seeming completely surreal to Noreen. "You know, if you weren't always in such a daze you would've noticed how Lawrence always looks at you," she winked, "unless you have noticed, and that's why you're always so tense."

She patted her apron with her free hand to wipe off her palm while she balanced a large tray full of beer steins above her head. Though Noreen considered Mags one of her closest friends, half the time Noreen could not make sense of what she talked about on the first try; she reckoned it was because Mags stole liquor from Lawrence as well but for her own consumption. "I don't really see where you're goin' with this Mags," Noreen commented.

Mags lowered her tray onto the table in front of her and began distributing the drinks to her customers, spilling beer on herself in the process. Noreen helped distribute the beer as Mags whispered into her ear. "Mr. Colt silly! He's always eyein' you like you're meat or somethin'. I'm just sayin', I think he likes you."

Noreen tensed; her friend did not know how Lawrence treated her since she always left the bar in the mornings before Noreen did in order to arrive home before her husband woke. "I mean, he is a lot," Mags chuckled again, "and I mean *a lot* older, but you're what, twenty?"

"Eighteen," Noreen corrected her.

"Really? Oh, that's not too bad."

Noreen could not tell if her friend was joking. "Don't be disgusting," she answered utterly repulsed. Not only was Lawrence a vile and inhuman creature, but he also was more than three times her age. Vomit regurgitated in her throat, and she forced herself to swallow it.

As Noreen went to give away the last beer on the tray, Mags grinned a cheesy, teasing smile and grabbed the stein out of her hands to take a drink. After several gulps, she wiped her lips and handed the beer to the absentminded customer. "HA, I guess you're right," she finally responded, "I mean what am I kidding, you'd never go for an old geezer like that. You have to admit, though, he is the sweetest, ain't he?"

Noreen glared at her, but Mags continued. She was visibly not in the right state of mind to argue with, so Noreen chose to ignore her. "Oh put a smile on your face ya sour puss! I love ya, but you need to lighten up every once in a while." Mags looked around the bar and then back at Noreen. She giggled slightly louder than before, as she turned to walk away with the tray under her arm. "See," she nodded to her side, "he's starin' at cha right now!"

Noreen tensed again, and she felt her hands beginning their nervous vibrations. She shoved them quickly into her apron pockets as she turned her head to the side and scanned the crowd for Lawrence. Unlike before, she found him standing beneath the large, antique painting that stretched across the entire width of the far wall. From end to end, the canvas portrayed an enormous creature whose actual size, Noreen was told, far greatened in length than the painting itself. To Noreen, the whale resembled more of a monster than a mammal, but whatever it was, she saw nothing but power as she looked at it, something she knew that Lawrence believed he had over her.

Scanning her eyes down the painting, she found Lawrence conversing quietly with a few of his customers just beneath the whale's stomach. Noreen watched as he handed each of the men shots of liquor while keeping one for his own satisfaction. His attention was not upon the men standing around him, though; his focus never left Noreen and neither did his toothy smile. He was a sly magician in Noreen's eyes. He hypnotized his audience with such a deceitful, attracting performance, while he disguised his wicked tricks far beneath the surface. He winked with his droopy eye at her and raised his glass, toasting her before taking a shot of the clear liquid and swallowing it down his throat.

Chapter 6

"*M*ags? Come on, wake up. Come on Mags, *please!*" Noreen shook her friend's motionless body, but it was useless; the side of her cheek leaned against one of the small tables beside the bar and her messy red hair covered her closed eyelids. Her arms lay on the table beside her head, her hand still holding the dirty rag she had been using to clean the table tops. The bar had only been closed for nine minutes, and Mags had already blacked out on the table's hard surface.

Lawrence usually stayed away from Noreen until after Mags left each morning, so he was busy in the backroom restacking the unused liquor back onto the shelves. The other two bartenders had already left, and John was sent away, leaving Noreen and Mags alone in the once crowded room.

Fear flooded through Noreen's shaking body at the thought of being alone with Lawrence while Mags remained unconscious on the table. She wished John was still there to protect her, but Lawrence had already sent him down the road to make an exchange with Irma for some of her expensive moonshine. Noreen knew the real reason he sent John away, though, and that reason made her stomach churn. With Mags, her only hope, now blacked out drunk on the table, Noreen knew it was all over for her and her friend. Noreen would be beaten, and Mags would be fired; however, with Lawrence busy restocking in the backroom, there was still a chance for Mags if Lawrence thought she had already left…

Deciding her friend's fate for her, Noreen lifted Mags under her armpits to drag her to an inconspicuous location.

As she adjusted her grip, a shooting pain surged throughout Noreen's lower back, causing her to drop her friend on the floor. Noreen cursed herself as she watched her friend's body flop onto the stones.

Pausing for a moment, Noreen checked around the room to ensure their privacy before grabbing Mags' hands and dragging her around the corner of the bar. The thought of Charlie dragging her from the hall flashed a sense of déjà vu across her mind, and she wondered whether Mags would be angry or grateful for being dragged over the rough, uneven stones. Another thought crossed Noreen's mind that swayed her opinion. *At least Mags is wearing shoes.*

Noreen hauled her friend behind the bar and gently set her arms down to her sides. She opened up the largest cabinet beneath the bar's long countertop and began removing the mugs and drinking cups from inside and onto the floor beside her. Each time the glasses touched, a clanking sound disrupted her silent process and triggered Noreen's hands to shake even harder. Suddenly, Lawrence's voice echoed through the bar as he called her name from the stock room. Noreen flinched, causing the glass mug in her hand to crash to the floor and shatter into thousands of tiny pieces.

A loud bang came from the stockroom and footsteps immediately followed. "What the hell just happened out there?" More footsteps followed. "Noreen, that better not of been you breakin' my precious china!" His voice was getting closer and closer and Noreen began to panic. Hurriedly, she rolled Mags' unmoving body and stuffed it quickly inside the cabinet, unintentionally allowing her friend's head to smack against the back of the cupboard as Noreen scrambled to hide her. "Nooreeen," Lawrence stretched out the vowels in her name as he called after her playfully, "come out, come out, wherever you are."

Noreen shut the cabinet doors and leaned against them, praying that Lawrence would not find her. She stared at her shaking palms and waited. Glass shards crunched beside her, and Noreen whipped her head toward the sound. As she did so, something hard smacked the side of her face, sending her entire body to the floor. "You gone clean that up?" The playful tone in Lawrence's voice was no longer present, and he now seemed to be barking at her.

Noreen opened her eyes to see a pair of brown shoes crunching more of the broken glass in front of her. Raising her eyes, Noreen caught Lawrence's malevolent grin focused directly upon her. "I said, are you gone clean that up?" His expression turned to a frown after he repeated himself for a second time. Noreen nodded, unable to speak. "Oh, I know you will," Lawrence took another step forward and crushed more of the glass beneath his boot, "and you know how I know?"

He stomped relentlessly on the broken glass, prompting Noreen to retreat backward with her arm shielding her face from the flying shards. She slid away from the beast, an arm's length at a time, but he continued to pursue her until he trapped her in a corner between the wall and the edge of the counter. He dropped down to his knees and viciously grabbed hold of Noreen's jaw in his fingertips. He yanked her toward him until her face was merely inches from his. "I said, do you know how I know?" His ghastly breath filled Noreen's lungs.

Fear took over her and she was unable to answer him nor call for help. She shifted her eyes helplessly around the room, in search of John, wishing he was still there to help her. Lawrence spat on her lips to refocus her attention back to him. "I know cause I gone show you how to do it!"

At Lawrence's threat, Noreen began squirming furiously in every direction, but he was too strong and she could not escape him. He maneuvered himself beneath her and cursed Noreen as he covered her nose and mouth with one of his hands, using the other to grab hold of her left wrist, just like he had when he broke it the first time. Noreen's frightened and uneven breaths became gasps for air under his palm as he forced her wrist down onto the broken shards. The pain from the glass piercing through her skin accelerated her breaths until they transformed into a repeated process of hiccups and chokes.

    She sat in Lawrence's lap unable to break free while the tears flooding her eyes blurred her vision. Each time she blinked, she saw more red cover the floor, more of her blood spilling from her wounds. "See we're workin' together you and me, cleanin' up the mess you made." Lawrence whispered in her ear, following his sentence with numerous vulgar threats he promised he would do to her.

    By the time Lawrence freed her wrist from the glass, it was too late; her **L** tattoo was covered in blood and filled with shards of glass that poked out of her skin. But as Lawrence adjusted his seating, Noreen found her chance to revolt. She grabbed the nearest shard with her uninjured hand and knifed it into the outside of his upper thigh. Lawrence shouted in pain and freed Noreen to pull the glass out of his skin. Noreen gasped for air as she dove onto the floor and started to crawl away from him. She felt more and more glass crunching beneath her as she used her uninjured forearm to pull her weight across the floor.

    Unexpectedly, she felt a hand grab hold of the bottom of her dress and tug her back toward her worst nightmare, back to Lawrence. Desperate to save herself, Noreen reached for one of the cabinet doors and grabbed its handle. In retaliation, Lawrence drove his fist down onto Noreen's spine and she screamed out in pain. She no longer cared if The Cove was discovered or if the Government found them, she screamed and cried as loud as she could, hoping that someone would find them and save her. As she screamed, Noreen kicked at her attacker, but her vision was worsening at every blink from the lack of oxygen and her eyes began to funnel at their corners to black.

    Noreen stopped fighting her employer as her breathing worsened. She thought about her wrist and the **L** tattoo she had been so proud of since it was engraved on her skin, the tattoo which was given to her by the Government and that represented who she was and where she belonged. The tattoo had distinguished her from those in the Town of East and from the Right Handers who resided there, but now it was erased by the wounds forever engraved over it. She no longer felt pride as a Left Hander but a sense of detachment from the fellow Left Handers of her town. She began to feel exactly how she perceived her friend John Doe to feel every day, disconnected from the rest of their small, abandoned world.

As Noreen's thoughts drifted, her consciousness did as well, hearing only her own wheezes hiccupping from within her throat. She allowed her eyes to close as she could no longer feel Lawrence's grasp on her dress or even the ground beneath her. She rather floated now above the surface, with her head bobbing like one of the buoys bouncing in the harbor, up and down and up and down, until she felt nothing at all.

Chapter 7

"*D*id anyone see you on your way back?" a hushed, yet distant voice echoed down the hall.

"No," a deeper voice echoed back.

"Good, good… Are you sure?"

"I believe so, it was still dark out since the sun hadn't risen yet."

"Good, good," the same first voice repeated itself, sounding increasingly more familiar.

"Before I leave, please give this to Mr. Satchell. I figure he is the reason why Noreen takes this stuff, and I agree he needs it more than Lawrence does," a short pause followed the deep voice.

"Yes, I will make sure he gets it. Thank you, Eli."

"I will come back in a few hours to see how she is doing, and I will bring some vegetables from my orphanage's garden in repayment for your hospitality."

"Oh Eli no, there is no need for that, you have already done more than enough for our family; we should be paying you!" Noreen could now make out her mother's and John's voices from the other room, but wondered why her mother was referring to him as Eli and why John had been staying at their home.

"I know how scarce food is, Mrs. Satchell." Noreen pictured his emerald eyes as she listened to John speak to his mother in the hall, keeping her own eyes closed beneath their lids. "I will be back soon." John ended the conversation.

Noreen's eyes fluttered open at the sound of the front door slamming shut to see the gray stoned ceiling above her. It looked much different during the daytime than at night. The stones were lighter in color, and Noreen could even make out the chipped imperfections of each individual rock. As she opened her mouth to yawn, she felt soreness in her throat. She started to lift her hand to touch her neck but stopped with her arm still lying on the cot. A terrible pain surged through her entire left side, and she remembered her fight with Lawrence.

Her pulse accelerated, and she blinked back the tears that welled at the corners of her lids. She attempted to sit up by pushing her palms into the cot, but she collapsed back down in pain. Noreen continued to stare at the gray above her, unable to move. After what seemed like a lifetime, she heard her mother walk into the room and gently sit beside her. The woman pushed Noreen's curls from her face with her cold fingertips as she sat in silence.

"Mom," Noreen cleared her throat as she continued to stare at the gray stones above her. The memory of Lawrence yanking her jaw flashed across her conscious. "What happened to me?"

Mrs. Satchell paused and placed a hand on her daughter's arm. Noreen winced and the woman removed her sympathetic touch, while apologizing to her daughter. "Noreen," she struggled to hold herself together, "I had no idea things were that bad. I am your mother, I should have known!"

"No mom, it's not your fault."

Mrs. Satchell cupped her daughter's face with her hands and turned Noreen's head toward her. Though her mother's actions caused her great pain, she wanted desperately to view something other than the dull shade of grey above her. "I love you so very much Noreen," her mother choked. She continued to talk, but Noreen failed to listen. She could only focus on her appearance, as the woman looked like a completely different person than the one she had always known. Rosacea darkened her cheekbones down to her chin and large puffy bags swelled beneath her eyelids. For the first time, her mother looked as old as her dying father. "And that is why I am forbidding you to work there again." Noreen heard her mother finish.

She removed her hands from Noreen's cheeks and placed them in her lap. Noreen followed her hands downward as she examined the rest of her appearance. She wore the same clothes since the last time Noreen had seen her. "You know why I-"

"Yes, I know why!" Mrs. Satchell raised her voice, silencing Noreen in an instant. The woman was breaking down for the first time in front of her daughter. "Noreen, you better listen to me," she choked again, "I don't care what your father asks of you, you are to never set foot in that place again, do you hear me? You mean too much to me."

Noreen nodded without lifting her head from the cot. "I'm fine, mother, really."

"No, Noreen, you are not fine," Mrs. Satchell shook her head, "I was the one who undressed you into that nightgown, so don't you think for a second that I didn't see all those cuts and bruises, some of which are already yellowing which means you've been cursed with them for some time now. How could you not tell me how much that man hurt you?" The question barely escaped her lips. "If the Government sees you like this, well, I just don't know. Why, you could pass as a…" she swallowed, "I mean who knows what they might think!"

"I'm not that bad, mother, I'll be better in a couple days, I promise!" Noreen tried to lift her head to show her mother her strength, but the tension in her shoulders caused her muscles to spasm. She laid back down on the cot in defeat.

Realizing what her daughter was trying to do, Mrs. Satchell stood and turned her back to her. "You are not strong enough," she began as Noreen gently turned her head in different directions to relieviate the stiffness in her neck, "you have been unconscious for two days and have not eaten."

Noreen whipped her head to look at her mother, "I what?" she winced at the pain from her reaction.

"Don't worry, I brought you something to eat." Mrs. Satchell lifted a small bowl off the wooden tray on the floor beside her and turned back to face the cot. Noreen's heart thumped rapidly, still in shock from the news, but she calmed slightly after seeing food for the first time in days. She had not realized how hungry she was until her mother began spoon feeding her the bean filled soup. The woman cradled Noreen's head with one of her hands to provide the support she needed to swallow the broth.

Noreen could taste kidney beans and lima beans, while the rest just seemed to blend into a single flavor. The warmth of the thick liquid eased the soreness of her throat and, somehow, she could feel the soup as it reached her chest and pooled in the empty pit of her stomach. There were chopped tomatoes in every bite and some sort of leafy vegetable that felt slippery on her tongue. It was the best thing she had ever tasted.

After finishing the bowl, Mrs. Satchell left the room for several minutes, only to return with her husband's bedpan and a rag in her hands. She wiped down the bedpan in a quick swipe using the cloth before she lifted the quilt off of Noreen's lower half. Noreen grimaced, "mother, I can't."

"Yes, you can," Mrs. Satchell corrected her, turning the three words into one, "your father does this every day, so you can at least do it for the next couple."

"But, I can't use *his*," Noreen accentuated the last word of her statement.

"And why not? I don't think he'd mind, he has no other choice *but* to share. Now, I'm going to lift your nightgown and take off your underwear and then I'm going to slide the pan underneath you as best I can, okay?"

"Okay," Noreen squeezed her eyes shut, not wanting to believe what was happening.

"Alrighty, once I get the pan under you, I'll tell you when it's safe to go," she paused as she noticed her daughter's horrified expression. "Don't worry, Noreen, I'll turn away when you do."

Noreen kept her eyes closed but peeked once before she relieved herself to ensure that her mother's back was truly turned away from her. When she finished, her mother slowly pulled the pan out from under her and placed it on the floor. She re-clothed her daughter and returned the blanket back onto her lower half. Noreen thanked her and watched as she walked toward the door with the filled chamber pot. Before she exited, Noreen called after her. "Was that John who just left?" Mrs. Satchell stopped halfway through the doorway and turned back to face her daughter. She nodded a 'yes' and Noreen continued. "Why was he here?"

Her mother's head cocked to the side, "do you not remember what happened that night?" she asked with a puzzled expression.

"Not really, I mean, I remember the fighting, and the 'ah' screaming," Noreen swallowed, "and Lawrence and how he-" she hesitated and lifted her arm painfully from under the quilt to examine the dried, bloody cloth that now covered it.

"I understand," Mrs. Satchell stopped Noreen from having to continue. "Something must be done, though. We need to find out how you can get another **L** tattoo without the Government getting involved."

"No, you don't understand," Noreen continued, though she was afraid of her mother's answer, "I need to know if my wrist was the worst thing that Lawrence did to me… I mean my dress was torn and I don't know if you would even know or not, but you said you changed my clothes, and I remember there being a lot of blood and-" Noreen lifted the blanket barely a foot to examine her body within her pale colored nightgown.

"No, sweetheart, he did not rape you." her mother replied. Noreen exhaled a shaky breath and half smiled back at her out of relief and embarrassment. "But your tattoo is destroyed, and that may even be worse."

"Mother!" Noreen protested in disbelief.

"Noreen, if the Government sees those terrible scars, they will think it's some kind of conspiracy or revolt against them or the Left Handers or something. Noreen, they would find a reason to take you if they saw you like this, I know it. God help us that that does not happen. It simply cannot happen because I just won't let it!"

Noreen was able to lift her head to meet her mother's gaze from across the room, now having the strength to do so with the food resting in her stomach. She knew the consequences of missing her tattoo and wished her mother would stop reminding her of them. "I am fully aware of what could happen if people found out that my **L** is gone or if anyone sees me like this, but I would take the label as an outcast or untouchable any day over what else could have happened to me that night!"

"Just look at your father you naïve little child!" Mrs. Satchell yelled at her. She breathed deeply while still clutching the bedpan in her hands. "Do you want the Government to destroy you like they destroyed him? Your father is sick and probably will not even last to the next Day 19. What Lawrence did to you WAS the worst thing he could have done!"

Noreen squeezed her eyes shut. "Can we just drop it please?" she begged.

"I am thankful nothing else happened to you, I am your mother, for God's sake," Mrs. Satchell persisted, "but we must be prepared for the future with you in such a condition."

"Please, just stop!" Noreen finally raised her voice to match her mother's. She opened her eyes just as she noticed her mother apologizing to her between silent lips. Noreen nodded once, accepting her apology, but also not wanting to fight with her any longer. After a pause, Mrs. Satchell left the room and Noreen heard the backdoor smacking closed. She knew her mother was somewhere outside tossing her urine in the grass. She waited for the woman's return to retrieve the wooden tray that still sat on the floor beside her to restate the question that had been left unanswered. "I still don't understand why John was here?"

Mrs. Satchell paused mid-step and shook her head. She smiled sympathetically at her daughter. "John carried you home from…Why, Noreen, that boy saved your life! He did not leave this room for the past two days, ever since he first brought you here! He stayed to make sure that you were going to be alright. I mean he barely slept or ate anything I fed him. He barely even told me what happened that night, I just…" she pointed to the hall, "before I came in here to see you, I finally got the chance to question him about it. He has just been so depressed and, well, I don't think he forgives himself for not being there for you sooner."

Noreen's eyes widened. "No, that can't be. It's not his job to protect me. He shouldn't feel that way!"

Mrs. Satchell sat alongside the edge of the cot once again, careful this time not to touch her daughter. "The only reason he left just now is to bring us food, to repay us! I mean, can you believe it? He saved your life and wants to repay *us* for feeding him, or try to repay us at least." Noreen's lips parted in disbelief as her mother continued, "I imagine he did not think you would be waking up so soon and that's the only reason why he left. He's a good man that Eli, a very good man."

"Wait," Noreen caught her mother's slip, "why did you just call him that?"

"Call him what?" Her jaw tightened.

"Eli, you just called John- Eli. I heard you call him that earlier, too!" Noreen pushed her palms into the cot like she had before, but this time she sat herself up completely until her back rested against the wall.

"I did?" Mrs. Satchell laughed cautiously. "Oh, my mistake, I meant to say John."

Noreen knew her mother was lying and wondered why but chose not press the conversation further since she knew her mother's stubbornness was unbreakable. "How is father?" she changed the subject.

Mrs. Satchell ignored her daughter's question and pulled the quilt up to her shoulders. "Get some rest, sweetheart. John will be back soon with something else for you to eat, and, you never know, Charlie might bring some fish home from the fishery, if it did not sell that is. I know that's rarely ever happened, but we can hope, right?"

This time, Noreen insisted on her mother answering her. "But you did not answer my question. I said how's-"

"Everyone is fine, just fine!" Mrs. Satchell cut her off. "Now get some rest like I told you." She kissed Noreen's forehead before exiting the room. "If you need anything, just shout, okay? I love you."

"I love you, too." Noreen mumbled after the woman closed the door behind her. She turned her head toward the light shining through the window. She could not understand why her mother was acting so strangely. So many of her questions were left unanswered and yet even more rattled inside her brain.

She wondered what time it was? And where was her sister and why hadn't she bothered visiting her? She wanted to know how long it would be until her brother or John came home and why John felt obligated to protect her. And if Charlie would be home soon, then why had John given her mother something to give to 'Mr. Satchell' instead of giving it to Charlie himself? *But what if that something was not meant for Charlie? Who else would it be for?*

Questions hit her like bullets to the brain, and her head began to throb. She hated not knowing what was happening around her and having secrets involving her kept from her knowledge. She wanted desperately to talk to her brother, knowing that his calmness would soothe her. She wanted to thank John but also question him. Most of all, she needed to see her father because she could not help but imagine the worst of what could have happened to him…

Chapter 8

*H*ours later, Noreen woke again. Her head faced the now dark windowsill while her body remained in a seated position and completely motionless. She tilted her head to relieve its stiffness and saw John sitting on the floor with his head leaning against the wall, his eyes closed. His presence startled her, but for some reason it comforted her at the same time. The first thought that came to her mind was that she hoped the floor was not as cold as her father's, as she remembered her conversation with Louise on the night that seemed like forever ago.

John's knees were bent in toward his chest and his muscular forearms rested on them casually. She was relieved to have him resting there, though she could not understand why. Judging his rugged appearance from the cot, Noreen decided that she liked the way the black hairs on his face shaped his jawline when normally she was fond of a clean shaven man. Something about his rough physique appealed to her, though she wished his face did not look so tense.

His eyeballs moved rapidly beneath their lids, giving Noreen the impression that he was awake, and when she whispered his name to test her theory, the Doe's eyes flew open. He turned his head toward her and nearly stumbled before he swung his legs under him and into a kneeling position alongside her cot. "Hey, how you feelin'?" he asked.

Noreen lifted the corners of her lips until they formed a smile. "Fine. I'm feelin' alright."

"Can you move any part of your body without pain?" John's face remained serious as Noreen's frowned in response to his question. John nodded, reading her expression. "You're probably just stiff from lying there for so long."

"Probably," Noreen hoped he was right. She paused, "thank you for everything."

John looked away, as usual when she thanked him, and he leaned back on his heels. Expecting this, Noreen also looked away from him and stared back up at the ceiling above her. The shadows dancing across the stones were a pleasing familiarity, but they could not distract her from her wandering thoughts. "John?" Noreen said his name in the form of a question. She continued to watch his silhouette on the ceiling. A sound grunted from John's throat acknowledging her question, but Noreen already knew he was listening. "There was a reason why Lawrence came after me," she started, having trouble voicing her employer's name.

"Mags is home safe," John interrupted her. Noreen darted her eyes back to John and found him staring at her. His gaze was absolutely mesmerizing and for a brief moment, she forgot to breathe. "I returned to The Cove, after bringing you here, to take care of some things, and I found her in the cabinet," he explained. "She was conscious and was able to tell me where she lived, so I took her home."

"Thank God," Noreen inhaled finally. She ignored the part where he had brushed over his reason for returning to The Cove, though she figured it had something to do with Lawrence. "He did not see Mags in there, did he?" she referred to the beast.

John shook his head. "Good," she felt relieved, "she can't afford to lose that job. She has been trying so hard to save money for her children, if they return home that is." Noreen spoke her thoughts absentmindedly. "I believe they are almost two now, so she should be finding out their handedness very soon. I just hope they are both left handed so they can return home to her. Otherwise, like you, they'll end up in an orphanage since they have no family on the other side."

John shifted his weight, becoming uncomfortable, "I didn't know she had kids."

"Yea, two, twins!" Noreen continued to ramble, oblivious to the Doe's sudden anxiousness, "I met her shortly after she gave birth to them, when she started working at The Cove. She told me about her children by accident, I think. You see, she was drinking then, and I don't think she would have told me if she were sober."

"Is that why she drinks?" John interrupted.

"I believe so, odds are that at least one of her children will be right handed, if not both, and that means they'd have to be sent to the Town of East into an orphanage like I said before." She did not filter her speech before the unidentifiable man.

"I know," John interrupted her again.

"I'm so sorry," Noreen realized she had gone too far. She tried to meet John's eyes but failed to do so. "I didn't mean to bring that up. I guess I'm just nervous."

"Why are you nervous?" He met her eyes once again. Noreen blushed.

"Well," she paused, unsure whether or not to continue, "this is the most you've ever said to me, and I just don't want to say the wrong thing."

His jaw tightened, "Is that because I'm a *Doe*?"

"Of course not!" Noreen shot forward despite the soreness aching through her muscles. She had never called an orphan a 'Doe' before, and his use of the derogatory term shocked her. "It's because we are so, well, I've never talked this much with…"

"With a *Doe*," John finished her sentence.

A lump formed in Noreen's throat from the guilt she had bestowed upon herself. He was right, and they both knew it, but she would never admit it nor would she ever acknowledge his remark. They sat in silence for a long time until Noreen could not bear the awkwardness any longer. "Um," she began, trying to change the conversation back to the one before, "How did you find her? Mags that is."

John eased a bit, obviously relieved Noreen had broken their silence. He breathed out hard, as though from a laugh, and his lips shaped into a crooked smile. "I thought she had already left, but I was wrong," he explained. "She had awoken in the cupboard, still drunk as before, not givin' a damn that she was stuffed inside a cabinet. That's when I heard her singin'."

Noreen smiled, thankful that John was not one to hold grudges for the foolish comments she made. "What was she singing?" she asked.

John shook his head, "I have no idea. I could barely understand anything she was saying. I'm surprised I even got an address out of her to take her home! Luckily, our addresses aren't that hard to remember."

"What was it, 12?"

"Close, house number 14."

Noreen burst into laughter as she pictured her friend singing aimlessly in the cabinet, but a shooting pain in her spine disrupted her joy and added a sudden tension to her breaths. John sprung up to reach for Noreen's hand but resisted grabbing hold of her wrapped abrasions. He crouched impatiently by her side, waiting as Noreen collected herself and forced a smile. "I'm fine, I am, really!" she lied.

"You don't have to put on an act in front of me," John shook his head. "You don't have to pretend to be so brave all the time, I won't think any less of you."

"I don't act brave, I am brave!" Noreen became suddenly agitated with him.

"I know you are. You wouldn't show up every night at The Cove if you weren't, and you wouldn't take all those beatings either. I am just saying no one is brave or strong all the time, but I respect you for trying to be." He looked down upon Noreen who held her back with a single hand, but she looked away from him before he could say anything further to annoy her.

She looked straight ahead at a crack cutting through the stones. "Is that why you baby me so much? Because you think I am not strong or brave enough?"

"Of course not!" John rebutted.

"Then how else would you know that I was in trouble that night? Huh?" Noreen could not help but return her gaze back to John. Her voice increased in volume as she built up momentum. "You left The Cove but came back. Why else would you come back?"

John clenched his fists and straightened his back, though his height already towered far above her. "I came back to check on you," he responded. Noreen remained quiet, forcing him to elaborate. "I don't trust Lawrence alone with you. I had a feeling that he sent me to make the exchange so he could be alone with you. I was trying to protect you, Noreen, I was trying to protect your honor! It had nothing to do with your capabilities; I know how strong willed and independent you are, but I also know what Lawrence is capable of, and he is someone you could never handle on your own!"

Noreen swallowed once John finished his explanation and bowed his head toward the floor. She could not respond to him, she had no idea how, so they remained silent again for what seemed like hours.

Legs crossed and shoulders relaxed, John leaned against the wall beside the small, rectangular windowsill as he stared out of its frame. He wore a serious expression that was accentuated by the sharp angles of his jawline and, with his eyes squinting into the darkness, Noreen guessed he was in search of something that did not exist. He wound two of his fingers in the loop of his jeans near his hipbone, bending his left elbow outward and his wrist in. She felt envious of his ability to bend and turn his wrist in every direction while hers was wrapped inside a tightly wound bandage. She had once believed that after Lawrence broke her wrist for the first time that it would never be harmed again. Her belief, however, was an ignorant fallacy she had foolishly trusted.

Peering up from John's wrist, Noreen found herself staring back into his eyes. He raised an eyebrow slightly and lifted his torso off the wall. "Here, let's see if you can stand," John said as he stepped toward her. He touched Noreen's arm, and she flinched. "I'm sorry," he quickly apologized.

Noreen inhaled deeply and lifted the corners of her lips to indicate her forgiveness, though she still remained in pain. "It's alright," she lied, "just let me try this on my own."

John nodded and gently removed the quilt before extending his arms out beside her ribs if she were to need his assistance. His arms remained in the air as he squatted beside her, though he kept them distant enough not to touch. Ignoring him, Noreen pushed her elbows into the cot, rather than using her left hand, and slid her legs over the edge of the mattress. John smiled at her efforts, but Noreen hardly noticed. Her focus concentrated on a single focal point in front of her, the second button down on John's black and blue checkered flannel.

Since the old mattress lacked a base, it rested against the uneven stones, making it lower to the ground and harder for Noreen to lift herself. By holding her bandaged wrist toward her chest, she attempted to use her right hand as a support while rotating herself to face the cot and balancing her weight on her knees. Not foreseeing such a horrific failure, Noreen gasped at the sudden sharp pain that pierced through her lower back and briefly paralyzed her twisted spine. She found herself tumbling downward, but before her body could hit the floor, John's arms wrapped around her and broke her fall. Once again John had come to her rescue, but as she gazed up at him, Noreen felt suddenly uncomfortable.

She had never been so close to a Doe in her entire life and as she continued to stare into his eyes, her heart raced faster and faster. She wondered if he could feel its thumping through his hold on her, but his expression did not seem to acknowledge it. He remained silent until he sat Noreen carefully back onto the cot and lifted the quilt over her. "Are you alright?" he asked as he shifted his chest over her to pull the blanket further up her torso.

Noreen did not respond or, rather, she could not respond to him. She could not understand why he cared for her so intently, unless, *maybe he cared more than she thought. That, of course, would be impossible, for he was a John Doe! He lived in an orphanage separate from the rest of the community because he had no family in the Town of West, no father here to pass down his surname, which meant that he had no identity! Any man or woman declared a John or Jane Doe from birth was forbidden to get involved with anyone other than a Doe like themselves, and both she and this John knew that. So what was his motive then? Why else treat her so generously?*

His gaze silenced her subconscious considerations out of fear that he could read her thoughts. She narrowed her eyes and glared at him with suspicions of her 'rescuer'. "John," Noreen muttered, "why are you still here?"

John's torso remained over her with his hands pressed into the cot at her sides. "What do you mean?" He narrowed his eyes to match Noreen's but out of confusion rather than anger.

"You know exactly what I mean." Noreen eyed the positioning of his arms and John immediately removed them. "Yes, I am thankful that you came back to save me and my honor, but why are you still here now? I don't even know you, yet you keep trying to take care of me like I'm some sort of child!"

John lifted an eyebrow. "Yeah, you're welcome," he responded sarcastically. He folded his arms over his chest while he rested his backside against the edge of the cot.

Noreen fumed with anger. "Oh now you say 'you're welcome'. Every other time I have said thank you in the past, you've ignored me!"

"So that's what this is about," John pushed himself away from the mattress and stood to walk away from her. He punched the wall with his fists before resting his head and palms against the stones. "Why can't you just accept that you've needed help from someone? That you aren't invincible, because no one is. I mean, look at you, Noreen. Lawrence would've torn you apart if-" He stopped mid-sentence and whipped back around to find Noreen staring at him. "That didn't come out right!" he renounced his statement.

"Yes, it did," Noreen removed her left hand from under the quilt and examined her bandages as she spoke, "I know how I look, John, at least how I used to look before the other night. My mom removed the mirror from this room while I was unconscious. But from what I can see of myself, I think I look just about the same as I did before. My skin is still dirty and covered in bruises. I still have scars, now enough to cover my entire body, but with each one of those scars, I can tell you exactly how and where I got them, because I don't forget who has tried to hurt me or my family!"

She looked down upon her body with disgust before she turned her gaze toward John's. Unlike anyone else she knew, he did not look as though he was suffering from malnutrition. In her opinion, there must have been some underlying reason for having such a muscular physique in a town where food was so scarce. "I can see that I am too thin, but that's because I don't get to eat much unlike you, who seems to be well fed in my eyes." Noreen verbalized her silent thought, "I do not know how that is either, unless you steal your food. But, again, I wouldn't know anything about that since you are still practically a stranger to me."

Noreen swallowed, feeling immediate guilt for her accusation. "Look, my intention is not to judge your character, I could care less about how you keep yourself in such good health. I am just trying to explain to you that my untidy appearance is not news to me, and I don't care either because I work way too damn hard to care what people think of me. The reason why I can't accept defeat, though, is because it scares me, John, it really scares me, alright? I don't like having to need anyone to look after me or to care for me. I have enough problems at home to worry about and I need to be strong for my family," she hesitated and inhaled a deep breath, "I am sorry John; I know I owe you my life, but I…"

"No, I'm sorry, Noreen, I shouldn't have said that. God, all we seem to do is argue, and we have barely ever talked to one another," John shook his head. "The truth is, you're not the only one who is nervous. We may have worked together for almost three years now, but I have always been afraid to talk to you. You, Noreen, are my biggest fear, because I think you are the bravest, most beautiful woman I've ever met." His declaration seemed to almost disappear into the unsteady rhythm of his breaths. He cleared his throat anxiously as Noreen simply blinked back at him at a loss of words. The soft deepness of his voice hypnotized her while his sincere words left her speechless. "And you don't owe me anything," John added, "I just want you to be safe."

Noreen rested her tongue on the roof of her mouth, not knowing what to say. "But, why John? You're not supposed to…?"

"I know I am a *Doe*, Noreen, you can say it," he said as he walked over to the windowsill and fully opened the already partially divided flaps. More of the moon's light shined into the room as a result and formed a shadow of John's figure across the floor. "But I must confess something to you, Noreen. I would not be here if not for your father.

I would never have had the bravery to be here facing you otherwise."

At his remark, Noreen jolted upward and threw the quilt off her, only to stumble to the floor in pain. John lunged toward her but was too late to break her fall. Her entire body ached as she lay motionless on the ground and as he gathered her into his arms. Mrs. Satchell and Charlie rushed into the room after hearing the crash of her body against the stones. Louise followed behind them, covering her hands over her mouth to hold in her scream, as she saw her sister for the first time since her return. "You fuckin' Doe!" Charlie pushed John away from Noreen and cornered him in the back of the room. Noreen's head hit the ground as John dropped her to the floor. "What the hell did you do to her?" Charlie screamed.

"What did I do?" John motioned toward Noreen. "Look what you just did to her!"

At his remark, Charlie punched John across the face, but John, for once, did not fight back. Instead, he glared at Charlie as he rolled down his sleeves to wipe the blood that dripped from his jaw. He was taller than Charlie, but not by much, so their glares met one another practically dead on.

Far below them, Noreen watched from the floor. She knew John was much stronger than her brother, she had seen him fight many men on numerous occasions at The Cove, but this time he did not fight back. *Why wasn't he fighting back?*

"Noreen," her mother's panicking voice broke her trance, "are you alright?"

Noreen reluctantly held her mother's gaze as she answered, not wanting to miss the fight between her brother and the Doe. "Yes, yes I'm fine. I'll be fine," she responded. Before she could turn her head back to find the two men, though, they were both already at her sides, ready to lift her off the floor and back onto the cot. Noreen protested as they lifted her effortlessly off the ground. "No, stop! Not there– take me to my father. I must speak with him!"

Charlie's jaw dropped open in disbelief and her mother tensed. John, though, showed no surprise and instead he stared back at her expectantly after a single nod in her direction. Charlie was the first to respond to his sister. "Are you out of your mind? Father is dead!" he lied.

"Take me to father, Charlie, now."

Charlie turned his head sharply toward John and then to his mother who had already begun walking out of the room with the ring of keys jingling in her hand. "Come now, boys, do as she told you," she paused to separate the brass key that opened her husband's door from the number of keys on the ring. "Let's take her to her father."

Chapter 9

*N*oreen could feel Charlie's glare on her as he and John carried her body out of the room, so she deliberately refused to look in his direction. Sconces illuminated the hallway on either side of the wall, providing enough light for her mother to find and lift the dark rug off the secret hatch and unlock the hidden door. The rickety stairs leading to their father's room creaked loudly as Charlie and John stepped down in unison while carrying Noreen in their arms.

A mattress lay in the center of the room on a wooden base that was attached to a semicircular bed frame. Noreen's father rested on the bed with a single, white sheet covering his body up to his chest. A larger, yellow stained blanket folded over his lower half and draped crookedly over the edge with a single tip touching the floor.

A dark red mahogany wardrobe stood in the furthest corner beside a small, matching wooden table with two cushioned chairs on either side. Hanging on the wall opposite the antiques were dusty picture frames and cluttered shelves filled with memoirs dating back to before the Infection. It was the only place in the cottage where they kept personal moments of their past, though Noreen never knew why nor did she ever question it. On the nightstand beside her father's mattress was a partially melted candle whose light battled with the darkness of the windowless room until Mrs. Satchell lit a second candle and placed it on the table beside the wardrobe.

The smoke from the burning wicks did not seem to bother anyone because the very small amount of smoke that emitted into the air rose toward the hatch. Mrs. Satchell walked over to her husband's bedside after placing the ring of keys in her pocket and motioning for Louise to pull up a chair for her sister. She took her husband's hand then and whispered for his eyes to open.

He was much weaker since Noreen had last seen him. His bones were far more brittle than before and his cheeks were considerably more hollow. She tried to picture him like her mother had once described, in the days prior to the Government leakage of the Infection. His stomach was plump, his cheeks rounded, and there was even the presence of a slight double chin that would appear each time he twisted his neck. Unfamiliar to Noreen, the man's hair was always kept short as was his dark brown beard that reached from his sideburns down to his neckline. He used to have dimples, as well, that were apparently identical to Noreen's; the dimples, though, were no longer present, and his beard now matched the grayish, white hairs that shed daily from his scalp.

He had always appeared this way to Noreen, but each day, the man appeared more and more like a lifeless skeleton. It killed her to see her father rot away so quickly before her, and she realized then why her mother had not told her of his condition; her father was going to die soon, much sooner than she thought. "My girl," Mr. Satchell's whispered, "your mother tells me you were in a fight! And from the looks of you, I believe she was tellin' the truth. I can't imagine what the other guy must look like!" He smiled pitifully, failing in his attempt at lightening the mood with his 'joke.' "Sit closer my child." he commanded.

John and Charlie started toward Noreen, but she waved them away, not wanting to appear weak before her father. She stood up slowly without their assistance and though her legs wobbled at first, she was able to press them forward. As she walked toward the bed, Louise lifted the chair and placed it behind her. She lowered herself down, and Mr.

Satchell smiled again pitifully at his daughter. "You're even prettier up close, my child."

Noreen wanted to cry, but she clenched her teeth together. Her father struggled to turn his head and look about the room. "Ah, and I see we have a visitor," he exchanged glances with the only non-family member in the room, "and you must be Elijah, or so I've heard you prefer Eli, correct?"

The three siblings looked at their father in disbelief as John responded to him eagerly. "Yes, sir. It's a pleasure to finally meet you, Mr. Satchell. I have waited a long time for this."

Noreen moved her gaze from her father to John, but she, along with her siblings, remained silent. "Well, we have met before, you just were too young to remember," Mr. Satchell continued to converse with John casually, not even considering to question his blood-stained sleeve and jawline. "I expect the orphanage is treating you well."

"Yes, thanks to you," John moved beside Noreen to get closer to her father. He kneeled on the ground and placed both of his hands on his thigh parallel to the floor. "I have thought many, many times about what I've wanted to say to you when I eventually got the chance to meet you, but my thoughts seem to have escaped me. I guess what I must tell you is that, sir, it is an honor, and I thank you for everything you have done for me!"

"I am pleased to see you again as well, Eli. Your father was a dear friend of mine, and I hope I have lived up to the promise that I had made him so many years ago."

"Yes," John nodded profusely, "You have done more than enough for me, more than I could have ever hoped for! Thank you so very much, sir."

"No need for thanks, a promise is a promise. A man should always stick to his word." Mr. Satchell emphasized each of his words, probably due to the frequent pauses he took to catch his breath. "A good amount of thanks is necessary for you too, though," he looked at Noreen, who stared at him with a puzzled expression, "thank you Eli, for watching over my little girl."

Noreen scowled at John. Not only was she confused, but for some reason she was offended and somewhat heartbroken. "What are you talking about father?" she gritted through her teeth.

"Noreen, there are a lot of things I have hidden from you, Charlie and Louise. And I think it is time that you all know, because I don't have much time left to tell you." Noreen swallowed the saliva that was practically choking her throat while her brother and sister inched closer to their father's bedside. Mrs. Satchell gripped her husband's hand even tighter in what appeared to be a caution, but he ignored her and used all of his strength to continue. "Years ago before the Infection," he began, "when I was around age seven, maybe eight, I befriended a boy who just so happened to be the same age as I was. William Foster was his name, always known to me as Will. He and I became best friends from the very start. It was not until a little over twenty years later or so that I met another important person who is still the most beautiful woman I have ever set eyes on. And eight months later, she and I married. This woman, of course, is your mother."

Noreen glanced at her mother to see her smiling as she held her husband's hand. For a moment, she looked ageless, completely free of worry and heartache, but that moment did not last. Her husband began to hack up blood onto his shoulder causing her smile to fade as she leaned over his chest and wiped the blood off his nightgown with his bed sheet. When she leaned back away from him, though, Noreen noticed that her mother's hand was still intertwined with her father's.

Mr. Satchell started again, reliving a memory of his past, as though his lapse never happened. "My friend Will had married a woman named Charlotte shortly after your mother gave birth to Charlie. And a year after their marriage, Will and Charlotte conceived a baby boy named Elijah, known now to you three as John Doe." He glanced at John briefly before looking back to his children. "A few months later on, August 19th, when your mother was pregnant with Noreen, the Government leaked an airborne disease that infected our entire nation.

Everyone panicked. Our borders were closed, and we were shunned and unwelcomed by every other country on earth. Our families were separated, Will's and our own, and we had to hide for weeks and weeks in this very basement. To survive, I would leave to find food, but what I saw was absolutely horrifying. Hundreds of disfigured people whose skins were covered completely in unrecognizable sores scavenged through the streets in search of food. Fresh bodies piled on the ground like garbage, and after a certain number of days, they were picked up by soldiers and thrown into Government trucks for experimentation. The Government named the disease the Infection because no other could ever be so disastrous.

After segregating everyone into two separate towns based on handedness, with Eli's mother forced to live on the other side, the Government required all Left Handers be marked with an **L** tattoo on their left wrists and the Right Handers be marked with **R**s on their right. This was done to distinguish those who could possibly be infected from those who could not. But the segregation and separation of families unfortunately did not end there.

To prevent any exposure to Right Handers in fear that the Infection would mutate further and destroy a far more prevalent population of peoples, the Government removed all children under the age of two from their parents' homes. Once their dominance was determined, children were either returned to their parents of the same handedness or sent to the opposing side to either live with family or become an unnamed, unidentified orphan forever.

No matter the probabilities, the fact that two Right Handers could bear a left handed child or two Left Handers could bear a right, the Government did not mandate any form of contraception to either group. The horror of losing our children, though, influenced many to refrain from having any at all, whereas a few brave souls attempted to have their children in secret." Mr. Satchell glanced over to his wife briefly without turning his neck, his speech still directed toward his children. "Your mother was one of the brave who gave birth in this very room and on this very mattress to avoid losing any of our children to the Government.

At her insistence, I placed a sock in her mouth to muffle her screams, but she had complications during the birthing process and I was forced to find a doctor to save her." He paused and winced at a sudden pain caused by his wife squeezing his hand with enough force to prevent the circulation of blood to his fingertips.

Noreen glared at the woman, shocked at her blatant attempt to stop her husband's explanation, but she refused to look in Noreen's direction. Mr. Satchell swerved his eyes slowly to his wife and closed them for several seconds in acknowledgement of her unspoken gesture before he turned his gaze back to his children and the Doe sitting before him. He continued again once his wife's grip loosened and his blood began flowing freely through his veins. "Two years went by and our beautiful, little left-handed Noreen was returned to us. But during the following year, whispers of experimentations on the living left-handed adults haunted us, and shortly after, Eli's father and I were taken."

"Does that mean you're a leper, father?" Louise asked. Mrs. Satchell turned her glare from her husband to her daughter. Louise caught her mother's stare, and she immediately bowed her head to the floor.

"No, no I am not," her father answered, "but they thought I was, Louise, because I tried hiding Will from them. My dear friend Will got infected, and *he* became one. You see, after the Right Handers were forced to leave, our food supply became even scarcer, and it was when I was searching for food that I found Will, alone and delusional, scavenging through a..." he hesitated and peeked a glance at Eli but soon turned his gaze away from him. "I will not describe how he looked nor will I explain his desperation any further, but to clarify what I meant, I shall note again that the Infection had taken over his mind and body. Desperate for food, he was no longer the same man that he used to be.

As soon as Will realized that the Infection was taking over his body, he took Eli to the nearest orphanage shortly after Eli was returned to him from the Government as a Left Hander. He did so in order to save his son's life, because they would have killed Eli if he was found with his infected father. My friend knew he was better off dead to his son and he made me promise to look after Eli and make sure he was safe and well cared for. If Will had given the orphanage Eli's birth name, I would have been able to adopt him, but he had not. As a leper, Will had not wanted to be seen and so he dropped off his son on the front steps of the orphanage and never went back. Because Eli was already labeled a John Doe, we could not take him in and raise him as our own."

"I don't remember him," Eli interrupted, "I try, but I can't picture my father's face."

"You couldn't, you were too young," Mr. Satchell concluded, "but, so you know, your father looked just like you! I shall tell you more about him when I speak with you later, alone." Eli nodded and, after a breath, the dying man continued. "The night I arrived back home after seeing Will, I told my wife what happened. I also told her that I planned to meet him at the same time and place the following day to bring him provisions. She did not want me to go and neither did Will, but I had made up my mind and no one could stop me. When I arrived at the community well to meet him, both Will and I were alone, but one of our neighbors spotted us and immediately informed the Government. Sirens sounded throughout the town, and we knew something was terribly wrong. I tried hiding Will by lowering him into the well, but it was too late. Soldiers swarmed us in seconds, and we were taken."

"Weren't you afraid to touch a leper?" Louise questioned. Noreen held her breath as she too wanted to know her father's response.

"No, I should have been, but I was not. He was my friend." Mr. Satchell stared blankly at the wardrobe, lost in his own memories. "We were taken and experimented on. They tested new drugs on us like we were animals," he closed his eyes at the painful memory. "After showing countless side effects from the drugs, they decided I was no longer fit for experimentation and that they needed 'fresher' Left Handers to test. They left me to die in the Forest of Lepers, where they had sent Will to live among the lepers months before. In the forest, I searched and searched for Will, but I could not find him. To this day, I have always regretted not having found my best friend," he paused to hold back the tears forming at the corners of his lids and to take control of his emotions. "Eventually, though, I found a way out of the forest and-"

"How?" Charlie stopped his father, "how did you get out of there alive and not get the Infection?"

Mr. Satchell hesitated and turned to his wife before answering with a sigh. "Some Left Handers never acquire the Infection, even after having contact with a leper. Others are less fortunate. So far, I am one of the lucky ones though the disease still lies dormant in my veins. When I was first left in the forest, Charlie, I did not know how the disease could affect me. I was so terrified. I had never been so afraid in my entire life!

For nights on end I would not sleep. I was too paranoid and afraid. It was so eerie there, everything was so... still. After some time, the forest began to play tricks on me, and I was talking to inanimate objects as though they were alive and my friends. In reality, there was no one there except the lepers. In fact, all land mammals in the forest were either killed or taken by the Government to prevent a potential spreading of the Infection through other species, something that I found out much later. What kept me sane was my constant search for Will. Regardless of the sores that covered the creatures I encountered in the forest, I was sure I would recognize my friend if I saw him, but I never did.

It got quieter and quieter as I went deeper into the forest, and I knew I was not safe. Every now and then, I heard the lepers moving through the trees and stepping on nearby twigs and branches. I could even see them sometimes, in the shadows, watching me. It did not take long before I realized the lepers in the forest had only survived because they had turned to cannibalism from the lack of wildlife. I found this out because I became their target.

I was attacked many times. Once here," he motioned for his wife to pull off the bed sheet to reveal the scars along his thigh, "and again here and here." His wife knew exactly where his scars were located, and she showed them to her children reluctantly. Louise covered her eyes and buried her head in her brother's chest. Noreen continued to look with disgust, as she was unable to look away from him. When Mrs. Satchell decided enough of his scars were revealed, she covered them back up with her husband's bed sheet.

Noreen peered over at John, or the so called 'Eli' as her father had called him, just as her mother concealed her father's wounds. Surprisingly, he did not appear unnerved in the slightest by the gruesome sight and his emotionless stare disturbed her greatly. She did not understand how anyone could look at such horrible images without becoming instantly repulsed; even her brother Charlie eventually looked away by nestling his face in his youngest sister's hair.

Mr. Satchell lifted his palm and waited for his wife to grab hold of it. "I wanted you all to see those scars because you children must know of the Hell I escaped. The only reason I am alive today is because I outran the lepers and hid from them in the trees. I had no weapons, no protection nor any shoes for my feet. All I wore was the hospital nightgown I was given at the experimentation laboratory. I drank from the streams and ate whatever plants, berries or even carcasses I could find to stay alive. I was lost in the Forest of Lepers for over six months before I found an exit and came across the barbed wire fence that still borders our town. Since I knew I could not climb the wire, I searched for a soft area of ground along the fence to dig my way under. I cannot remember how long I searched, but just as I was about to give up, as I laid beside the fence with my face half-buried in the dirt, I discovered a large hole along the bottom edge of the wire, and I began to dig.

    I dug and dug for I don't know how long until finally I made a tunnel thick enough to climb through to escape my misery. I made it back home over six years after I was taken. I remember thinking about how much our town had changed in my absence, and that is when I began my search for your mother.

    When I finally found her, she took me in without hesitation, not even caring how broken and sick I was from all the testing and from living for years in the wild. When she took me in, I found a small six year old girl I did not know, sitting on the floor of the kitchen. You see, I did not know your mother was pregnant with Louise when I left, but thankfully, Louise, was born a Left Hander and had been returned to her mother." Mr. Satchell tried the best he could to smile at Louise, crying helplessly in her brother's arms. "If after the first two years of life, the Government determined that you, Louise, were dominantly right handed, you would have been sent to the other side to live with your Aunt Clara just like…" His wife squeezed his hand once again, forcing Mr. Satchell to refrain from speaking. He inhaled deeply, still lost in thought, his sunken eyes staring off at nothing in particular.

    His disturbing glance caused Noreen's hands to shake, so she quickly lowered them into her nightgown's pockets, hoping that no one would notice their spasms. Mr. Satchell started to mumble again after a long pause while his wife continued to eye him carefully. "Once I returned home, I made your mother lock me in this very room because if the Government found me here, you would all be taken. I know I am a burden on the family, but I never had the courage to end my life. That is why I am thankful that my time is finally up. I am dying my children-"

"Father, please, don't," Charlie interrupted.

Noreen barely heard her brother's voice; the only one she could clearly hear was her father's. After so many years of being told lies and trying to believe them, after so many years of not knowing what had actually happened to him, why the Government had taken him or where he had gone for such a long time during her childhood, the pieces were now finally fitting together. Noreen realized, then, that it was the first time her father had told her anything about his past, and she realized that in actuality, she had never known the man at all.

Taking her trembling left hand out of her pocket, she tried to tuck a strand of curls behind her ear but couldn't. The mitten-like bandages that wrapped around her hand prevented her from grabbing them, so she placed her hand on her thigh in defeat. To her surprise, another hand appeared in front of her and pushed the curl away from her face and behind her ear just as she had wanted. Following the hand with her eyes up the arm of its owner, she realized it belonged to John, Eli. He cautiously reached over to Noreen's thigh and grabbed hold of her bandaged hand. Its warmth eased her, and while his touch was light enough not to cause harm, she wondered what he inferred of their incessant shakes. Clenching her jaw, she tried not to think about it.

Despite her anger toward Eli, she did not want him to let her go; it comforted Noreen to have someone hold her, especially since none of her family members noticed. Charlie and Louise had their eyes closed, with Louise's head buried in her brother's chest, and Charlie's still nestled into his sister's hair. Her mother was kneeling beside her husband, caressing his cheek with a pained expression as she stared into his eyes, but, from Noreen's angle, her father did not seem to notice her touch. The skeleton kept his gaze toward the ceiling, and had it not been for the rising and falling of his chest, Noreen would have thought that her father was dead.

Her eyes moved to Eli, but they failed to meet his gaze. His head was down, and his hair masked his expression. Glancing down at his hand and back to his face, Noreen could not help but question his intentions. She wondered if his hold on her was for her comfort or his, for her father's approval or for her liking. Whatever his motive, she removed her hand from his grasp and tucked it back into her pocket.

Eli immediately peered over to Noreen with a worrisome expression, but Noreen refused to look back. The comfort she had briefly felt vanished. She no longer wanted the Doe's comfort, but rather wanted nothing but to hear her father's voice and his long overdue explanation. Glaring directly at the skeleton before her, Noreen began her inquiry. "Father?" she began. She waited until his pupils moved in her direction before she continued. "Why didn't you tell us sooner? Why are we just finding this out now?"

The man shifted his gaze toward Noreen's mother who responded for him. "Because of your father's condition, Noreen, and yours."

"I don't understand, what condition? What's wrong with me?" Noreen demanded to know just as Charlie and Louise opened their eyes to watch and listen to the conversation.

"Your father never planned on telling you, any of you, but now that Noreen has gained such a condition, he felt," she corrected herself, "*we* feel that it is a good time to tell you… now that we have the chance."

"What condition? Mom, I will be fine in a few days, maybe a week or two, I told you that! My scars will fade, I promise, and I will cover myself as well. See. There is no need to worry!" Noreen took her now stilled hands out of her pockets and waved her arms above her head to confirm her mobility, though it caused her a great deal of pain.

"Yes, I believe you," her father's distant voice echoed throughout the room. Noreen tensed at the sound of his voice, and she placed her hands immediately onto her lap. "I know how tough you are, Noreen, I know. You will recover quickly, I am sure of it, because of your mental strength and courage. That is also how I know that you are capable of letting the Government take you based on your appearance alone. They will assume, most definitely, that with all of your bruises, you must have internal bleeding and with all of your scars, you must have tried to scratch away your bumps and sores, though we all know you do not have any of those symptoms. By letting the Government take you, it will enable you to reach the Forest of Lepers and from there find and cross over to the other side."

Noreen shook her head as everyone in the room had their eyes on her. Charlie moved Louise off him then before he crawled toward his other sister. "Father no," he answered for Noreen while he placed his arm around her.

Their father continued despite his son's rebuttal. "If you make it, you will need to be branded with an **R** on your right wrist as soon as possible, but obtaining the tattoo won't be an obstacle until you reach the-"

"That is far too dangerous dad, and you know it!" Noreen's brother cut him off. "Why should she go over to the other side? We don't even know if she is immune to the Infection! We are fine here. We are all fine!"

"Charlie be quiet!" Mrs. Satchell snapped at him suddenly. She no longer kneeled beside her husband but stood as far from the bed as possible while facing the large wardrobe in the corner. She cried hysterically with her arms crossed over her chest, prompting Louise to rush over and wrap her arms around her mother's waist. Mrs. Satchell stroked her daughter's hair gently without glancing in her direction.

"Mom, dad," Charlie's voice was quieter, "what's going on?"

Mrs. Satchell started to cry even louder causing her to break from Louise's hold. She climbed up the steps quickly to escape the others in the room. Louise raced after her, almost missing her footing on the wooden stairs, but she made it out of the basement before her mother could close the hatch.

Noreen turned her attention back to her father. He lifted a hand off the bed, raising a limb for the first time since his company had entered the room. He held the hand out for his daughter and, reluctantly, Noreen leaned her right hand forward. "No." her father stared at her left.

Noreen understood the man's request and intertwined her right arm back with Charlie's before leaning her left hand gently onto the bed. Mr. Satchell laid his forearm down on the mattress, breathing harder from his effort. He pointed to her scarred wrist wrapped tightly beneath the thick layers of bandages. "Going to the other side is a risk you, and only you, must be willing to take," he whispered to her. "This is your ticket out of here, Noreen. This will enable you to go to the other side and reunite with your twin sister!"

Chapter 10

Noreen felt as if the room were spinning, "I...I have... a twin?"

Her father's expression was emotionless. "Identical," he said, "her name is Nicole and she is a Right Hander."

At the word 'identical', Noreen felt nauseous. She could taste the beans and tomatoes she had eaten earlier that evening already climbing back up to her throat. "Get me out of here," she stood up slowly while holding her stomach, "I'm gonna be sick."

Instantly, the Doe rushed to her side and raised her arm around his neck before unhooking her arm from her brother's. Meanwhile, Charlie's face went blank and his senses were no longer tuned in to his surroundings. Eli noticed how his tensed position meant that he was incapable of helping or even do anything at all, so Eli pushed past him with Noreen stumbling by his side.

Noreen's legs gave out as she began to dry heave onto the floor, causing Eli to lose his balance and send them both crashing to the floor. "Charlie!" Eli yelled for Noreen's older brother to help him as he watched vomit begin to pour out of Noreen's throat. Charlie did not move, though, and instead he remained motionless in shock.

Eli bent over Noreen, pushing the curls from her face like before, but this time to prevent them from becoming drenched in vomit. She stopped heaving for a moment, long enough for the Doe to lift her off the ground. Careful not to step in the liquid that blocked their exit, Eli tip toed steadily around it and carried Noreen up the steps. He shouted over and over as he stood just under the hatch with Noreen's limp body in his arms. He used his head to bang the door blocking their path until Louise finally opened the hatch. Eli rushed past her, out of the basement and through the kitchen. He kicked open the backdoor causing its hinges to loosen further as he stormed outside.

"John, what's happening? What's wrong with Noreen?" Louise ran after them.

"Get water from the well and boil it fast before she gets too dehydrated!" Eli demanded.

Louise stepped back timidly, "but I'm not allowed to get water from the well, Noreen usually goes-"

"Get it now!" Eli shouted. He lowered Noreen's body to the dirt.

Louise started for the well but raced back when she realized she had forgotten the buckets. She retrieved them quickly from beside the wood pile before leaving for the well in the darkness. Meanwhile, Noreen's vomiting ended. Her cheek dropped against the dirt, and she curled her legs toward her chest to shape her body into a ball.

The acids that swirled inside her stomach added to the pain that ran through practically every limb and muscle in her body. Eli kneeled above her, one hand in the dirt and the other on her side. She wanted to say something to him but couldn't; no words could escape her throat. Eli sat quietly listening for Louise's return until he could hear the sloshing of the pails coming toward them. He jumped up from his position beside Noreen to run toward the sound of spilling water to take the buckets from Louise's arms.

Noreen could hear them speaking softly as they rushed past her, but she refrained from looking up at them or even moving at all. Two more voices joined the conversation, and Noreen knew her mother and Charlie had come back to their senses.

"I started a fire to boil the water, now go ahead and pour it in!" Mrs. Satchell demanded. "We must purify the water before giving it to her or else she will get even sicker."

"We should probably give her something more than water, she no longer has any food in her stomach." Charlie murmured, still in a daze.

"All she needs right now is water," Mrs. Satchell disagreed, "and then, later on, when she can handle it, we will give her more soup." She turned to Eli. "What did you bring from your garden?"

"Six potatoes and some carrots. I'm sorry, but that is all we had." He pointed toward the counter.

"That'll do for now." Mrs. Satchell followed his gesture to find a bounded cloth sitting on the countertop. She walked briskly over to it and untied the rag to discover the food hidden inside. "Alright, you and Charlie start peeling these potatoes," she told the two men as she removed the vegetables from the bag. "Louise, go check on your sister."

"But Mrs. Satchell," Eli interrupted her, "Charlie is right. Noreen needs actual food in her stomach, not just soup."

"No, well yes and no." Mrs. Satchell corrected herself. She turned to face Eli. "Right now all she needs is fluids. In a day or two we shall give her solid food, like some of those potatoes. We are working with what we got, Eli; Day 19 is four days away. There is no meat until then, if we even get any meat."

"I will get her meat before Day 19!" Eli announced, halting Louise in the back doorway. Noreen tilted her head enough to see her sister staring off into the kitchen while she strained to listen from the outside.

"Eli, how on earth do you propose to do that? Hunting is against the law, we do not own any weapons and, even if we did, there is nothing to hunt."

"But you're wrong," he disagreed with her. Noreen could see Eli's arm pointing to the outside as he spoke. "We have birds, lots of them! How else do you suppose I am so well fed? Mrs. Satchell, I know where I can get a shotgun!"

"What? That is crazy talk," she disapproved. "You are not going to risk your life, all of our lives, to shoot at a bird with a gun you don't even know how to use!"

"I will not put your lives in danger. That is a promise," Eli swore. Noreen curled her fingers into the dirt and crawled forward until she could fully see Eli as he stared into the boiling water in the fireplace. He motioned to Mrs. Satchell in the direction of the hearth. Reading his thoughts, her mother took a mug from the cupboard and a ladle from the drawer below it. Hurriedly, she dipped the ladle into the pot and poured some of the purified water into the mug as Eli continued. "I will go to the farthest south western edge of the harbor, as far from Government headquarters as I can get. Once I am there, I will hunt for seagulls," he explained. "I can go to the rocks, where the waves crash hardest at the right time of day. The sound of the waves crashing against them will muffle the sound of the shotgun. I have done this before, Mrs. Satchell, I know what I'm doing." Noreen noticed Eli's hands ball into fists as he nodded to her mother.

"That's ridiculous!" Charlie argued with him. "You don't know where to shoot. There are civilians and fisherman all around the harbor. They will see you and someone will catch you, or hear your gun go off, and they *will* inform the Government! We depend on the Government for survival, our town has no other choice but to do so. Our friends, coworkers and neighbors will turn you in for any chance of repayment from the Government regardless of how close you were to them or how much of a friend you thought they were. It is all a game, Eli, a game of survival."

"I have no friends, Charlie, no family here either, so I *can* afford the risk!" Eli stepped in front of Charlie, who sat beside the kitchen table, and broke his trance. "I am an outcast. I live in an orphanage. Your father was the only one who has paid for my survival and care since I was an infant because of his friendship with my father. Your mother has risked her life for me every third month to come to the orphanage and pay the director so I could receive things like a bed of my own, a toothbrush or even a pair of shoes for my feet! I owe your family my life, and I made a promise to your mother and father to protect your family's secret and to protect Noreen so someday she could reunite with her twin sister. I have kept every secret, every promise I agreed to keep, and I will never break those promises. I will die with those secrets, Charlie. My real name may be Elijah Foster, but here I am a nobody, nothin' but a 'fuckin' Doe, remember?"

 Charlie stood up as though accepting Eli's challenge. "Yeah, you're right. You are a nobody, and you have nobody either, but I do. I have a family and a fiancé. I have people I care about!" He paused to take a breath. "That is why I am going with you, because I have a *family* to look after. But let's get something straight. Just because our fathers were friends, that does not make us friends as well!"

 "Stop this talk right now!" Mrs. Satchell demanded as she handed Louise the mug of water for Noreen. "What is wrong with you boys? Neither of you are going anywhere. I will not risk losing either of you!"

 "So what then, mother?" Charlie crossed his arms. He eyed Louise through the window as she helped her sister drink the water under the moonlight. Louise was oblivious to her brother's argument as she pestered Noreen to drink the liquid from her cup in a forceful tone. Noreen obeyed and drank the fluid, though she strained to listen to the conversation that intensified in the kitchen. "I never thought I'd say this, but the Doe is right," Charlie admitted, "Noreen will die and never be able to meet her twin sister. And then you will have lost not just one, but two of your daughters and my respect for you all together if you don't give us this chance to save her, to save all of us!"

Mrs. Satchell gripped the ladle in her hand tightly to collect herself while Eli stepped forward and spoke to her in a softer tone. "I have gone hunting many times, Mrs. Satchell, and I have yet to be caught. We can do this!"

Charlie stepped beside Eli without looking at him. "And I work at the harbor, mom, so I know where and when we can go to shoot the birds! And John, I mean Eli, he knows how to shoot them." He placed his hands gently on his mother's arm, and she lowered the ladle to her side. "Mother, I am a fisherman; I know about a cave entrance just below one of the cliffs on the southwestern edge of the harbor. Eli will stay hidden behind the rocks, and he can tell me where he will be shooting. By the time he shoots and kills the birds that fly over the mainland, I will collect them as soon as they hit the ground. I can also be the look out when Eli isn't shooting, so we will know if someone hears the gun's fire."

"That is absurd, why don't you just fish like you always do?" Mrs. Satchell interrupted her son.

Charlie shook his head, "I'm not allowed to be seen fishing in the harbor unless I am scheduled to. Besides, there are not enough fish for us to catch; the Government traps most marine life in their nets to give to those in the Town of East, and we get their leftovers, as usual."

"Fishing would take too long anyways. We don't have time to wait around for a bite." Eli added.

"Yeah and if we hunt, we will be protected because the mouth of the cave I know faces the harbor. Most don't even know of the second entrance in the back that faces the mainland! I only know of it cause Madeline and I would…" Charlie's face reddened, though his mother did not seem to notice, and he quickly refocused his argument. "No other fisherman will be able to reach us by water either because it's illegal to own a boat unless you are an official."

"And what about the Government, what if they come by boat?" Mrs. Satchell tried desperately to find reasons for the young men not to go.

"They will come by boat, mother, every two hours, because that's when they make rounds."

"How could you possibly know that, Charlie?"

"Because every day as I sit and wait to catch something, I watch their boats from the mainland. They come every two hours, I am sure of it, while keeping far away from us, far enough for them not to see me and John inside the cave. When we go that is. It can work, mother, we *can* pull this off!"

Mrs. Satchell looked away from her son in defeat and poured a second mug of water for Noreen. She blew at its steam to cool the liquid and walked toward the back door. Before exiting the kitchen, she stopped in the doorway, blocking Noreen's view of the kitchen. "Don't get caught, please, I can't afford to lose you, either of you. I cannot afford to lose any more people I care about. I have lost too many of those already."

The moment she moved out of the doorway, she knelt beside Noreen and cradled her daughter in her arms. Noreen did not look at her, though, but at Charlie and Eli who now faced one another in the kitchen. While her brother appeared angry, the Doe seemed calm and unaffected by his glare. "So, you're the fisherman, when do we leave?" the Doe asked.

"That depends," Charlie narrowed his eyes, "when can you get that gun?"

Eli glanced outside to see if the sun had peaked over the horizon. "Right now," he said. "We have to go as soon as possible or we have to wait until tomorrow morning at this time when it's still dark. Wanna come?"

"Yeah. Where do we have to go?"

"The Cove. The gun is Lawrence Colt's. He keeps it in the backroom with the alcohol in case a fight breaks out." He hushed his voice and Noreen strained to hear him as her mother and sister hovered around her. "Lawrence was the one who taught me how to shoot since I'm like The Cove's bodyguard. I haven't had to use it, though, so no one else knows about the gun but me, and now you and your family."

Charlie raised an eyebrow. "How did Lawrence get a gun?"

Eli took a deep breath in preparation for Charlie's reaction. "He used to work for the Government years ago but got fired for substance abuse and sexual harassment. He kept his guns, though, and started an underground bar in retaliation. He needed someone like me to know how to use a gun to protect his bar from the Government and anyone else who got out of hand. And I needed the money, well, I *need* the money, so I agreed."

"I see," Charlie nodded slowly as he walked around his father's hatch and toward the front doorway. "You say he has guns? More than one shotgun?"

Eli nodded, mimicking Charlie's movements as he followed him around the hatch. Charlie lowered himself enough to disappear from Noreen's line of vision. As he stretched out a foot at a time, he came back into her view, tying his hemp shoelaces tightly against his feet. "And what if Lawrence catches us?"

Eli smirked. "Well, he can't tell on us, we've got too much on him."

"The Government doesn't give a shit about Noreen, Eli, they don't care who gets hurt as long as no one tries to revolt."

"I wasn't talking about that, he owns an illegal bar and illegal weapons. The worst he can do is *try* to stop us from taking his guns. After the other night, I don't think he will."

Charlie nodded and raised himself to his feet. He disappeared from Noreen's view only to reappear again moments later wearing his black, multi-pocketed jacket. "You have anything else at the orphanage you can wear?" he asked while studying the Doe's appearance.

"What's wrong with what I'm wearing?" Eli became defensive.

"Calm down Doe," Charlie ordered. "I meant do you have anything darker you could wear? Something without that damn bright blue in it." He nodded to Eli's checkered flannel as he fastened the buttons of his coat.

Eli looked down to his flannel and noted its colors. Though half of its checks were black, the remainder were a vibrant teal. "I'll see what I can find," he grumbled.

Charlie peeked out the shutters of the front window as Eli glanced back out the kitchen doorway to find Noreen staring at him. She sipped the purified liquid from Louise's mug as she sat cradled in her mother's arms. Her chest was covered in dried vomit, and her hands were clasped loosely by her neck. They shook violently as they pulsated against her throat.

Eli stepped toward her with a longing expression, but Noreen failed to match his sympathetic gaze. Though she had heard their conversation, she could not comprehend most of what they were saying. Her thoughts were preoccupied within the world of her own subconscious and Eli could do nothing to help her.

Charlie opened the front door and slipped through its crack, but before Eli turned to join him, he crossed his heart with the index finger of his left hand to gesture his own soundless promise to Noreen. Noreen understood his vow but did not acknowledge it. A chaos of petrifying visions jumbled through her brain as she envisioned such a terrifying and hellacious fate in her near future. It crept nearer in her mind like the progression of her father's death inching closer and closer.

Chapter 11

"When are Charlie and John, I mean Eli, coming home?" Noreen stared out the open window from her seated position on the cot. She explored with her eyes through the daylight. "They've been gone for almost two days."

"I don't know, but I hope it's soon. You're not the only one who's hungry." Louise placed one hand on her stomach to exaggerate her declaration. "I mean the beans and potatoes we've dug up are enough for now, well especially the beans, but I don't know when I was last full."

Noreen smiled sympathetically at her sister with closed lips. "I know, I'm sorry. I wish I could help out around here somehow or even leave this house, but you know, mom won't…"

"Yeah, I know 'mom won't let you!'" she pretended to mimic Noreen in a nasal voice. "You know, it's a lot harder to garden without the extra hand, and I also never realized how hard it was to carry water back from the well like you always did. It takes a lot of strength." She paused to flex her nonexistent biceps, "ha-ha, now I *would* say that you're pretty strong too but look at you. Ha! With my growing strength and your laziness, I'm like a super woman compared to you now!" She shoved Noreen's arm playfully and laughed.

"Whoa, watch it! Your super strength is gonna shove me off this cot!" Noreen laughed with her while pulling the patterned quilt higher toward her chest. "And laziness? How am I being lazy? It's not like I can do anything besides walk around the house."

"Yeah, yeah. Excuses!" Louise joked. "But really, I am glad you're doing better cause now I can shove your arm again without always havin' to see that ugly face you made when you were in pain. HA!"

"You're so hilarious, Louise," Noreen remarked sarcastically.

"Yeah, I am pretty funny, aren't I?"

Noreen ignored her and smirked at her sister. "Alright, so in all seriousness, why are you in here? Really, is it to get out of your chores or just to make fun of me?"

"Well, mom originally locked me out of here when you first came back cause she said you were too horrifying and ugly to look at," Louise confessed. A teasing grin formed deep expressive lines in her cheeks. "So I am just here to have the comfort of my bed back! But I also think that I've gotten quite used to your disturbing look."

Noreen shook her head. "You can never be serious with me unless we are arguing, can you?"

"Yes I can!" Louise's smile faded. After a long pause, her expression became serious, contradicting her sister's last accusation. She waited until Noreen's eyes gazed back out the window before she revealed her honest reason. "I just want to talk with you like we always used to. I mean, since you can't garden yet or even go on a walk down the street with me, we haven't been able to, talk that is."

Silence followed while Noreen turned her attention back to her sister and interlocked their palms as one. "We can talk whenever you want, about anything!"

"…even about mom and dad?" Louise asked. "You haven't visited father since what happened two nights ago even though you have the strength to walk over and see him. And you haven't spoken a word to mother either."

"Your point?" Noreen felt a pain in her heart. She was still angry at her parents for not telling her sooner about

Nicole, but she also could not explain the situation to Louise; Louise had not yet been told about her right-handed sister and probably never would for her own safety. The night Noreen was told of her twin sister, her mother made Noreen promise not to mention anything about her. Noreen and her mother both knew that Louise would never be able to ever meet Nicole, so it would be best if she never knew about her at all.

At some point after Day 19, her mother was planning on telling Louise, that Noreen was killed during the fight for meat instead of telling her the truth that Noreen was to escape while the massacre was occurring to leave for the Town of East and reunite with her twin sister. Once again, the lies would be for Louise's protection. While Noreen hated the secrets she was forbidden to share with her younger sibling, she knew they protected her from the Government. Louise's life would be much safer without them, and without Noreen.

"Well, my point is that I don't think it's fair to them," Louise pressed. "We both know father's condition and mother was obviously upset that night, and she still took care of you regardless of her feelings." She shook her head, "come on, Noreen, don't you think you're being a little selfish?"

Noreen bit her lip to keep from arguing with her sister. She could not afford to tell Louise the true reason behind her anger, so she decided to alter the focus of their subject. "You know, you're starting to sound more and more grown up every day."

Louise raised her eyebrows in surprise at her sister's response. A hint of a smile fleetingly changed her sister's expression, but she was quick to pretend to feel otherwise. "Who me? No way! I never wanna grow up; I already have too much to think about."

"Ha, yeah, I guess you're right," Noreen looked away from her, hating how they faked their emotions with each other. Their family was bound by secrets and an endless number of lies. Not once could she ask her sister for advice, yet she continued to feel utterly torn making decisions. To Noreen, solitude at that moment seemed most appealing, yet Louise's presence oddly soothed her. She desired quiet, but she was also afraid of silence. And while her options needed to be considered, she wanted nothing more than to delay them for as long as possible.

Worst of all, Noreen desperately wanted to meet her twin sister, but she could not decide if reuniting with her other half was worth never seeing the rest of her family again. So many conflicting feelings and so many heavy contemplations tugged Noreen's brain in opposite directions; however, she knew they needed to be faced or she would never truly find peace. But the absolute, unquestionable willingness of her parents to send her off to never be seen or heard from again killed her inside. *Do they really have that much faith in me? Or do they care so little about me to let me go?*

Louise disturbed her unspoken concerns with a nudge in her side. "You guess? No, I *know* it's true by 100%. The only good part about being an adult is, well I don't know, I guess maybe falling in love? But like that'll ever happen." she remarked sarcastically. "People don't go on, what did mom call them? Dates? Yeah, that was it," she answered her own question, "dates. HA! Like anyone has time for those. Lucky for Charlie, though. He found someone real special, and hey, that means we're gonna have another sister!" Louise smiled and Noreen bit her lip once again at her reference to having another sister. *If only she knew.* Noreen thought. Louise winked at her unexpectedly. "And lucky for you too, I guess."

"What do you mean?" Noreen frowned.

"You know exactly what I'm talking about, so don't try to hide it," she paused and waited for her sister to understand, but Noreen remained confused and silent. "Eli, duh!"

"Are you nuts?" Noreen could not believe what she was hearing.

"Yeah! I mean no," Louise smirked once she corrected herself, "I see the way he looks at you. He likes you, I can tell, but I don't know if that's necessarily a good thing since, you know, he's a *Doe*." Louise hushed her voice as she whispered the derogatory term for orphan.

"Stop it, Louise, don't you dare call him that!"

"I can't call him what he is? Come on, Noreen, before you heard all that stuff dad told us, you called him a Doe too!"

"No. I never called him a Doe. I always called him John, because he did not have any other name, at least not one I knew. Besides, I would never disrespect my friend like that."

"Ahem, friend?"

"You heard me!" Noreen snapped.

"Whoa, I'm just teasing you!" Louise laughed. "God, you need to relax. We both know that you'd never fall for him anyways. He is beneath us."

"Beneath us?" Noreen repeated Louise's words as a question. Her sister, somehow, continued to shock and irritate her in every way possible. "How could you be such a spoiled brat when you don't even own a second pair of shoes to walk in? He has done more for this family than you will ever do in a lifetime! He has not only saved my life once but on multiple occasions. He deserves to be called Eli, not by that offensive word!"

"Oh yeah? Well at least I know where we stand in this community and that is above all John and Jane Does. Those nobodies keep people like us from being at the bottom in the eyes of the Government. Besides he's only protecting you because father paid him to!"

"What are you talking about?" Noreen's eyes narrowed. The memory of the night she vomited was now a blurred vision deep in her subconscious.

"You didn't hear? Oh that's right, you were outside when this happened. You see, Eli was telling Charlie, mother, and me all about it. Well, mainly Charlie because mother already knew since she was the one who delivered the money to him in the first place!" Louise smiled vindictively. "Eli was like your paid bodyguard."

"You're lying!" Noreen shouted. She had never considered Louise's theory before, and it weighed on her heart like thousands of coins piled on her chest.

"I am not! Why don't you just ask mother and find out for yourself?" Louise's grin grew wider as her voice became sarcastic. "Oh wait, she left for the barter's market. Too bad you can't leave the house to go see her. Darn!"

"Watch me," Noreen bluffed, slowly standing up from her seat on the mattress and walking to the door. Her strides seemed far less draining since she had been taking short walks several times a day around their cottage to build up her strength.

"No! What are you doing? You know you can't go outside yet!" Louise yelled as Noreen's hand wrapped around the door's handle. "I was kidding, I mean, part of what I said was true, but I was just messing with you. Come on, Noreen, you can't be that heartless to risk my life like this!"

"Is that all you care about?" Noreen whipped her head around. "Your life? If I left this house, now, before I am ready and strong enough to leave, wouldn't *all* our lives be in danger?"

Louise stood up angrily, having been fooled by her older sister. "You tricked me! You aren't gonna leave!"

"Oh yes I am! I am going to leave this God damn room to get away from *you*! But, of course, not this house. Really, Louise, do you think I'm that dumb?"

"Well it is you," Louise stuck her tongue out of her mouth.

Noreen clenched her fist tighter around the door handle but did not turn the knob. "Tell me what really happened when I laid outside that night, Louise. I know Charlie and Eli left to get us food, but what else did you hear Eli say? Tell me the truth."

Louise was quiet until the silence in the room became unbearable. She told Noreen the truth about what Eli said to Charlie, and the once blurred memory in Noreen's head became a clear.

"It all makes sense now." she turned away from her sister as Louise finished her explanation.

"You really thought he did it out of the kindness of his heart, didn't you?" Louise's inquiry was more of a statement of pity than of sympathy. "If it helps, Noreen, I only lied to you at first because, well, I was jealous, because I still think he likes you, despite everything, and I guess I just want someone to like me, too."

"No, Louise, that does not help." Noreen's voice lacked intonation. She twisted the doorknob finally and escaped the room, practically in tears, in search of her mother. Regardless of the anger she felt toward her parents, Noreen needed to see her mother. She needed to hug her and hear her say that she would make it to the other side and find Nicole; to tell her that boys like Eli did not matter, that her father would be cured, that she would be able to see her brother marry, and that everything would be alright. Though Noreen knew most of the things she wanted her mother to say to her were not true, she needed desperately to hear the words spoken out loud so she could pretend to believe them and feel normal for once in her life.

"Mother?" Noreen called down the hall. She could hear voices by the front doorway, so she followed the sound hoping that her brother had returned. She began to jog lightly, feeling the strength building within her as she turned the corner. She prayed Charlie would be there, but he wasn't. It was his fiancé who stood in the front room with her mother instead.

Madeline gasped at the sight of Noreen and immediately flicked her heel up and ripped off her shoe to hold it out defensively in front of her. "Leper! Get back! Get back I say! I'm not afraid to hit you with this!"

Noreen backpedaled slowly, coming to the realization of what she had just done. Her sister peeled around the corner after hearing the commotion, but it did not take long for her to comprehend what was happening either. She quickly stepped in front of Noreen to protect her sister. "No, no! It's not what you think!" Mrs. Satchell also stepped in between Madeline and her daughters, "Noreen is not a leper. She had an accident, but she is fine, I promise you!"

Madeline shook her head in a nervous habit. "But look at her! She, she must be a, a leper! And you of all people," Madeline glared at Mrs. Satchell, "you are protecting one of them! The Government must know of this."

"NO!" Mrs. Satchell and Louise yelled in unison while Noreen remained speechless. Noreen's mother knew that Noreen was not yet strong enough to be taken; she needed more time, more food to give her strength. Mrs. Satchell continued to ramble on to Madeline out of fear. "If you tell the Government anything, even if it is not true, then they will discard you just the same as they will us. There is no doubt in my mind they will. And Charlie! They will get rid of him too if you even say a single word to them!"

Madeline remained in a guarded position by tightly gripping her low heeled loafer in her hand. Her eyes widened as though coming into a realization. "Is that why I have not seen Charlie? Is that why he did not show up at my house yesterday when he was *supposed* to meet with my father? I thought he was having second thoughts; that's why I rushed over here in the first place, but he's a leper too, isn't he?!"

"No, Madeline, no. Don't blame Charlie!" Noreen finally gained the confidence to speak. Madeline jumped back at the sound of her voice, but Noreen continued. "You have it all wrong, please, let me explain!"

"Don't you come any closer, you leper!" Madeline screamed as she waved the shoe at her.

Noreen flinched, but pressed further, "Madeline, I'm not a leper! I swear!"

"You swear, huh?" Tears gushed from her eyes. "Well, how about this. I swear I will never marry Charlie, EVER!"

She retreated toward the front door and opened it, never turning her back on Noreen. Before she exited the room, though, she tugged on her left ring finger until a brown band slid off and she threw it to the floor. She slammed the door behind her and walked quickly down the street, careful not to run from the cottage and call attention to herself.

Noreen ignored the door's harsh slam and focused on the neatly braided hemp as it hit the floor and rolled to a stop over the black mat covering her father's door. Its soundless drop pinched a nerve inside her chest as she remembered her brother's excitement the evening after he had presented it to his now ex-fiancé, Madeline. Noreen swallowed and walked away from her sister and mother as though in a trance. She eased her body to the floor alongside the mat to pick up the handmade engagement ring between her fingertips. "This is all my fault," she whispered.

"No, Noreen, you did not know." Mrs. Satchell bent down beside Noreen and placed a hand on her daughter's back. "It was bound to happen at some point. That is, people are going to wonder about you and wonder about Charlie's whereabouts as well," she paused. "Madeline will take Charlie back. She loves him, and he loves her. Once she understands the truth, then she will…"

Noreen shook her head as she continued to stare at the beautiful artistry of the ring's perfectly interwoven loops. "But mom, we can't tell her everything, you know that!"

Mrs. Satchell sighed. "Yes, I know, but we will have to tell her something."

"You don't think she'll go to the Government, do you?" Louise interjected.

"Honestly, I don't think she'd have the courage to face them," Mrs. Satchell said, "I think we are safe for now, but we must remain careful and on guard for anyone who could walk through that door." She nodded in the direction of the front entrance. "When Charlie returns home, though, we must break the news to him, gently; who knows how he will cope."

"He is coming home soon, right?" Noreen purposely left Eli's name absent from her question.

"I hope so, dear, I really do." She held both of her arms out for her daughters and immediately, Louise dropped down to the floor and melted into her mother's side. Noreen hesitated, with the ring clenched between her fingertips. Rather than cradling into her mother's arms right away, she reached her hand up until it touched one of her mother's open palms. She curled the hand-woven ring inside the woman's grasp and lowered her empty hand back to her side.

"I'm tired of being so strong all the time, mom," her voice broke. "I'm really scared." It was the first time she had ever admitted weakness to her mother, but she felt torn in so many different directions that her body could not handle the stress or the physical pain any longer.

"No, Noreen, you are wrong. You *are* one of the strongest people I have ever known." Mrs. Satchell used her free hand to tilt Noreen's chin upward. "You have done so much for this family, done so much to protect us. It is okay to be afraid sometimes. Everyone gets afraid every once in a while, but if we do not face our fears, then we will be afraid for the rest of our lives. Everything will be alright, I promise."

At her mother's final words, Noreen leaned forward to feel the warmth of her mother and sister surround her. She buried her head into her mother's chest, and the three women huddled together in silence. Without knowing it, her mother had said the exact words Noreen needed to hear.

Chapter 12

*I*t was the evening and the sun was on the verge of setting beneath the horizon. The wind was lifeless, yet the cool spring air of May hovered over the earth. Within the Satchell household, flutters of movement trailed throughout the cottage in preparation for the evening meal. Once again, the stockpot over the fireplace boiled violently with a mixture of peeled potatoes, greens and herbs combined together in a harmonious blend. The blissful aroma of rosemary emitted from the pot, but its perfume failed to vanquish the stench of the three women pacing the room.

Preparations for the meal had long been completed, but the three anxiously moved about the kitchen, resetting and rearranging items on the table in an obsessive manner. It was the eighteenth of May, merely one day before the monthly massacre, and with Charlie and Eli's absence carrying over to the third day, none of the women knew if the men would make it back before Day 19 arrived.

Though Noreen experienced some mild dizziness as she paced the small cottage, her strength gradually returned to her with every meal. She had resumed all routine chores that kept her within the house, but due to her condition, she was prevented from exiting into the outside world.

Noreen stopped pacing and stood within the shadows of the window's rightmost panel as she stared out to the fields of grass. She imagined Irma Anderson gossiping about her disappearance, or rather, her confinement in their home. Her neighbors probably assumed she gained the Infection and had been transformed into the horrifying and diseased leper of their worst nightmares, but that was exactly how Noreen wanted it. Her **L** tattoo was destroyed, and the rest of the wounds covering her body would undoubtedly leave scars. Without even having to face a mirror, Noreen knew what her appearance meant for her future; unless she wanted to be trapped indoors for the remainder of her life, she could not stay in her town. Neighbors would talk, and the Government would quickly become involved. It would be too much of a risk to stay and both she and her parents recognized that.

    The thought of leaving for good, though, terrified her more than the Infection itself, but her decision was finalized when she visited her father that morning for the first time since he had told Noreen of her twin sister. Her anger toward him had eased over the course of the past few days, and when she visited his room early that morning, Noreen could tell how pleased he was to see her. While they conversed, her father sipped the alcohol Eli had apparently stolen for him, as he was the one who delivered the small bottle to the home and assumed correctly for whom the liquor was intended.

    She was forced to help him sip his morphine, but at first, some of the liquid missed his mouth, dribbled down his chin and soaked a patch of his nightgown. The wasted morphine angered her father immensely and thus triggered wheezing breaths to vibrate within his chest. Watching him struggle, Noreen temporarily refrained from pouring the remaining liquor down his throat, only to return the bottle to his lips after his insistent pleads and begs.

    Of all the negative qualities the man possessed, she hated it most when her father begged for his numbing addiction. It made him seem so desperate and so weak. Thankfully, his pleading had not lasted very long during their short time together in the damp, windowless room of the basement. Once the liquor was gone, he insisted on telling Noreen the details of how he survived the Forest of Lepers.

Since the forest separated the Left Handers from the Right, Mr. Satchell told Noreen that she needed to let the Government take her in order to reach the forest and eventually get to the other side. He advised her to reveal herself as soon as the militants turned their trucks and began to speed back into the safety behind the gates. If she were to reveal herself too early or too late, the people of the town would go into a massive state of panic, far worse than anything ever seen on Day 19 before.

As explained by her father, if the Government determined that Noreen suffered from the Infection, they would most likely take her to the center of the forest and leave her there to die, just as he was. Unlike her father, though, Noreen would hike east in order to reach the other side. To locate her destination, Mr. Satchell gave her a brass, pocket compass with the cursive initials A.C. engraved into its back. The compass was the same one given to her father right before he entered the forest out of pure mockery by one of the scientists in the experimentation laboratory.

Patting the oversized pocket of her nightgown, Noreen felt her father's compass resting against her thigh. The key to her father's survival, and the only thing small enough Noreen could bring on her journey, had been passed down to serve her with the similar purpose of guiding her through the green covered death trap. Its presence so close to her gave her a sense of comfort as she knew that she needed the device to survive.

Taking her hand off the pocket, Noreen brought herself back to the present. She stepped away from the open windowsill and sat in her chair alongside the table. She dunked her spoon into the bowl of soup steaming in front of her as she continued to replay the conversation she had with her father. "How is it?" Mrs. Satchell interrupted her thoughts.

Noreen answered her mother with a mouth full of starches. "Delicious," she swallowed, "it's absolutely delicious mother, thank you."

Mrs. Satchell smiled in return and placed the small pot of potato soup on the table for the three of them to share in case anyone wanted a second helping. Both sisters knew, of course, that they'd consume as much as possible until the pot was empty. Despite the fact that their mother prepared liquid based meals to trick their stomachs into feeling fuller, Noreen and Louise never felt fully satisfied, so when multiple portions were available, there was never any food left behind. "I will be right back," their mother said. "I am going down to feed your father."

Noreen and Louise nodded, aware that the man no longer had the strength to leave his bed to eat with them at the table. Death no longer crept forward but rather accelerated the skeleton's fate down a vicious spiral with a dark force that seemed to be sucking their father's life completely out of him. Both sisters had long ago accepted his fate, but neither understood how to prepare themselves when his time officially ran out.

The two waited until their mother opened the secret hatch and went down the rickety stairs before they devoured the food in their bowls. Chunks of cubed potatoes were packed together with pieces of finely chopped cabbage, soy beans and brown lentils. A slight hint of onion enhanced the soup's flavor, as did the freshly picked basil crumpled overtop. The soup's taste lingered on Noreen's tongue even after swallowing, encouraging her to consume more and more until her bowl was practically empty. As she and Louise scraped the bottoms of their bowls, a piercing siren wailed suddenly.

Noreen felt as though her heart stopped. The Government's siren screeched out from the tops of the tall poles uniformly placed along the property lines of every third cottage and though the nearest stood far from her home, its pitch did not fail to rattle her eardrums. Noreen turned to her sister. Louise's jaw was hanging open with a mouthful of food that eventually dropped from her tongue and onto the table. Without pause, she used her fingers to shove the chewed glop back into her mouth and swallow it down her throat.

Noreen ignored her sister and turned her attention to her father's secret door in the hall. Her mother was running up the narrow staircase with a melting candle dripping wax over her fingers. "Noreen, come quickly!" Her breaths were hard and her voice sounded winded as she yelled over the siren's volume. She motioned for Noreen to come to her. "You must hide, now!"

"What's going on?" Noreen stood from her chair. "Why are there sirens?"

"I don't know, but it can't be good. You must hide, Noreen. The militants that ride through the town when the sirens go off are not the same ones that deliver the meat. They will kill you, Noreen, without thinking twice about it!" Mrs. Satchell rushed over to her daughter and yanked her arm toward the hall. "Louise, go out back to the garden and pick every vegetable, anything that can last us for the next few days! If the Government comes, we must save at least-" Sound escaped her throat as she caught Noreen's blank expression.

"You alright, mom?" Louise asked. She followed her mother's gaze toward her sister. "Noreen?"

Noreen stared out the back window in horror. She lifted her index finger and pointed to the outside. "Something is in the grass!"

Louise ducked and covered her head as she hid behind the protection of her mother. "Where?" she shouted.

"I just saw something moving out there!" Noreen's hand trembled midair as she held out her arm.

At her daughter's statement, Mrs. Satchell clenched her fist around the sleeve of Noreen's nightgown and tugged her toward the hall. "Quickly! You must hide!"

Noreen spun around, not needing her mother's pull to force her to move as she ran toward the hatch. She only had a short distance to travel, yet her destination seemed as though it were getting further and further away from her. Abruptly, she heard the back door push open and the noise temporarily muted the siren from her consciousness. She pressed herself to the side wall, hoping that the safety of its shadows would protect her.

At the same time, her mother blew out the candle and closed the hatch in the cottage's darkness, without Noreen safely secured inside. She concealed the door beneath the protection of the mat and leapt to her feet. As Noreen squinted to see the woman, the blare of the sirens returned to her attention, yet they still seemed as distant as her father's secret door. Turning away from it, Noreen watched her mother race into the dimly lit kitchen where Louise was alone with their visitors. Noreen caught a glimpse of a man's figure facing her direction and instantly, she whipped her head around to lean it against the stone barrier that supported her back.

She breathed abnormally through her nostrils as she listened to the voices shouting over the sirens. Louise's shrieking ended and a continuum of hysterical sobs followed. Noreen held her breath. A part of her desperately wanted to sprint into the kitchen and see what was happening, but she knew that was impossible. She contemplated running in the opposite direction, but she had nowhere else to go. She was trapped within the shadows, hiding like the innocent criminal she was, an ill fortune Lawrence had happily cursed her with. Just as Noreen exhaled a long held breath, the sirens ended and her gasping huffs echoed in the abrupt silence. Straightaway, she covered her mouth with a single palm and sank down to the floor. *They heard me. They know I'm here. They-*

A man's voice called her name unexpectedly from the kitchen leaving Noreen without thought. She remained still with her knees bent and one of her arms tightly grasping her opposing shin. Her name was called again from just around the corner, this time with more familiarity. Curious, Noreen uncovered her mouth and slowly removed her arm from around her legs. She gathered her hair into a tight fist to conceal them behind her as she leaned her face around the corner.

She peered around the barrier to find her inquirer standing directly in front of her. The man's boots were covered with thick clumps of dried mud that covered his laces. Tucked into his shoes were light blue jeans, also stained with dirt. As Noreen raised her gaze up the man before her, his familiarity became recognizable. "Charlie?" Noreen looked up at her brother. She released her hair from her grasp as Charlie bent down beside her. Immediately, Noreen wrapped her arms around him. "You made it…" she whispered in disbelief. Her words seemed to flow out with her breath. She could hear her brother crying on her shoulder as she gazed at the crowd of people in the kitchen behind him.

Her mother sat on the floor smiling with her hands clasped together, barely touching her chin. She mouthed cryptic words of prayer as she closed her eyes and tilted her head back toward the ceiling. Her position was static, whereas Louise moved about the room with a determined expression. Within seconds, the girl flew out the back door hauling the two empty buckets in her hands, presumably taking them to the well.

On the kitchen table lay four small, lifeless seagulls, while two larger birds rested over Eli's shoulder with their twig-like ankles clasped loosely in his palms. Noreen stared at Eli with sudden butterflies fluttering in her stomach. He stood behind the table, waiting patiently and out of the way of those around him, while Noreen's family rejoiced for his and Charlie's return.

He still had on the same dark jeans but now also wore a black hoodie that Noreen had never seen before. The hood was pulled over his hair, though its messy strands spiked out from beneath the edge. The whites of his eyes gleamed through the hood's shadows and illuminated his heavenly green irises. The corners of his lips lifted upward in a smile as he gazed down at the seagulls resting on the table.

Noreen's stare was interrupted as Charlie removed his arms from her sides and used his hands to wipe away his tears. He sniffled before helping Noreen stand and leaving her side to revisit their mother. Noreen stood motionless with her hands by her sides, not once looking away from Eli. More than anything, she wanted to run across the room and into his arms, but she felt as though her feet were cemented to the floor. Without looking away, Eli matched her stare and held her gaze. His smile widened to show his teeth, and he took a step toward her after removing the dead carcasses from his shoulder and placing them beside the others on the table.

As he walked toward Noreen, she could feel her heart beating faster. At that moment, she forgot the anger she held toward her 'body guard' and her previous desire to want nothing to do with him. Now, her emotions took over her, and she stood involuntarily weak at the knees. Afraid of losing her balance, she placed her right palm on the wall beside her, leaving her scarred and bandaged limb by her side. Eli stopped walking once they were about a foot away from each other. He pulled down his hood to reveal his entire face and head out from within its shadows, and he reached out to take her hand.

Gently, he held her wounded palm and brought its bandages to his lips, kissing the inside of her wrist where her **L** tattoo had once been located. In response, Noreen took her right hand off the wall and placed it on the back of his neck to lessen the distance between them, inviting Eli to wrap his arms around her waist. He rested his head against hers as they embraced, and after a few moments in each other's arms, Noreen looked up at him with a smile. She felt a strange desire for their lips to meet, but Eli leaned away from her. "You look well," he said. His words came out more awkward than he had hoped, or so Noreen supposed.

Before she could respond, the muscles in his forehead tensed and his face became serious. "The Government heard our gun shots and are looking for us," he confessed. "They sounded the sirens for me and Charlie, but everything will be fine as long as we eat those birds as soon as possible to get rid of the evidence."

Noreen dropped her arms from around his neck. "Where are the guns now?" she inquired just as the sirens ended.

"I kept one for safe keeping," he twisted his torso and lifted his sweatshirt enough for Noreen to see a handgun tucked in the back of his jeans. He turned to face her as he continued his explanation in a softer tone. "But we returned the hunting rifle and shotgun to the backroom of The Cove where we found it. Lawrence, ah," he paused, "well he wasn't there and neither was anyone else, so returning the guns was easy."

"But...?"

Eli smirked, "but Charlie and I *accidentally* left the entrance way to The Cove open as we were leaving."

"What? The Government could find it! Why would you do that?" Noreen exclaimed. Eli waited for her to understand and after a short pause she did. "You want to blame Lawrence for the shootings, don't you?"

Eli smirked again. "That's the plan, but just in case it doesn't work we have to get rid of the evidence like I said."

"And the glock?" Noreen gestured toward the gun hidden beneath his clothes.

"No one will ever know; none of Lawrence's guns were kept in special boxes or in a safe or anything; they are all tucked away on a high shelf behind some liquor where no one can see them. When the Government finds the entrance to The Cove and walks into that backroom, they will not only find the liquor but the guns as well, and Lawrence will be taken away before he notices that one of his guns is missing!" Eli looked proud as he finished illustrating his plan.

"Let's hope so," Noreen bit her lip. "No one else saw you running did they?"

"I don't think so, we were very careful," Eli could still see the concern on her face regardless of his assurance. "Just relax, we are fine, everyone is fine, and we brought home food remember?"

Noreen nodded as she looked away from him and over his shoulder. She could see Louise waddling back into the room carrying the heavy buckets toward the fireplace. Eli followed her eyes and half smiled with closed lips before he started toward Noreen's sister. Noreen touched his arm to stop him. "Eli?" she paused as his eyes locked with her's. "I'm glad you're alright."

Eli smiled. He leaned forward and kissed Noreen's cheek before running over to Louise and grabbing the buckets from her arms. In response, Noreen lifted her bandaged hand to her cheek as she watched Eli help her sister by hanging the grips of each bucket on the hooks above the fire. As she continued to stare, she decided that Eli had changed considerably in the short amount of time since they last worked together. While his kiss on the inside of her wrist was a common gesture signifying pride and dignity in their town, the one on her cheek was far bolder and more surprising to her. She believed the reason behind the John Doe's outwardly noticeable charm involved the shared knowledge discussed among Eli and her family, but she could not be entirely certain since he in fact had always cared for her in a respectable fashion. Before she could ponder further on the matter, though, a deliberate cough sounded beside her.

Noreen looked in the direction of the sound to find Charlie standing beside her. She smiled as her brother lifted her in the air and spun her in his arms. "Oh Noreen, I must tell you everything that happened!" he exclaimed. "You have no idea how thrilling it was to hunt! Well, Eli did all the shooting, but, aw man, Noreen, I'm a lawbreaker!"

Noreen couldn't help but laugh at her brother's enthusiasm. He had never done anything wrong, to an extent, and his excitement for doing something deemed bad in the eyes of the Government amused her. "I'm so proud!" Noreen continued to laugh.

"Charlie!" Mrs. Satchell yelled over to her son. She was no longer in a state of prayer but was now plucking away one of the birds' feathers while she shouted orders to them. "Tell your father the news; oh, he will be so excited to hear it! And tell him we will be celebrating you and Eli's return with a feast of our own!"

Responding to his mother, Charlie removed his jacket and tossed it onto a chair beside the table as though claiming his seat for supper before starting for the hall. Once at the entrance to his father's hatch, he tugged away the mat and opened the secret door. Mrs. Satchell called after him again and he paused with his body already halfway through the entrance. "Bring up one of those chairs in the basement, so Eli can join us for supper!"

At her command, Charlie and Eli exchanged glances with Charlie being the first to nod a sign of respect toward Eli before escaping down his father's steps. Mrs. Satchell ignored their interaction and continued to give directions excitedly. "Louise, help me pluck these birds, quickly. And Noreen, you close the shudders and reset the table. Now Eli, I need you to go out the back door and around to the front. You must warn us if anyone comes, but stay hidden! We must keep an eye out for, well, for anyone really."

"Yes ma'am." Eli smiled briefly at Noreen before leaving out the back door. As he ran from their cottage, Noreen peered after him through the small frame of the window sill. She followed his silhouette in the darkness until it disappeared in the grass.

Chapter 13

"*I* bel- I believe… a toast is in order," Mr. Satchell murmured. He breathed deeply as though trying to gather his strength. Before he could begin his toast, his head drooped toward his chest, and he struggled to raise it. Noreen leaned over to help him, but the man huffed angrily in objection, prompting her to lean back timidly into her chair. She continued to watch him discreetly from behind her drinking glass.

The man's back was hunched over, and his small inflated stomach rested over the belts Charlie and Eli had strapped around his waist and chair to keep him from sliding out of his seat. He had not touched his meal since being carried to the table, but he had laid a flask in his lap, grunting every so often for his wife to open the bottle and pour the liquor down his throat. The initial appearance of the flask confused Noreen because she thought only a single bottle had been retrieved from the bar, but after Eli gestured to his gun from his seat directly across from her, Noreen understood that he had stolen the flask while returning all but one of the weapons to The Cove.

Mr. Satchell smiled briefly when he entered the room, but Noreen could tell he was greatly depressed. She could see it in his eyes, the embarrassment and pity he felt from having to be carried into the room by men, having to be strapped to his seat like a toddler in a high chair and from having his wife feed him his liquid fuel. Noreen watched her father, thinking how the Government destroyed him, and how things would have been so different if the Infection never existed in the first place. Time seemed to have reversed for the man she barely knew, and he was now like a helpless child once again. She hated herself for what she wanted for him, but she knew the ailing man called her father would be better off dead.

"Darling," his wife interrupted him softly, "maybe you should try eating something first." She leaned over to Mr. Satchell to cut a sliver of the dark meat resting on his plate, but after a moment's delay, the pitiful man grunted back at her with disapproval and a noticeable amount of embarrassment. Mrs. Satchell moved away from him and placed one of her elbows on the table to rest her face in her palm. She did not appear angry but rather disappointed and helpless. The man she once knew was now almost entirely unaware of his surroundings and was no longer able to gesture or speak in a meaningful or courteous manner. Persuasion was useless on the man lost in his own world.

"I juss' have one 'ing to say," Mr. Satchell stared at the water in his untouched drinking glass until his wife leaned over for a second time to wipe his chin with his napkin and raise his glass for a toast. He grunted at her again, and she quickly replaced his glass with the flask positioned between his thighs. His head drooped, but he lifted it painfully in order to speak to those around him. *"Throats burn for the east, stomachs yearn in the west, one turn of the moon after this feast, and no return of a half child put to the test."*

He coughed and grunted for his flask, and Mrs. Satchell poured the alcohol into his mouth until he consumed every ounce left in the bottle. He grunted again, and his eyes rolled back as his head drooped to the shoulder closest to the hall. Charlie and Eli stood from their seats in acknowledgement to his gesture and approached his sides.

Charlie wrapped his arm around his father and supported his weight while Eli unstrapped the belts around his waist. When the belts came undone, Mr. Satchell's body slid downward briefly until Charlie got a better hold around his sides. Eli gently wrapped his arms around the man's lower half, and they lifted Mr. Satchell from the chair to take him back to his chamber. Before the three men reached the hall, Mrs. Satchell was at the hatch with the ring of keys and a candle in her palms. She unlocked the basement door quickly and guided the men down the steps.

As soon as the door shut behind them and the candle's light was extinguished from view, Noreen released the breath she had long been holding. At the opposite end of the table, Louise stood with tears in her eyes and raced toward the privacy of their bedroom. Noreen watched her sister run down the hall, and a tear rolled down her cheek.

More tears left trails of water along the curves of her cheekbones, prompting Noreen to lift her bandaged hand and swipe the wetness off her skin. She winced at the harsh cloth's touch on her cheek, and quickly brought it away from her. Raising her left arm, she was able to examine her bandages and the rainbow of red that now tainted them as she turned her arm in different directions. After taking a breath, she lifted her other hand and began to unravel the bandages.

Her injured hand throbbed as the final wrap of cloth was freed from her wounds. Without bending her wrist, Noreen flexed the muscles and curled her knuckles inward. Her once open wounds had become scars with dried blood bordering their edges. Her **L** tattoo was buried beneath them, now completely indiscernible to the naked eye. It was the first time she had removed the bandages from her wound, and it was also the first time she saw the damage they hid. With her arm raised high, Noreen's hand began to shake uncontrollably. She lowered her appendage to allow her blood to flow back into her fingertips, but, glancing at her other hand, she noted that it too trembled with equivalent force.

Noreen dropped the bandages from her shaking grasp just as her father's hatch creaked open and closed again. Footsteps followed and, within seconds, she saw Eli walking toward her. She placed her hands under the table and out of sight as he took the seat across from her. Unsure what to do, Eli laid his forearms on the table and clasped his hands together, but Noreen hardly noticed. She refused to look at him and instead looked through him at the grey stones that lined the wall at his back. She was silent at first, not even acknowledging his presence, until he started to speak, "I-"

"It was about me, you know," Noreen cut him off before he could speak a second word through his lips. "That stupid, stupid rhyme was all about me. Dammit, why did he have to toast to me? I am not his only child!" She choked back her tears and continued to stare blankly at the wall behind him. "That man needs to die. Oh God, I can't believe I am actually saying that out loud, but that- *that* rotting skeleton in there is not my father!" She pointed blindly in the direction of the hall. "My father would not let that happen to him. He is strong. He is... Oh, Eli, he wasn't always like this."

"I know," Eli said.

"No, you don't know. You did not know him or who he really was. He has been physically weak and- and mentally strained ever since he returned from that forest!" Noreen emphasized different words as she spoke, "but my father, he was always a stubborn ass... You know, I hated it when my mother called him that- "stubborn" because I always considered him the bravest and strongest person I ever met. I wanted to be just like him.

He never used to let anyone treat him...like a child. Not until tonight. He had never even showed that he was in pain, at least he tried not to in front of me or Louise or Charlie. He was never this bad, not ever. He shouldn't have been so stubborn tonight, with all his grunting and crying and begging and pleading. I heard it all from the kitchen while Charlie was in there with him after those stupid sirens ended and after you went outside. Oh how I wish those stupid sirens hadn't stopped so soon. Then I wouldn't have heard all that garbage! I wish I had never heard my father beg or cry or be in pain. He just needs to die; he is in so much pain. I want him to die!"

Eli half stood to lean across the table and cup his hand around Noreen's cheek. "He begged because he wanted so badly to enjoy this meal with you and your family. He wanted to celebrate with us tonight because he does not have much time left. He is brave, Noreen, and you are just like him in that sense." His hand fell from Noreen's cheek, and she finally looked at him rather than through him. He leaned back from the table and sat back down with his hands clamped together. "You are right, though, Noreen, I don't know him like you do, and I never will, but I do know how great of a man he is."

"He is a great man and I know that because I have lived with him and cared for him for the past eight years, but you only think so because he has paid for your-for your-"

"Dammit Noreen!" Eli said harshly and walked around the table. He knelt in front of her, gripping the arms of her chair to force her to turn in his direction. "Yeah he helped me out. He provided me with things I needed, things that a John Doe like me could never get, like a pair of shoes or even a God damn roof over my head. I should have been kicked out of that orphanage once I turned sixteen years old, Noreen, sixteen! But your father paid for me to stay there so I would not end up on the streets, homeless like all the other Does that reach of age.

In return, he had your mother ask me to watch over you because your father saw the marks of Lawrence's beatings on you night after night. The first time your father asked, though, I declined, and I told him you should not even be working in such a place to begin with!" Noreen's eyebrows raised. "I only worked there myself because Does like me rarely even get hired. But after watching you come in night after night and never quitting or giving up on your family," he paused, "I realized you were just as stubborn and brave as your father, so I agreed to look out for you. It wasn't until after I agreed, that I realized you also worked there to get the booze for him too, so most nights when you were in the back, I distracted Lawrence to keep him from catching you. You needed the distraction, because, well, he was always watching you.

Noreen, your father protected my father. He protected my family and saved my life. I would do anything to help him in return, but I would not do anything to help you because of that; I would do anything for you because of how much I've grown to like you!" Eli reached for her hands, but hesitated as he finally noticed the uncovered scars across her left wrist. To Noreen's amazement, their horrifying appearance and evident quivers did not deter him. He reached out and took hold of her hands, continuing without alteration in his tone. "I am going with you tomorrow, Noreen. I am going with you so I can reunite with my family on the other side. And I am also going with you because I don't want to lose you either."

Noreen stared at him. She took her hands out of his hold and pressed her shaking thumbs onto his wrists. "No, I'm sorry Eli, but I don't think that would be a good idea." Eli was silent as she continued. "You've been branded a Left Hander. My **L** has been destroyed and covered by these scars. They will know you don't belong on the other side. If we make it, they will send you right back, or do something much worse."

He leaned his face closer to hers. "Then I will remove it."

Noreen shook her head. "It's a tattoo, there is no pain-free way of doing that, Eli, and you know it." She pressed her thumbs down harder onto his wrists, with her right finger located over his black inscription. "My father has always glorified our people and said that we must stay strong and unite against everyone who is against us or else we will not survive. Our **L**s mark who we are. If you destroy it… Eli, I had no choice, I have no choice, but you do!"

"Unite?" Eli ignored the second half of her statement, "we must unite against anyone who is against us? Noreen, everyone is against us! I don't even know why the Government hasn't just killed us all already. We mean absolutely nothing to them except to provide them with people they can experiment on for their next God damn national failure." Noreen opened her mouth to speak, but Eli pressed further. "How do you expect us to unite when our 'people' are ready to kill and beat each other, completely guilt free, for their own personal advantages? People like that are not 'my people' and that is exactly why I do not participate in Day 19 because it is just a savage bloodbath between our own neighbors. And that is also why I have no friends here and trust no one here either. I have no one here, Noreen, no one except you and your family. But more importantly, I am no one here. In the Town of East, I am a Foster. Here I am just another Doe."

Noreen paused. "I understand," she whispered back to him. She wanted desperately to tell him how relieved she was to hear that he wanted to come with her, but she refused to do so. She did not want it to seem like she needed him or his help in any way, even though he helped her many times in the past. She too liked to have him around but would not admit that either. "I should go check on my sister," she said to change the subject.

Eli nodded and bent down to gently kiss her scarred left wrist once again before she stood and walked away from him. Her heart raced in her chest, yet her hands, oddly enough, had stilled during the course of their conversation. She stopped just outside the bedroom and placed her left hand flat against the wooden door. She stared at the spot on her arm where he had just kissed her and replayed the moment his cool lips brushed against the inside of her wounded forearm. Just thinking about it made her entire arm tingle, and she felt as though her pain had momentarily vanished. She wondered what it would feel like to have his lips on hers, but the thought drifted away from her as she scanned her wounds.

A tiny shard of glass poked out of one of her scars, and she used the nail of her opposite hand to dig into the area and remove the glass out of her skin. She winced at the stinging it caused and pictured her mother picking out shards of glass while she was unconscious days before. She was thankful her mother had done so while she was unconscious since the pain of digging the glass out felt like the tip of a sharp knife stabbing into her. After several tries, Noreen stopped and brought her nail away from her wrist, unable to retrieve the glass.

She turned around in defeat to find a tool that could assist her, but she halted when she reentered through the kitchen doorway. She gasped Eli's name, feeling as though she had been punched in the stomach as she watched him sitting before the hearth. He sat in a chair pulled up close to the fireplace, holding the poker in his hand. He pressed its hot, reddish-orange colored tip to the skin of his left wrist. Hair covered his eyes, but Noreen could see him trembling in agony.

Noreen rushed over to him and ripped the poker from his grasp, surprised at his lack of resistance. She shoved its burning tip into the bucket of water sitting on the floor beside them and hurried back to his side. "Eli, no, Eli, please, let me see it. Please?" She grabbed his forearm and brought it closer to see the inside of his wrist.

The top layer of his skin including his **L** tattoo, was gone. It was replaced by a pinkish-orange under layer of skin with a gruesome bubble floating over it. She looked up at his face and swiped his hair from his eyes. Tears filled the corners of his lids, but he refused to let them fall down his cheeks. The wetness of his eyes made his irises an even brighter green than usual, however their color was far from Noreen's attention.

He turned away from her after their eyes met, and Noreen turned to the bucket of water beside them. Instead of retrieving her dirty bandages from under the table, she tore the bottom of her nightgown. She dunked the ripped fabric into the bucket and squeezed out the excess water. Kneeling before Eli, Noreen took his wrist and wrapped it gently in the cloth. He clenched his jaw, as though holding back his screams, but Noreen continued to wrap his burn until the entire wound was concealed.

She tucked the end of the fabric into the swathed layers of material to secure the bandage in place before she lowered her hands to her knees. Eli shifted his jaw from side to side twice; he still would not look at her. "Thank you for that," he mumbled. He wiped the tears from his eyes with his undamaged hand.

"Of course," Noreen's voice cracked.

Eli hesitated before finally glancing in her direction. "I guess this will be the first and last time I go to Day 19." He failed at his attempted joke.

'Mine too' was all Noreen could respond. Eli motioned his hand at her, but Noreen nudged herself away from him.

"I'm sorry you saw that," the John Doe whispered to her, now staring into the fire, "but I'm not sorry I did it. I want to go with you, Noreen, and now, after this, I have to go with you. And I think you want me to go, too."

The two caught each other's eyes and held the gaze. Noreen pursed her lips before she spoke. "What I want is for you to never hurt yourself ever again, do you understand me?"

"I had to do it, you know that."

"You don't *have* to do anything," Noreen objected, "I don't want you hurting yourself for me, ever!"

"Normally, I would never do something like this on purpose, Noreen," he kept his voice even, despite that she raised her's considerably. "If I didn't get rid of my tattoo, I wouldn't be able to go with you."

"I never asked you to come with me. Even if I wanted you to, I would never ask."

"And I never asked to get a tattoo imprinted on my wrist, but somehow, I was forced to have one!" Eli snapped. "And now I don't, so what's done is done. It's too late to change it back now."

"Okay, fine, let's say you come with me, but what if we continue to argue like this. How is that gonna work?" she refused to take their disagreement lightly.

"We will make it work," Eli rebutted, "we've gone through so much together already that I definitely think we can handle each other when we are completely alone!"

"I don't want us to have to 'handle' each other in order to stay pleasant. I don't want to argue with you at all. We are just two different kinds of people!"

"Who is gonna look after you then when you need it, huh? What if you are attacked when you're all alone out there?" he raised his voice louder than Noreen's. "Listen, we have talked about this before, and I know you're tough, but if you can't handle Lawrence how do you expect to handle a leper?"

Noreen stood and smacked him hard across the face using her right hand. She waited for him to speak, but he would not look at her. Instead, he faced the floor with his long, dark bangs covering his eyes. Noreen inhaled deep breaths to calm herself as she waited for him to meet her gaze. When he finally looked up at her, his glare matched her's perfectly. "You know somethin?" The softness in his voice surprised her, despite the significant amount of anger that growled within it. "You're right. We are two different kinds of people. I'm a Doe and you're a hypocrite!"

"A hypocrite?" Noreen breathed.

"Yeah, a hypocrite. You just told me you didn't want me gettin' hurt because of you and then you smack me across the face!"

"Well you deserved that one!" Noreen declared. She paused to swallow, feeling guilt despite that his comment still upset her. She cleared her throat and attempted to alter her aggressive tone. "Look, I'm sorry, but I-"

"No, don't apologize. You're right, and I deserved it." Eli cut her off again. Noreen furrowed her brows, unable to read his thoughts. "I'm sorry I brought him up again," Eli referred to Lawrence. "I know you're not a hypocrite, but you are right that we are two completely different people. But you gotta understand, I wouldn't care if you were a Doe like me or if you were even a leper! I will always be there for you, Noreen. You just need to realize that, even though the journey to find your sister will be worth it, it's not gonna be easy...

What I'm saying is that going up against lepers will be easier in numbers. If I go with you, we can help each other and comfort each other along the way. We can stay out of each other's way if we want that, too. Hell, if you want to be angry at someone, I can be that guy!" Eli looked up at Noreen and broke the seriousness with a crooked smile.

Noreen could not believe how quickly their conversation turned nor how much he was willing to do for her. No one had ever cared for her that much before and, though that comforted her, it was also quite terrifying. She bit her cheek as she stared into his eyes. "Then come," she choked.

Eli stood and wrapped his arms around her causing Noreen's breath to escape her lungs, as a cluster of butterflies erupted inside her stomach. "So what do we do first?" he asked as he stepped back and away from her.

Noreen took in a deep breath before beginning her explanation. "Well, as you know," she took another breath. Eli nodded for her to continue. "Well, the trucks drive through the most eastern side of town along the fence line to patrol the area before they start picking up speed about two miles from the gates leading to Government headquarters. From what Charlie has told me, they start throwing the meat once they start picking up speed. He said it's always at 5pm, and the mass that assembles to fight for the food doesn't form until the first piece of meat is thrown. I will need to stay hidden until then."

"What can I do to help?"

"Uh, you can help me stay hidden and help me get the Government's attention before their trucks reach the gates."

"Of course," Eli responded as Noreen glanced toward her bedroom door. She had forgotten about her sister's troubles until then. "What are you going to tell Louise?" Eli regained her attention.

"I, um, I thought of something during dinner," she paused to back toward the kitchen table and sit on the edge of one of the chairs that surrounded it. "Since the Government is looking for someone with a gun, and since Madeline, Charlie's fiancé, came by yesterday and saw me and how I look..." Eli raised one eyebrow, hearing of Madeline's visit for the first time, but he remained quiet. "I will ask my mother to tell Louise that Madeline told the Government what happened, and when they came for me, they saw us together and took you as well because they found the gun in your possession? I think that could work."

"It sounds believable to me," Eli agreed. His voice stopped at the sound of a creaking door hinge coming from the hall. He turned his head quickly in the direction of the noise, but Noreen did not move her's from its positioning. She knew from many past and painful memories, that the sound was her father's hatch being pushed open very slowly, most likely by her mother. Several moments later, as Noreen guessed, her mother was by her side, and Eli's bandaged hand and wrist were already hidden inside his sweatshirt pocket.

She felt her mother's hand gently squeeze her left shoulder, and in response, Noreen reached up and placed a single hand over it. The woman squeezed back in return. "How is he?" Noreen asked, watching Eli stare into the fire like before. She waited for her mother to answer her, but there was no response, just the sound of muffled sobs coming from her throat. Noreen let go of her mother's hand, and faced her.

Mrs. Satchell did not attempt to conceal her emotions, unlike in the past, nor did she wipe the tears that drizzled down her cheeks. Somehow, she appeared even older than when Noreen last saw her, hardly in an hour's past. Although nearly every time Noreen saw her, she aged considerably, this time was different. Her skin was dry and, like her lips, there were an endless amount of cracks that accentuated her wrinkles. No color existed on her cheeks and her flesh matched that of Noreen's father's. The woman looked twenty years older than her true age and, for once, she seemed weak and vulnerable.

A pinch twisted inside Noreen's chest, and she suddenly felt alone. She bowed her head in defeat as she absorbed the unspoken information conveyed by her mother's sobs. At that moment, Noreen knew her father was dead.

"May I see him?" her voice a whisper.

Mrs. Satchell nodded, continuing to cry as she fell into the chair behind her. Footsteps echoed in the room, and Noreen lifted her head to find Charlie coming out of their father's chamber. He made eye contact with Noreen but merely shook his head as he rubbed away the tears spilling from his eyes. He turned into the room Louise had escaped to, and, as he closed the door behind him, Noreen caught a glimpse of her sister's body curled up on the floor. She too had already foreseen their father's fate.

Scanning her eyes across the inside of her family's cottage, they subconsciously attracted to her father's hatch in the floor of the hall. Noreen knew it would be her only time to see him and her last, but as she stared at the door, she felt immobile; her entire body went numb and she no longer could feel her legs beneath her. Eli's voice brought her attention back to the room. "Will you be alright in there, alone?" he asked.

    Noreen did not remove her eyes from the door. "I won't be alone," she disagreed with him, "my father will be with me." At her own confirmation, her blood began to pump faster through her veins and she felt her mobility return to her. "He always will be," she finished, planting both feet on the floor. She lifted her left foot off the ground and began her journey toward the dimly lit steps of the basement. She listened to her mother's sobs fading away in the background as she reached the stairs and carefully lowered herself down into the cold, damp room beneath the floor.

Chapter 14

𝒯he corpse of her father was pure white, whiter than the feathers plucked off the seagulls, now in heaps on their kitchen floor. His stomach and chest appeared deflated, though Noreen had the lingering feeling that his chest would rise at any moment and he would shoot up to suck in the stale air that emanated off his loosely hanging skin. His eyes were shut, and although Noreen was disgusted and rather terrified by her father's corpse, from the look of his delicately closed eyes alone, she knew he was at peace.

Unsure what else to do, she knelt beside the body and gently touched his wrinkled hand as it lay peacefully over the thin white sheet draped over his chest. Noreen shivered at the initial touch; his body was still warm. After a few moments of silence, she cleared her throat as quiet as she could manage, almost afraid she would disturb him, before she began to speak to the familiar man she had barely known.

"Hey there, Dad. I know your eyes are closed and all, but in case you don't know, it's me, Noreen." Noreen took a deep breath and bit her lip, feeling dumb for the words she had just spoken to her deceased father. She started again, this time speaking much slower and with more fluidity. "Father, please forgive me, I am having a lot of trouble trying to find the words to say to you because I really don't want to mess this up or say the wrong thing. You just-you just need to know how much mother, Charlie, Louise, and I are gonna miss you." she paused to stare at her father's wrist as it lay face up over his bed sheet. She scooted her knees forward and reached her arm out to graze her fingertips over the single lettered inscription forever engraved onto the inside of his forearm. Suddenly, the memory of her father's return to their home overwhelmed her, and she felt as though her mind and body reversed in time.

She was running through the yellow fields of grass once again, in the land extending far out from behind her home. She had not been allowed to leave her mother's land, but her desire for play led her off course until she reached the open terrain surrounding what she had once called 'the giant stone toilet'. It was the first time she had ever seen a well, so her curiosity drove her closer. With its height reaching to her chin, she inserted her toes onto the stone blocks and climbed up the sides of the shaft to peer inside. At the top, she curled her toes over the edges of the stone to hold her in place as the wind blew against her back. She stared into the blackish muck, and allowed her urges to flow through her. Turning her back to the well, she lifted up her dress and squatted into the hole. Unexpectedly, she heard something rustling through the meadow, and the grass began to shimmy in a curving line that seemed to be heading straight for her cottage.

Curious again, she released her dress and stood from her squatted position, only to lose her balance and fall back toward the well. With her arms flailing, they smacked the edges of the stone. She immediately locked them so her body formed an X over the hole, but she was not strong enough to hold on forever. Her bottom began to droop downward until it was submerged into the liquid. She screamed as loud as she could, knowing it would not take long before her entire body sank into the darkness.

Out of nowhere, two hands reached around her sides and a strange, unshaven man lifted her from the well. She continued to scream at the wild man holding her in his arms until she heard her mother's voice beside her, hushing her cries to silence. The wild man carried her back home to safety. This wild man was her father.

Returning to the present, Noreen removed her fingertips from her father's wrist and allowed drops of water to fall from her tear ducts. She lowered her tongue off the roof of her mouth and parted her lips, feeling their stickiness as she ripped the two apart. She knew exactly what she needed to tell the man lying before her. "You need to know that you were never a burden to this family," she began, "but I do admit that I did dislike you very much at times. I mean, I will always love you, dad, but I always hated, I hated how much you drank and how you would whisper to me the type of alcohol you wanted. Most of all I hated how alcohol became your- your outlet from the world. You-you shut us out, dad- you shut me out! I know you were in pain, but you have to know that I needed you and most times you weren't even aware of anything around you, so you were never there for me to help me when I needed you most!

You drank away your sorrows and your pain, and you made me suffer every day by having to deliver those-those awful drinks to you. You *knew* what I went through to get it and yet you continued to ask for it. And instead of doing the noble thing and facing your own battles, you hired me a 'bodyguard', Eli, who I had always known as just another John Doe. You used him because you knew he practically worshipped you for helping his father. I will never understand how someone could be that selfish!" Noreen panted as she cried and yelled at the corpse, "I had to keep you a secret; I had to keep so many secrets for you, even from my own sister. Do you realize how hard that is? I will never have a strong relationship with Louise because of that, nor will I ever in the future because I am leaving tomorrow because you failed to tell me I had a twin sister. How could my own father not tell me I have a twin? An identical twin?

And do you know what else, dad? I blame you for Madeline breaking off the engagement with Charlie! If it wasn't for you, I would never have worked at The Cove, I would not look the way I do now, and Madeline would never have thought of me or Charlie as lepers. And even after everything that has happened, Charlie still has no idea he is no longer engaged!" Noreen's anger was building as she felt more and more tears streaming down her cheeks.

"I used to worship you, father. Mother would tell me stories about you after you were taken. Her stories made you seem invincible, so I would sit outside and talk to the moon and the-the stars every night like the young, naïve little girl I was, believing you would hear me and follow my voice back home. Like mother, I, too, used to think that you were invincible. But after you came home, dad, after I watched you die ever so slowly and painfully, I knew my young mind's thoughts were that of fairytales.

Oh how I began to resent you for not trying hard enough or fighting the pain enough, but now I look back and think how stupid I was to have even thought something like that," Noreen's voice became quieter as most of her anger dissipated out of her. "You see, I could never understand why you wanted to die and I was forced to accept your state of mind because I knew I could do nothing to change it and that-that killed me!

But towards the end, I too wanted you to die. I will always hate myself for thinking that because even after all the things I resented you for, you will always be my biggest hero. You may have been weak and fragile toward the end, but all of your pain and suffering was for the people you loved. You were taken for trying to save your friend, but you came back to the family you were forced to leave behind and in my eyes, that makes you the bravest and most heroic person I have ever met!" Noreen stopped to calm her hyperventilating gasps as she felt her hands tremble violently from the lack of oxygen. She leaned away from her father and looked away from his corpse. After some time, she was able to stand and walk slowly back up the steps. Looking over her shoulder at her father, she whispered *I love you, dad* before lifting the hatch and exiting his room for the last time.

Chapter 15

Staring into the mirror, Noreen barely recognized herself. It was the first time she was able to see her reflection in a mirror since her mother removed it from their bedroom after her last return from The Cove. Though her mother initially removed it to protect Noreen from her own appearance, Noreen insisted on seeing herself before her final departure later that evening.

She evaluated herself closely. She could not remember the last time she wore her jeans and was surprised to find that they still fit her, despite that she always had a slender build. Her jean jacket, on the other hand, was a size too big since it was her mother's old one from over fifteen years ago, but she insisted that Noreen wear it to protect her arms and chest from anything sharp or unexpected in the forest.

Underneath her jacket, Noreen wore an old, brown, sleeveless top; under that, her mother's only sports bra. As expected, the support fit rather well since she and her mother were both exceptionally flat chested. Her long, blond curls were pulled back into a messy ponytail to reveal her severely bruised face and neck even further while her face purposely lacked any sort of makeup to accentuate the yellow and brown bruises covering her skin.

Flapping her jacket open and closed, Noreen fanned herself to cool down while the thick, hot air seeped through the cracks of the window sill and into her room. The air was humid, wetter than the sweat that perspired from her hairline and dripped down her neck. It was 4pm, one hour before the trucks came and one hour before her entire life as a Left Hander would be over.

 She thought about her younger sister then, the sister she had known all her life, the sister she would be leaving behind in search to of the other. She spoke with her mother that morning and the plan they discussed was already set in motion, unable to be reversed. Although every person in the town had the day off work and no one normally went outside their homes before five in the evening, her mother sent Louise to go to the harbor with Charlie and told them to wait there and mourn their father's death.

 Meanwhile, Noreen would leave for the edge of town with Eli. When the trucks disappeared behind their gates and the sirens marked the end of the massacre, Louise and Charlie would return to a mere empty household, with only their mother waiting inside. Since Charlie was told the news that morning, Noreen said her goodbyes to him without Louise around. She could only imagine, though, how devastated her sister would be when their mother tells her that the Government came to find and kill Eli, the 'hunter', and along with Eli, they found Noreen and killed the 'leper' as well.

 Shaking her head at the thought, Noreen placed her hands onto her hips and moved her eyes down to the shoes on her feet. She wore a pair of Charlie's boots that he had grown out of during his years of adolescence. Since her feet were much smaller than her brother's, she had to tuck the bottoms of her jeans into her boots and wear two pairs of socks so that her feet fit comfortably inside without sliding around.

 She bent down to double knot her already tightly fastened shoe laces as they were too thin to support Charlie's current pair but perfect for her own use. A knock thumped gently on the door and Noreen called her visitor into the room. Rather than gazing upward, she continued knotting her shoe laces while also fighting the pain it caused in the turning and twisting motions of her left wrist. When her visitor did not speak, she looked up to find Eli waiting patiently with his hands resting in his sweatshirt pocket.

The darkness of his clothes seemed to emphasize his features, both his sweatshirt and jeans the color of ebony. His hair had been finger-combed to each side of his forehead, and Noreen wondered if he had just combed through it seconds before entering the room. "Come on in," she motioned for him to enter.

Eli remained in the doorway, keeping one hand firmly gripped on the doorknob. "Are you almost ready?" he gripped the knob even tighter.

Detecting apprehension, Noreen walked toward the door but stopped when she was less than a meter away from him. "We have time, Eli." she responded.

Eli nodded, moving his jaw from side to side a few times out of a nervous habit. Noreen raised her eyebrows; she could not believe the amount of anxiety he was showing and it frightened her. "But yes I am ready," she added.

"You have the compass?" Eli spoke quickly, again, appearing nervous. Noreen patted her jacket pocket. She had told him about the compass the night before, after he and her brother, Charlie, had buried her father in the backyard beside the garden and far from the family's outhouse.

Noreen swallowed. "Do you know where my mother is?"

"She's outside ripping weeds from the garden," Eli responded. "I think she is trying to distract herself." Noreen gave him a half-hearted smile in return, but Eli only mimicked her expression for nearly a second before turning the knob forward and back in his palm. He left the room during the pause, leaving the door cracked behind him.

Noreen did not bother chasing after him and instead glanced back in the mirror at her reflection. She rolled her shoulders back and slipped her hand into her pocket. The cold touch of her father's compass soothed her. She took another deep breath. It was her time to be strong, for her own sake and her mother's.

She exited the room but left the door cracked behind her so the click of the door latch would not call attention to the John Doe pacing the front of the hall. She walked quickly into the kitchen and out the door to find her mother sitting on her calves with her legs and feet tucked beneath her. To Noreen's amazement, the woman was not pulling the weeds violently out of the ground like she envisioned; she pulled each handful slowly and carefully to guarantee that each root was removed from the soil. Noreen called to her mother but did not move from her stance within the doorway.

Mrs. Satchell gazed up at her child. The skin of her eyelids was red and swollen, but her eyes were completely free of tears. "Is it time already?" She stood slowly, calmer than Noreen expected.

"Almost." Noreen leaned her head on the door frame while hiding her shaking wrists behind its barrier.

"Well, you look ready," Mrs. Satchell said. "I'm glad my jacket fits you so well." She placed her hands on her hips after patting some of the dirt off her apron. "Would you like some water? I just boiled some for you and Eli in the kitchen. You probably won't get any for some time since it would be a waste to carry any with you."

Noreen swallowed the dry lump in her throat, wishing she could take her knapsack with her, filled with canteens of water and other necessities she would need for her journey. Her mother explained earlier that day, though, that bringing anything other than the small compass hidden inside her jacket pocket would be pointless because the Government would take any of her additional items and discard of them immediately. "I'll have some in a moment, thank you, but I wanted to talk to you alone first."

Mrs. Satchell became fidgety as she played with the strings of the apron that wrapped twice around her stomach and tied in front of her waist. "About what, hun?"

Noreen narrowed her eyes in confusion. "What do you mean 'about what'? I want to say goodbye to you, just the two of us."

"There's no need for that, sweetheart. I'll always be with you, just as your father is with us right now." She gestured toward the five stones that created a circle in the dirt beside the garden where the body of Noreen's father rested.

Noreen peeked over to the grave as she shook her head in disagreement. "No, you're wrong, there is a need, mother!" she turned back to the woman before her, her voice building with tension. "I *need* to say goodbye to you! I *need* to know that you will wipe Louise's tears after you tell her I'm gone, that you will comfort Charlie when you tell him he is no longer getting married because of me. I *need* you to tell them how sorry I am for not being here for them when we *need* each other most! Please, mom, I *need* you to make sure everyone will be alright, including you. I *need you* to be strong. You don't understand, I *need* closure!"

Noreen blinked back tears as her mother took her in her arms. "I will be, honey, I will. I will tell them, don't you worry. And they will understand because we are a family, and we love each other, always and no matter what, right?" She patted Noreen's hair and they both cried onto each other's shoulders.

Noreen wanted to say so many things to her mother, but no words escaped her lips. She wanted to laugh one last time with her, to hear one more of her stories. She wanted to stay in her arms forever and never let go, but like all her mother's stories, there was an end, and this was theirs. It would be their last goodbye and their final embrace. In a matter of minutes, her mother would become a memory and her face, over time, would be forgotten.

Mrs. Satchell pulled from their embrace to look into her daughter's eyes. "I will miss you so much, my child," her voice remained even despite her unsettling expression, "I know you are not a little girl anymore, but you will always be my little girl." She wiped her daughter's cheeks with her thumbs. "Letting you go is the hardest thing I have ever done, but I know you will be okay because you, Noreen, you are so strong and so brave, just like your father."

Noreen's bottom lip twitched and she nodded back to the woman. "I love you, mom!"

"I love you too, Noreen, I always will." Mrs. Satchell kissed her daughter's forehead, and they both took another glimpse at the five stones encircling the grave beside the garden. Taking her daughter's hand, Noreen's mother led her back into the kitchen to locate Eli and drink the final sips of the well water before their time together ran out.

Chapter 16

*N*oreen was sweating profusely beneath her clothes. She inhaled choppy, shallow breaths as she fanned the flaps of her jacket to circulate air through its sodden material. Moist air sent goose bumps down her spine while the exhausting heat also gave her an overall sensation of lethargy.

Eli stood in front with his arms folded across his chest and his feet shoulder width apart. He rolled his shoulders back to straighten his torso whereas Noreen hunched over with her forehead nearly touching his back. Despite her drowsiness, she kept her forehead from leaning against him, though it hung just inches away from his sweatshirt.

She wondered if Eli's expression revealed any signs of fear like it had before, but luckily, the shade from the projected roof above them hid their faces in the darkness. "I don't understand," Eli mumbled over his shoulder. "It's almost five; why is this place so empty?" The shakiness in his voice answered Noreen's previous speculation.

Taking a breath, Noreen peered around him to view the empty dirt road before them. She looked in each direction but saw no one. She whispered back to Eli in a voice much calmer and more relaxed than his own. "Charlie told me that no one shows up until after the sirens go off. The sirens are what signal when the trucks are coming through the gates." Noreen watched Eli nod several times before she glanced up at the clock that hung above the Government's gates by a single piece of wire. It was less than thirty seconds until the clock struck five. "Remember what I told you earlier," she swallowed, "I cannot be seen too early!" Eli reached back and grabbed hold of Noreen's hand, squeezing it tightly as they watched the clock in silence. Five, Four, Three, Two,…

The clock struck five. Sirens blasted their eardrums, and the gates to Government Headquarters flew open. Three massive trucks drove past them at racing speeds, leaving tire marks and waves of dust in the trail of dirt behind them. Eli's grip became even tighter as they watched their neighbors run out of their hiding spots like savages. People who Noreen thought had the most innocent souls screamed horrifically as they carried tools like gardening shovels and kitchen knives and used them to beat their neighbors in a massive frenzy. Pools of blood spread across the ground, turning brown as it mixed with the dirt. The effects of the starvation and hunger in their town were revealed to her, within a single hour, for the mere possibility of getting meat.

Scanning through the crowd, Noreen recognized many of her neighbors beating one another for the carcasses being thrown off the trucks. Many of them even nibbled on the raw meat greedily as they fought off their neighbors and strained to take every piece for themselves. A familiar woman holding a log of firewood above her head caught her attention.

The woman grasped the wood with both hands and brought it down on an elderly man's back as she attempted to retrieve a leg from one of the deer's' rotting carcasses. She left the man to cry out in pain and fall into the dirt. As the girl bent over to rip the appendage off the dead animal, Noreen recognized her. With her hair pulled back and her face streaked with blood, the woman had appeared different to Noreen at first, but she soon realized that it was, without a doubt, her brother's ex-fiancée, Madeline, and the man she had attacked was her father. Noreen closed her eyes to avoid having to witness Madeline return to her elder and dangle the appendage before him in a teasing manner.

How could she do such a thing? Noreen thought. She could never imagine hitting anyone, especially her own father, for a piece of rotting animal as Madeline had just done. The girl absolutely disgusted her, and Noreen became incredibly thankful then that Madeline had called off the wedding with her brother. *What did Charlie ever see in her?* Noreen thought of the sweet, innocent girl that she had only met on a handful of occasions. *Why hadn't any of us seen this side of her?*

... But what if Charlie also became like this, like a savage, on Day 19? No, he couldn't. He was her brother, and she knew him far better than she knew his ex-fiancé. Charlie would never harm anyone except in self-defense. Never.

The memory of the night she left for The Cove for the last time, thankfully, surfaced in her conscious. Charlie had attacked her that night. He attacked her to protect their father because he thought she was someone from the Government, but he had also jumped back just as quick once he recognized Noreen and he proceeded to weep hysterically for nearly injuring his sister. That night alone proved that her brother was not, nor could he ever be, a savage. Charlie was nothing like the people in front of her.

Noreen let go of Eli's hand and plugged her fingers into her ears to block out the screams and cries, the sounds of objects being thrown and animal limbs being torn apart. She wondered how Eli could watch such horror and have such a strong stomach when it came to viewing such terrible images. A hand thumped on her back just then, and Noreen jumped away from it, pressing herself against the stone wall behind her. To her relief, the hand belonged to Eli, and he was reaching back to get her attention.

He looked back with an expression that lacked any hint of fear, unlike before. "You must watch this with me, or at least focus on the trucks themselves!" he demanded. His voice was much louder and far more even than she expected. "We need to know when to reveal ourselves or when to reveal you and where!" Suddenly, the sound of a truck skidding in the dirt disrupted their brief exchange, and they turned to see the vehicles heading back toward the gates. "It's time!" Eli grabbed her hand once again, and they began to run, side by side, out of shadows and into the sunlight.

    Noreen ripped her hand free of Eli's to move herself faster and faster past the violent crowd. She pumped her arms violently, using all her strength to sprint as fast as she could while watching the trucks to the right of her. Eight men wearing gas masks and body suits half stood in the bed of each of the three trucks while carrying large guns in their hands. Each time the cars swerved to dodge the bumps and dips in the dirt road, the men gripped the sides of their truck to avoid being thrown from the vehicle.

    Noreen tasted the sweat that dripped from her upper lip as she watched her neighbors glaring at her from the corners of her lids. With her damaged skin now fully revealed in the sunlight, the screams of her neighbors changed from that of anger and pain to sheer panic and terror. "Leper!" "She's a leper!" Their yells and taunts broadcasted loudly over her raging breaths. The first rock thrown hit her hip causing Noreen to shriek out at the unexpected pain. Another rock hit her chest and another to her thigh. More rocks began to bruise her already yellow tainted skin.

    Running diagonal to the trucks, Noreen's legs began to feel heavy, and she felt herself slowing down despite her determination to push herself further. Eli was in front of her now running faster while unknowingly lengthening the distance between them. The trucks flew past. It was too late.

    The people of her town were going to stone her to death, and their attempt to reach the Town of East would have been for nothing. She was going to die before ever getting a chance to meet her twin sister and to see the other side. Her mother would no longer have to lie to Louise but would be telling her the truth that Noreen did, in fact, die on Day 19.

Her run slowed to a jog and eventually she stopped. A few of the townspeople had vanished out of fear, but many still remained along the dirt road and continued to throw rocks at her, including Madeline. *It's all over.* Noreen gasped for air while her hands trembled in fear. She covered her head as more and more rocks flew in her direction, though no one would dare come close to her.

Through her sheltering arms, Noreen could see Eli stop as well and turn back to face her. She squinted her eyes to see exactly what he was doing. He seemed to be reaching for something beneath his clothes only to reveal the glock that had been tucked in the back of his jeans. He raised the weapon in the air and fired a shot. And then another. He continued to fire shots until the trucks slammed on their breaks and turned back in their direction. At the deviation in the truck's usual path, the people throwing rocks screamed even louder and quickly scattered out of sight. Noreen lowered her arms to her sides, no longer needing them to defend herself against her final attacker, Madeline, who disappeared through a cottage doorway while dragging her father close behind.

Noreen started for Eli, but the trucks too pushed forth with equivalent resolve. Suddenly, the bullets in Eli's gun ran out and his arm lowered. He took a step toward Noreen, but another shot fired. Noreen blinked and the Doe crashed to the ground with his face hitting the dirt. She screamed and she ran toward him, but the trucks swerved between them and blocked her path. More trucks entered through the gates carrying men and women with machine guns all pointed directly at her. Her heart raced with thumps pounding larger than what she believed her chest could handle. They surrounded her, and she had no escape, but that was what she wanted, right?

Her throat was the only part of her body to go dry as the guns inched closer and closer. Claustrophobia overwhelmed her, and the stench of death increased in potency. She was becoming the animal she had been told stories about; like in her mother's tales, she was now the doleful sheep being herded away, away from its own kind.

Turning in circles, Noreen deliberately spun herself to see every angle of space she had left between her and each of the muzzles pointed in her direction. She began to feel dizzy, but before she could rotate herself any further, a bag was thrown over her face and down the rest of her body until she was completely encased in it. She clawed at the small circle of light above her while gasping for the little air that seeped through its seams. A boot began kicking her repeatedly in her side and Noreen tumbled to the ground. She squirmed desperately inside the bag, clawing for the light above her but careful not to block the air coming through the same opening with her fingertips. The light she sought was getting smaller and smaller as the strings of the bag were being tightened until she was surrounded by complete darkness.

The only air available to breathe was the unpleasant stench that seeped through the threads of the sack. She could feel herself being dragged away, and she began to scream and kick defiantly as the bag scraped against the lumps of rocks in the dirt beneath her. Another boot kicked her side, forcing the air to escape her lungs. Noreen's screams ended. She gave up fighting in order to calm her breathing and hopefully conserve the little oxygen she had left seeping into the bag.

Around her, no words were spoken, so she was unable to hear any of her kidnappers' voices as they dragged her away from her home. For a long time, Noreen could only hear the bag scraping against the ground and her shallow breaths filling up her lungs. She tried to breathe as quietly as she could to listen for anything that could get her mind off the moment the bullet pierced through Eli's shoulder. Every time her bag scraped over a rock, she ignored the pain and subconsciously pictured Eli holding the glock above his head and pulling its trigger. She could have been stoned to death, but he saved her once again, only to be shot from behind in his right shoulder. He protected Noreen, this time without anyone asking him to. Eli had risked his life for her.

Finally, Noreen heard the squeaking and scraping of the gates as they closed behind her. She was now in Government territory. "Clear the gates!" A woman's voice projected, "the second fence will turn on in 3…2…" The sound of a loud zap vibrated, and Noreen flinched. She did not know a second fence existed behind the first, but the zap had something to do with it. Muffled voices came from all directions, and though she could not make out exactly what the voices were saying, she knew they were deciding what to do with her.

The shouting stopped abruptly and Noreen felt multiple pokes all over her body from what felt like giant forks stabbing her as if she was one of their lifeless carcasses. Without warning, the forks shoveled under her and lifted her from the ground. She was being carried to a different location but was unable to see where. Her overheated body sizzled inside the bag until it unexpectedly touched a tremendously cold surface under her.

The forks were removed from beneath her body, and Noreen felt herself cooling down instantly. She was surprised she had not passed out when she was being hauled into the Government's headquarters, with the lack of oxygen and the thick burning heat of the sun roasting her alive, but she felt almost better now that her body was cooling down against what felt like the glass lens of her father's old spectacles.

She was lowered to the ground, though her body never left the cold surface. A latch turned when the floor beneath her stilled and Noreen squirmed forward, following the sound until her head hit a wall of glass. Confused, she twisted her body and inched backward until her feet hit another wall behind her. Terrified, Noreen began to roll herself around inside the bag, but a wall stopped her in every direction. She was trapped inside what appeared to be a glass container.

The sounds around her faded until everything went quiet. Noreen could no longer hear anything except the sound of her own movements and breaths. Her ears rang in the silence, and she started to panic. Terrified that the crate was sealed air-tight, she began kicking and clawing at the sides of the box in desperation. She pushed her hands out in front of her until she could feel its slippery walls from within the threaded sack. Through the cloth, her fingertips grazed over a few round holes in the sides of the container, and to Noreen's disbelief, she felt cold air flowing through them and into her crate, as though a late winter blizzard had interrupted their early summer.

Hours later, the clanking of the container's latch disrupted the elongated silence as it opened the glass lid. A swiping sound of ripping thread lasted merely seconds before Noreen heard something placed onto the glass beside her. Before she knew it, the latch sealed her container once again, and there was silence. After a few moments of waiting, she squirmed around in her bag only to realize that the strings that tied its knot had been cut. Without pause, Noreen tore open the top of the sack with the little room she had inside her container and shimmied herself free of its darkness. The cool air that seeped through the holes of the crate seemed even cooler once she was free of the bag, but she took off her jacket regardless. While she could not see through the glass itself, the holes that chilled her space also illuminated the box.

She blinked several times to adjust her eyes from the complete darkness of her sack to the now pure white that nearly blinded her. As she rubbed her eyes, an unidentified scent trickled up her nostrils. She opened them instantly to find the source of the delectable aroma venting through the same holes on the sides of her container. While sniffing the air, Noreen flipped onto her stomach and raised her body until she was on her hands and knees with her head nearly touching the top of her container. All Noreen could do was blink at the sight before her.

She felt as though her mind was playing tricks on her or that she was hallucinating a terrifying nightmare for her already starving gut. A glass plate rested in front of her, a tall, glass cup at its side. Both were completely empty with no food on the plate nor any water in the glass. Yet she could smell something cooking, something delicious she had never smelled before. *This must be some sort of trick.* Noreen thought, *they are just trying to get to me. Yes, that is exactly what they are doing- they are trying to trick me or tease me or something, but it won't work. No, I am not like the others of my town. I can control my hunger. I can control myself!*

Despite her attempt at willpower, Noreen lunged for the cup and lifted it to her lips, but no water came out, nor did any other sort of liquid drop between her lips. Irritably, she threw the cup at the wall in front of her, and it broke into thousands of pieces. Noreen gasped as the memory of Lawrence and her final night at The Cove flooded her consciousness. She grabbed her left wrist with her opposite hand and fell forward onto her elbows. She closed her eyes in remembrance, unable to stop and unable to forget. *"I gone show you how to do it!"* Lawrence's voice echoed in her memory.

Noreen opened her eyes and grabbed her jean jacket to wrap it around her palm. She began cleaning up the shards of glass in front of her like she had at The Cove. *"See we're workin' together, you and me, cleanin' up the mess you made."* Noreen continued to hear his whispers as though he were still standing over her. She covered the shards with her jacket and combed her fingers through her hair, stopping midway to plug her index fingers into her ears. She sat on her legs with her body hunched over.

"What have I done?" Noreen shook her head, speaking to herself out loud. "This is all my fault, everything is all my fault. I would not be here if it had not been for that night. I would not look like…like this had it not been for that night." She unplugged her ears and began to rub her arms repeatedly. "And Eli. Oh God, Eli would still be alive right now. He would be here suffering with…" Noreen shut her mouth.

She could not believe those words were about to come out, yet she knew exactly why she had thought them. She was thankful Eli did not have to suffer with her, and thankful he would not be poked and teased like an innocent, doleful sheep being sent to the slaughter house, the same sheep of her mother's harsh and unlikeable narratives. But despite her gratitude, Noreen was terrified of being alone and having to face her biggest fears in solitude. At her home, she had always felt that she needed to be strong for someone else, so her family or friends would not be afraid or get hurt. Now, as she sat hunched inside the lonely crate, she was forced to be strong for herself and only herself. She could not afford to let anything or anyone break her.

Noreen stopped rubbing her arms and lifted her weight off her elbows. "I did not come all this way for nothing," she whispered quietly. She curled her fingers inward until they formed tight fists and, while staring blankly at the white floor beneath her, Noreen slammed each fist simultaneously against the glass. "Whoever is out there better listen up!" she commanded. Her breaths quivered, yet her hands were still. "I am not afraid of you. Do you hear me? I said I AM NOT AFRAID OF YOU!"

She waited for a response, some sort of sound, but there was only silence. Scooting forward, she kneeled onto her jean jacket over the shards of glass. She pushed against the side of the crate near the latch, but it would not budge. Desperate, Noreen cupped her hands around her eyes and pressed the outside of her palms against the glass, but all she saw was white, absolutely nothing but white.

A flood of emotions rushed through her. She did not understand why she was in there or how much longer it would be until someone came for her or responded to her cries. One thing was certain, though, all she could do was wait. Scooting back again, Noreen laid down with her stomach facing up. She hummed to distract herself from the appetizing smell that still haunted her breaths while she pressed her toes against the far wall of the crate in a rhythmic motion with her throat generating its beat.

Chapter 17

'Stop, please, I beg of you!' Her body lay flat on the ground while a large unidentifiable man jammed his boots onto her spine. The weight of the man imprisoned her against the ground keeping Noreen completely immobile and helpless. A second, thick-bodied man stepped onto her back and pressed his bare feet down hard onto the lumps of her spine. *'You're gonna break my back, please, no!'* Noreen wailed as a third man joined the others on top of her. It was getting harder and harder for her to breathe as the weight of the men crushed her lungs. *'Get off of me, please, my back, it's gonna break!'* Her desperate pleas were meaningless to the strangers who purposely shifted their weight to the center of her spine and heckled maliciously as they waited for it to break.

Just moments later, a piece of bone ripped through Noreen's skin as her spine snapped midway down her back. Before she knew it, the men had disappeared leaving Noreen stranded and alone with no one to hear her despairing cries.

―※―

Noreen flinched from the shooting pain that darted through her back. She jerked her body forward but hit her head on the white, glass ceiling above her. She shouted words of profanity as she eased herself back to her prior positioning on the cold floor. She touched her spine subconsciously to check its condition before even considering checking her head. Her spine was still intact; she was alright. *It was only a dream.* Noreen assured herself, though her chest and limbs were still damp with the sweat triggered by her nightmare. She shivered from the moist perspiration that clung to her skin along with the unnaturally cold air blowing at each of her sides.

She wondered how long she had slept, reasoning it must not have been for long since the delicious scent still lingered in the air with an even stronger potency. Noreen sniffed and followed the nearby scent as she slowly turned onto her stomach and lifted her body into the same hunched position as before. To her amazement, the shards of glass were gone and her jacket was neatly folded beside an unbroken glass cup and plate. Unlike before, though, a clear liquid filled the cup to its rim, and on the plate sat a single, perfectly round blueberry.

Noreen hesitated. *I'm still dreaming. This is some sort of trick again, I know it!* She leaned forward despite her contemplations and, using her finger, Noreen poked the fruit causing it to roll off the plate and onto the floor. *It's real!* She lunged for the little, blue ball as it continued to roll away from her but trapped it with her fingertips after it bounced off the opposing wall. She pinched the blueberry and lifted it to her lips, swallowing the fruit after a single chew. Its flavor came and went faster than the time it took Noreen to chug the chilling water from the glass. Once again, the cup and plate were empty, leaving her even hungrier than before.

Holding her stomach, Noreen hunched over and waited for a second blueberry to come. She closed her eyes, believing that if she closed them long enough, another would magically appear, but one did not. As time passed, she found that it was only when she slept could she awaken to a single serving of some fruit or vegetable with a cup of water in the adjacent glass. It was not a guarantee, though, that the 'meals' would always be provided.

At times when she awoke, she would find a scrap of food and a cup of water, at others, there would be nothing. With hopes that something consumable would be waiting for her, even if it were just a small blueberry, Noreen slept as often as possible. She participated in the ritual of sleeping and eating and sleeping and starving for what seemed like an endless amount of time with the lingering scent of some unidentifiable yet delicious substance relentlessly rising up her nostrils.

She lost track of the number of meals she was given after her eleventh, she also lost track of time altogether. She had no way of knowing if it was day or night, but to Noreen it did not matter since her sleep patterns at home were just as unusual. All she could think about was her next meal and when it would arrive, but never did the food match the haunting scent, never did it consist of more than a few bites, until now…

Noreen woke, half expecting to see a meal in front of her. To her surprise, she found more than she ever hoped for. As usual, the cup was filled to the rim with water, but unlike all the other meals in the past, the plate steamed with a warm snack that seemed to be just waiting for her.

Raising her left hand, Noreen poked her finger into the mushy bread steaming on the glass. Like the first fruit she had been given, she found that the bread was also real. Something was off, though, and she wondered why after so long that the meal would be changed, that it would be bread rather than fruit. Noreen sniffed the air. The unidentifiable scent was closer than ever before; it was coming directly from her sandwich. Curious, Noreen peeled off the top layer of toast, pausing as she gazed down at the source of the unidentifiable odor.

While she recognized the piece of white bread topping the sandwich, she had never seen the white and yellow goo that separated the two pieces of toast. It looked like an eye staring at her with the yellow surrounded by a thick white blanket of more unnatural goo. She lifted the sandwich, nevertheless, and took a bite. It was something she had never tasted, but she liked it. She shoved more of the sandwich into her mouth, finishing it off in seconds.

Noreen looked over to the top layer of toast as it rested on the floor beside her and considered ripping it apart with her teeth, but decided against it. Instead, she pulled her jacket to the side until it fell off her shoulders and tucked the bread into the pocket of her coat, opposite the one possessing her compass. She patted the material to make certain that both the compass and the bread were safely secured inside before she pushed her arms through the sleeves and put on her jacket. The piece of toast she saved rested close to her stomach and warmed the skin beneath her top.

Noreen lowered her body down even lower to the floor of her container to lick the remaining crumbs off her plate. She swiped the cup once she was finished and tilted the glass to her lips. Cool water touched her tongue, eventually filling her entire mouth and throat. She smiled as she swallowed the clean, refreshing liquid, continuing to tilt the glass against her lips until no more liquid dripped from the cup. She craved more like always but refrained from taking the piece of bread from her pocket.

She began to hum once again as she stared blankly at the colorless wall before her. She rocked herself back and forth to her throat's dull and dreary rhythm in order to distract herself from the slice of bread that called to her from her pocket. *Just one bite, I could have just one.* Noreen twitched. *No, I must save it for when I need it. But I want it now, I must have it now.* "No!" Noreen finally screamed out loud. Her indecisive thoughts were controlling her as she subconsciously rested a hand over her pocket. She turned to the clean plate sitting beside her, picked it up, and licked it over and over. Her tongue eventually made its way off the plate, down to the floor, and onto the walls of the crate as she licked the already spotless glass.

As she ran her tongue over the surfaces of the container, little by little, the lights illuminating the box dimmed and the white around her cleared. It was then that Noreen witnessed the unimaginable. The box became translucent for the first time, and she could finally see the silver room her container was enclosed in. Immediately, Noreen pulled her tongue back into her mouth and closed her lips. She leaned away from the wall and stared back at the dozens of men and women in long, white coats as they surrounded her.

A few of the men and women sat behind thin, silver boxes, using their fingers to tap fast paced ticking noises on their tables as they observed her. Others stood even closer to Noreen, scribbling with their right hands on clipboards that were piled with stacks of marked papers. Noreen stiffened as she realized that the strangers in the white coats had been watching her the entire time…

Focusing on the Right Handers before her, Noreen heard a loud tapping noise echo through her crate and found an elderly man standing along the right side of her container. She flinched at the sight of the white haired man calling for her attention but chose not to respond verbally to his gesture. His brown eyebrows formed variations of wrinkled lines across his forehead as he moved his lips in a cumbersome motion, but Noreen still heard nothing.

Recognizing her predicament, the old man turned and waved to a younger man standing behind an angled desk on the opposite side of the room. He cupped his ear as the younger man turned a large dial counter clockwise until the old man removed his hand to press the tip of his index finger and his thumb together in an 'ok' symbol. As he did so, the sound of distant voices began to volumize inside her crate. They became louder and louder until Noreen could finally hear the white coated Right Handers with absolute clarity. "Can you 'ah' hear me now?" the man hovering over her asked with a mechanical voice. A simple glance from Noreen prompted the man to continue. "Very well then. I must 'ah' put on my glasses before the start of the 'ah' verbal examination."

Noreen scrambled to the opposite end of the crate from where the old man hovered and peered over to the audience watching her. Every move she had made, everything she had said or done, the white coated Right Handers noted and recorded down onto their stacks of papers or coded into their silver boxes. She had become one of their experiments, an unfortunate Left Hander just like her father.

Feeling her chest tighten, Noreen began to hyperventilate. She watched the old man with bile as he remained indifferent to her gasps. He motioned calmly to one of the females sitting behind him, as Noreen clutched her throat with her dominant hand. "Turn the valve counterclockwise approximately 'ah' twenty degrees to give the subject more oxygen." the old man commanded. A dark skinned woman behind one of the silver boxes nodded back to him before she stood and walked out of the room.

Noreen continued to wheeze, but the old man ignored her by simply removing his eyeglasses from his collar and blowing hot air over their frames. He rubbed them on his coat after several breaths and adjusted them over his lids. Noreen cursed the man under her breath, but before she even had a chance to call for his assistance, the woman reentered the room and air circulated faster into her container and her lungs. Noreen's breathing calmed, and the man cleared his throat to gain her attention.

"To start my verbal examination, I shall 'ah' introduce myself to the subject and give a basic explanation of its whereabouts to formulate a type of communication that involves less tension between myself and the 'ah' subject." Noreen could not tell whether the old man spoke to her or to the crowd of people behind him, since his eyes looked above her crate as he talked. "My name is Dr. Allen Conroy, and I am an 'ah' epidemiologist."

Allen Conroy. Noreen repeated his name in her head. *Allen Conroy… A.C.* Noreen raised her eyebrows as she came to yet another realization. She placed a hand on her pocket and began to feel unsteady. His initials were the same ones engraved on her compass. The man before her was the same man who had given the mocking gift to her father, meaning he was also the same man who had experimented on him over eight years ago.

"That basically denotes that I 'ah' study infectious diseases, with my focus, like all of my colleagues, being on the most life threatening and dangerous disease, the Infection." Dr. Conroy stuttered as he spoke while the pauses he took between each of his words caused his speech to sound choppy and unemotional. "As the 'ah' subject under examination, you must know exactly what I am talking about." His smile revealed a set of perfectly white teeth surrounded by two drooping lips. Noreen could tell that the doctor spoke to her now, though not once did he look directly at her.

"Now," Dr. Conroy continued, oblivious to Noreen's apprehension, "we shall begin with a 'ah' series of questions that are the least difficult for the subject to answer. Then the 'ah' questions will become increasingly more difficult. Everyone," the old man turned away from Noreen to face the crowd behind him, "please remember to take notes and observe carefully."

The same man who had turned the dial to allow Noreen to hear rushed over to Dr. Conroy and handed him a clipboard. Noreen watched him hustle back to his slanted desk before she peered at the others in the room. The woman who had increased her oxygen was now in the back behind one of the silver boxes. Like the woman, not a single person in the room, other than Noreen had a single blemish on their skin. Even the old man before her had no scars or discolorations visible on his body, other than the red blotches covering his cheeks. "So, as I established, here is an easy one," Dr. Conroy paused to lick the pen he retrieved from his coat pocket, "what is your full birth name?"

Noreen hesitated. She knew she could not tell him her real name. Dr. Conroy would know of her father, and he could send the Government after her family. The old man looked up from his papers and above Noreen's head. His eyes blinked more often than usual. "Is the subject unresponsive?" he asked. Noreen remained quiet. "We know you can talk and, to answer your question from earlier, the one you obnoxiously shouted, we not only can hear you, now that we have increased your volume, but we have been able to hear you throughout your entire duration inside my laboratory. So, let's refocus our 'ah' attention on the examination, shall we?" Dr. Conroy shifted his head to the side to yell over his shoulder. "Please, delete and/or erase the previous 'ah' fifty-five words I have just spoken to the subject from all notepads and computers and we shall start again with the initial question." He licked his pen again before jotting sentences on his notepad. He bent over Noreen's crate to get a closer look at her. "What is your full birth name?" he asked a second time.

Noreen swallowed and whispered back to him, "Jane Doe."

"May the subject please speak loudly and 'ah' clearly for the entire staff to hear?" Dr. Conroy commanded.

"My name is Jane Doe." Noreen said louder. She hoped her voice did not sound as shaky as it felt rumbling out of her throat.

"Interesting, but will the subject please state its *real full birth* name since no individual is born a Doe."

"I don't know my real name," Noreen lied, "I grew up in an orphanage and-"

"As I noted earlier," Dr. Conroy cut her off, "your statement is an 'ah' interesting one, but I presume it is false, wouldn't you agree, Mr. Colt?" Noreen froze as Lawrence was guided into the room with his hands tied behind his back. He lashed his body violently as the guards pushed him forward, but once he realized that it was Noreen who was trapped inside the cage, he smiled and walked forward without resistance.

Noreen could not believe her eyes. She thought she had left her abusive employer behind as a nightmare of her past, but here he was, walking toward her while undoubtedly wanting to kill her. The guards stopped Lawrence about a foot away from her container, but he still managed to spit at Noreen, and create a long streak of saliva across her wall of glass. In response, one of the guards punched Lawrence hard in the stomach. A skinny, young man wearing gloves and a face mask rushed over to her container then and wiped away the saliva with a cloth and disinfectant.

By the time the man cleaning the glass finished and carefully enclosed the cloth inside a small bag with an airtight seal, Lawrence was standing upright again, and was fuming with anger. Watching him, Noreen was thankful for the first time to be inside her container. But while the glass protected Noreen from her worst nightmare, her entire body still shook with fear. "I also presume that you 'ah' know Mr. Colt. Is that correct?" Dr. Conroy asked.

Noreen was unable to respond with Lawrence's hungry smirk fixated upon her. "I presume that you do know Mr. Lawrence Colt since your friend was the one to confirm his identity," Dr. Conroy assumed. Noreen looked away from Lawrence and stared at the old man who spoke to her. "Mr. Colt has given me some useful information concerning the 'ah' John Doe you were captured with," he added.

Captured with? Noreen thought to herself. *That means they must have taken Eli as well.* Noreen couldn't help but smile from relief. "He is alive?" she asked.

"He is currently under investigation by agents in a different sector of the building but shall be brought in here when they are finished with him. Ahem, Mr. Colt-"

"Finished with him?" Noreen interrupted the doctor for a second time in a voice that no longer quivered with fear. "What are they going to do with him?"

"The Doe's whereabouts are up to the agents, I have no further knowledge on the matter," the old man continued to look over her crate as though he were lost. "Now, back to my 'ah' explanation. Mr. Colt has been held for a crime he did not commit. The guns in his 'ah' possession were stolen four days before the nineteenth of May by the Doe currently under investigation.

This was confirmed, because the handgun used by the Doe during the food distribution, in fact, belongs to Mr. Colt." Noreen peeked at Lawrence who laughed beneath his breath. "Although guns are illegal for all 'ah' Left Handers to have in their possession, Mr. Colt has agreed to tell us everything he knows about you and the Doe. In exchange, Mr. Colt will not be sent to the Forest of Lepers as punishment."

"So what'll be the Doe's punishment then?" Lawrence narrowed his eyes as he restated Noreen's previous question in a callous fashion.

"That is confidential information. Now, Mr. Colt, if you would be so kind as to tell me," Dr. Conroy glanced above Lawrence's head, "what is the subject's name?"

"Noreen." There was a hint of enjoyment in Lawrence's voice as her name was spoken.

"And her surname, Mr. Colt?" Dr. Conroy continued, blinking habitually.

Lawrence scrunched his eyebrows, "I never knew her full name."

"Interesting. And I say that is interesting because you 'ah' look as though you know this 'Noreen' very well. I am correct?"

The old man waited until Lawrence responded. "Yeah, I know her well, I know her real well," he winked his droopy eye at Noreen causing shivers to trickle down her spine.

"If you would elaborate, Mr. Colt, we cannot decrease your sentence unless you give us the information we need to continue our examination."

Lawrence smirked, showing a few missing teeth that had been present when Noreen last saw him. She wondered if his teeth were missing from a beating by the Government or by Eli on her last night at The Cove. Whatever the reason, they gave him an even more disturbing and threatening appearance. "You see," Lawrence started, "this one here was, well to be truthful and all, she was a little obsessive about me." Noreen clenched her teeth together. "She would come by after work and try to lure me with her thin, little body practically screamin' at me from under that tight, peach dress of her's. But I, the gentleman I am, would never take advantage of such a sweet, young thing like that. No sir, I am, well, I am some years older than she and me goin' after her would not be right. But Noreen, she would not stop throwin' herself at me like the tramp she is. It was almost embarrassing."

"You son of a bitch," Noreen glared at him, wishing she was not stuck inside the crate so she could hit him as hard as she could directly in his drooping eye.

"Will the subject please 'ah' refrain from verbal communication until Mr. Colt has finished his explanation?" Dr. Conroy's right hand never paused as he jotted down endless scribbles across his notepad without ever glancing down to the paper. "Mr. Colt, can you please inform us when you realized the subject became a leper?"

"A what?" Lawrence cocked his head in confusion.

"The scars and sores that cover the subject's skin, they are symptoms of the form of leprosy caused by the Infection. When did you first notice them?" Dr. Conroy restated his question while also providing further explanation.

Noreen held her breath. She needed Lawrence to lie this time. She needed him to tell the Right Handers that he had no idea where her scars came from; she needed them to believe that she was truly a leper. "I 'uh'," Lawrence straightened his back as he considered his response.

"He saw me in the alley!" Noreen chimed in before Lawrence could answer. She changed her tone enough to sound believable. "Outside his…work. I was wearing my peach dress because I knew how much he liked it on me. I hoped he would look past my… sores and love me for what is on the inside, because it's what is on the inside that counts, right?" she wanted to vomit at the thought of loving a man like her employer, but she held herself together.

"I see," Dr. Conroy noted, blinking abnormally fast. "And why didn't Mr. Colt turn you in? Why did you 'ah' turn yourself in?"

"Because, well," Noreen paused to think of another lie. Out of the corner of her eye, she saw Lawrence raise an eyebrow at her quizzically, though he remained quiet. "Because I promised him I would!" Noreen paused again until the old man prompted her to continue. "I promised him I would turn myself in because I was devastated that he would not love me back," Noreen hoped she would be able to remember all of her lies. "But I still loved him, so that meant I did not want him to get in trouble for knowing about a leper like me. That is why I showed up on Day 19 and-"

"And will the subject please explain where the 'ah' John Doe comes in to her explanation?"

"E-John, was in love with me," Noreen answered him, "and I did not love him back, but he was willing to go anywhere I was. It's all a…'um' messed up love triangle." Noreen clenched her teeth again, waiting for the old man's response.

"Interesting," Dr. Conroy concluded. Noreen hated how the old man continued to use that word. "Is the subject truthful in her statement, Mr. Colt?"

Left

Noreen hoped Lawrence was smart enough to say 'yes' to Dr. Conroy, so he would not receive further imprisonment for abuse on top of his charges for possession of guns and alcohol. If he agreed with her, then she would still be regarded as a leper by the Government. To her relief, Lawrence eventually nodded his head in support of her false explanation.

"Very well then, Mr. Colt. We thank you for the useful information you have provided. Would the guards please escort Mr. Colt back to his cell?"

"My cell?" Lawrence repeated Dr. Conroy's request in the form of a question. "I told you everythin' you needed to know. Why the hell am I goin' back down there? You said-" Lawrence squirmed around in the same fashion as when he first entered the room. For the first time, Noreen noticed he limped on the same leg she had stabbed with the shard of glass on her last night at The Cove.

"I said your punishment would be lightened, and it is! Nevertheless, you still violated the law and that is never acceptable, especially for those of your town. As a matter of opinion, though, I believe you should be 'ah' thanking me for not sending you to the forest." Noreen looked back and forth from the old man staring disturbingly above Lawrence's head to Lawrence, as he struggled to be freed. "In that cell, Mr. Colt, you will never have to worry about lepers ever again, because you will be in there for the remainder of your life."

"You no good," Lawrence spit, "piece of-" A bag was thrown over his head and his voice was muffled before he could finish his statement. The two guards at his sides dragged him toward the double doors and out of the room while the skinny man with the mask and the gloves rushed over to disinfect the floor. Noreen watched Dr. Conroy's smiling face as they heard Lawrence's struggling, even after the silver doors had long been closed. The man did not seem to have a conscience, and that terrified her.

Dr. Conroy fluttered through his papers until he found a clean page. "Now that we know your first legal birth name is Noreen, will the subject please tell us its birth given surname?"

When Noreen did not answer his question, the doctor continued. He paced slowly around her container, and Noreen crawled in the opposite direction to stay away from him. "If the subject refuses to answer the examiner's questions, the examiner will be forced to use rather 'ah' extreme measures to retrieve the information. Do you know what we are capable of 'ah', what was it, Noreen?" Noreen hesitated again and Dr. Conroy raised his voice out of impatience. "Did the subject not comprehend the question?"

"I understood, yes," Noreen answered quickly.

"WELL?"

"No!" Noreen shook her head in terror, "no I am not sure what you are capable of, but I would-I would rather not find out."

Dr. Conroy smiled at her confession. "Then will the subject please answer the question: what is your real last name?" He placed his pen into his coat pocket and leaned over her crate, slamming his clipboard onto the glass. Noreen jumped and covered her face instinctively without responding to him. Dr. Conroy cleared his throat and stood up once again. "Oh, Mrs. Jackson?" His voice sounded far too calm and cheerful. It was as though his emotions had flip-flopped in another direction. "Will you please send for the 'ah' Doe?"

Noreen uncovered her face and watched the middle aged woman stand for a second time and walk over to a small, black box that hung against the wall beside the silver doors. The woman pressed a button beside the box, and she parted her lips to speak. Moments after she returned to her desk, the doors to the room were shoved open and a half naked, broad chested figure entered the room. A bag was draped over the man's head, and a large, white bandage wrapped around his shoulder. Noreen pressed her palms against the glass as she shook her head in disbelief and in pity. The man before her was Eli.

Chapter 18

*T*hough he was taller than the four guards escorting him into the room, Eli's head drooped forward, making him appear shorter that he actually was. His jeans were covered with dirt and his sweatshirt and flannel were both missing from his upper half. The white bandage stretched across his right shoulder and tied on the opposite side of his chest beneath his left underarm. His right arm was immobile, but the rest of him appeared to function smoothly and was unharmed. Noreen almost cried with joy for the life of the man she thought was dead, but she kept herself composed. Dr. Conroy blocked her view of Eli by walking between them, but Noreen quickly scrambled to the opposite end of her cage to keep her guardian angel in sight.

"Lift the Doe's bag, please," Dr. Conroy demanded of one of the guards that restrained Eli by his wrist.

The bag was lifted, and Eli's head rolled to the side. Drool dribbled from his lower lip and onto his chest. His eyes were half open, yet he squinted them even further and looked in the direction of Noreen's container. "Eli!" she shouted to him as he struggled to stand. His mouth parted and a moan sounding like her name rumbled from of his throat.

"It is time the subject starts answering the examiner's questions," the old man smiled. While still gazing upward, Dr. Conroy raised his index finger and moved it in a circular motion to prompt the men holding Eli to turn him until his back faced her. As they did, Noreen's jaw dropped in horror. An uncountable number of multidirectional scars covered his entire back.

A man wearing a metal vest entered the room then, and Eli was forced to his knees. The man in the vest removed a large, brown ring from his belt buckle and slowly unwound the coil into a long, flexible rope. He whipped the air several times as though warming up his arm, while tormenting both Left Handers in the room. Tears rolled down Noreen's cheeks. "No, please, no. Please don't hurt him anymore, please!" she begged, but the man in the vest whipped the air again. "NO!" Noreen screamed louder. "I beg of you! Please don't hurt him!"

Dr. Conroy laughed and clasped his hands behind his back, leaving his clipboard on her crate. The man in the vest nodded in response to the doctor's snicker, and he whipped Eli as hard as he could against his back. Blood squirted across the floor and Eli moaned. He leaned forward, attempting to place his head against the ground, but he was forced to maintain a kneeling position by the guards who surrounded him. The man in the vest held his whip by his side, waiting for another of the old man's signals. "You sick bastard!" Noreen screamed from her container. She began shoving her body against the wall of glass in attempts to escape her entrapment.

"We know you care about the Doe, Noreen," Dr. Conroy ignored her efforts to break free of the glass. His words were less choppy sounding than before. "We heard you in that crate talking about him, thus concluding that everything you just said about Mr. Colt is a lie," he smiled sadistically, "Tell us, Noreen, what is your last name?"

Noreen hesitated, and the man in the vest lifted his arm for another swing. "Wait!" she shouted before the man could lower his whip. "If I tell you my last name, will you stop hurting him?"

"It is a 'ah' possibility," Dr. Conroy responded as the man with the disinfectant rushed over to quickly remove the Left Hander's blood from the otherwise immaculate tiled floor.

"It's Foster. My last name is Foster." Noreen inhaled a deep breath, hoping he would believe her, while also hoping that Eli's father never disclosed his identity to him. Although it would not particularly matter, since the leper had probably long been deceased and Eli did not have any other family on the Left Handed side, she still did not want Dr. Conroy to remember him. "My name is Noreen Elizabeth Foster and I am his wife," she concluded.

The old man raised his eyebrows, forming deep lines across his forehead. "So you're telling me," his smile caved into his cheeks further as he prepared to laugh, "that the Doe's last name is Foster?" Noreen nodded, feeling slightly relieved that he had not recalled Eli's father but also quite disturbed as his upper lip curled distinctively to reveal his gums. "Oh, how fitting." the old man scoffed.

"If you let us remain together, we will go to the Forest of Lepers voluntarily and cause you no further trouble!" Noreen blurted out, ignoring his last comment. Her words silenced the old man instantly, and his grin disappeared.

He looked down and straight into her eyes for the first time in the entire examination. Noreen tensed but refused to let go of the Right Hander's glare. He whispered to her then, in a volume purposely too soft for the others in the room to hear. "There are many, very interesting points you have made, *Mrs. Foster*," he paused and opened his eyes wider as though struggling to focus. "The first point I will touch upon is in the form of a 'ah' question, a question I dare not care to know the answer to. This question is why someone with status like you marry a Doe? Simply does not make sense, does it?" Noreen swallowed but did not reveal tension in her expression.

"The second point I would like to make concerns the Infection itself. You see, the aftermath of the initial leakage of the Infection is genetic, Mrs. Foster. What you may not understand is that *every* left handed person is a genetic carrier of this disease, but only some, very unfortunate, Left Handers have it mutate into the specific form of leprosy, while others develop leprosy from close contact with other lepers. The lepers who have come through this building, many of whom were transported in the same crate you are locked in now, were all sent to the Forest of Lepers where there are no animals to hunt or any food to eat.

They have no choice but to become cannibals, Mrs. Foster, and if I send you there, to live in the forest, I am sure you would share their fate. I am also sure that those lepers absolutely terrify you, because I know for a fact you are not one of them!" Noreen raised her eyebrows at his declaration, finally revealing concern in her expression. "I have seen my fair share of lepers," Dr. Conroy continued. "They all have the same yellowed skin you do, but I have watched you closely, Mrs. Foster, ever since you were first brought here twenty-six days ago. I have examined the scars and sores covering your skin, and I have a sharp eye for noticing things out of the norm. For instance, your color is fading, you are no longer the same shade of yellow you once were. And the bruises that once covered your hands and neck have, for the most part, disappeared since your arrival into my laboratory.

So the question at hand is why the subject would want to go to the Forest of Lepers when the subject is completely free of leprosy? There are many possible reasons, all of which I do not care to know. But the truth is, I do not care what happens to you. You interfered with a Governmental organization by interrupting Day 19's monthly ritual, you withheld information from the Government when you knew that a Doe stole and possessed an illegal weapon, and my simplest reason is that you are a Left Hander, and I have no sympathy for anyone of your kind. That is why your request to go to the Forest of Lepers is definitely more than a possibility."

He pushed his glasses closer to his face as he grinned. "Oh, Mrs. Jackson?" He gazed above Noreen's head once again as he called for the woman behind the desk for a third time. "I shall leave my decision up to you. You are a married woman, and my most trusted assistant. You shall decide the subject and her spouses' fate." Dr. Conroy grabbed his clipboard and stepped away from Noreen's container. "Let me know your 'ah' final decision, Mrs. Jackson." He nodded to the woman and walked briskly toward the double doors. Everyone in the room watched him except for the man in the vest who glared at Noreen as he marched behind the doctor. As Dr. Conroy pulled open the doors, he paused to shout back to Noreen. "Good luck to you, Mrs. Foster, wherever you wind up. You'll need it!"

By the time he disappeared behind the silver, the married woman Dr. Conroy instructed stepped toward Noreen's container. As she came closer, Noreen noticed the wedding band on the ring finger of her coffee colored hand. Her lips were pursed and her eyebrows were somewhat raised. She wore no makeup on her face other than a layer of skin-colored powder, that Noreen assumed was to hide any possible blemishes. She did not appear as old as Dr. Conroy, but she was at least in her early fifties. The woman examined Noreen as Noreen examined her back. "How old are you?" Mrs. Jackson finally asked.

"Eighteen," Noreen answered.

She raised her eyebrows even further. "And your husband?"

Noreen felt more comfortable talking to the woman than she did to the old man. "He is nineteen," she responded.

Mrs. Jackson nodded, looking down before raising her gaze again. "You are both very young and very naïve." Mrs. Jackson paused and, to Noreen's surprise, she truly looked concerned for her and Eli. "You have no idea what you are asking for or what you have gotten yourself into."

"But I do know, Mrs. Jackson," Noreen corrected her in a careful tone. "We would like to go to the Forest of Lepers so we can be together."

She could see the other staff members from the corners of her eyes. Each of them stared at her as though anticipating Mrs. Jackson's final decision. "I am sure there can be some arrangement made for you and your husband here, so you can both stay to-"

"No," Noreen interrupted, "please, let us go! We do not wish to be experiments any longer. We are asking to go to the Forest of Lepers." She turned her head toward Eli, who was now lying flat on the ground with his stomach and chest resting against the tiles beneath him. The four guards no longer held his limbs to keep him detained but were now standing beside his battered figure, knowing that the Left Hander could not escape them. She watched as the John Doe's blood-stained back rose and fell as he breathed unsteadily. "I cannot lose him." Noreen heard the truth of her words as she spoke them.

"Very well then," Mrs. Jackson sighed. Noreen turned her attention back to the woman standing before her. "I shall make the arrangements as soon as I can for you and your husband to leave Government headquarters and enter the Forest of Lepers by tomorrow morning. It is only fair to give you and your husband some time to rest before you leave here, especially for the sake of your husband." Mrs. Jackson peered over her shoulder to see Eli's body lying on the floor.

Noreen shuffled toward the edge of the glass nearest to where Mrs. Jackson was standing. The woman did not flinch nor did she appear frightened by Noreen's sudden movements, though she took a single step in the opposite direction. "Thank you, Mrs. Jackson, thank you!" Noreen cried.

The woman refused to look at Noreen and instead she watched the others in the room and their reactions to her decision. She walked briskly toward the small box against the wall. Again, Noreen watched her lips move as the woman spoke into the square. Unlike before, her soft voice was projected throughout the room. "Subject B9996-5162 verbal examination is now complete."

Unanimously, the sound of scribbling pens and unhuman clicks stopped, and the staff members all stood and began marching toward the exit. Mrs. Jackson stood beside the door and nodded to each of them as the fifty or so staff members marched past her. She pulled one of them aside and whispered into her ear before dismissing her with the others down the colorless hall.

Noreen, Mrs. Jackson, the four guards, Eli, and the thin man with the disinfectant remained in the laboratory. Mrs. Jackson walked toward the guards. "One of the sealed chambers is currently being prepared for Mr. and Mrs. Foster," she informed the other Right Handers. "They will be confined in the cell overnight before they leave tomorrow morning. Please bring Mr. Foster to cell number 1225."

As the four guards lifted Eli off the ground, Mrs. Jackson walked over to the thin man with the disinfectant. Noreen ignored her, and stared in Eli's direction, watching his head fall below his shoulders as he was carried away from her. "Please send for some guards to transport Mrs. Foster to cell number 1225." Mrs. Jackson's declaration to the little man did not seem to get Noreen's attention until after Eli disappeared from her view.

"Yes, ma'am," the man responded in a squeaky tone. He hustled out of the room with the disinfectant in his hands and the sealed bags half-tucked into his back pockets.

When Noreen and Mrs. Jackson were the only two left in the room, the woman ran to her desk to tap the keys behind her silver box. "I cannot have anyone watching us," she said. The lights in the room dimmed as her fingers continued to tap rapidly across the table. "I need to ask you something without any cameras recording our conversation." She clicked one last time before rushing back toward the glass container centered in the room.

"My name is Shaun Jackson, and I am a mother," Mrs. Jackson started. Noreen tilted her head in confusion, but before she could lean away, the woman reached underneath her buttoned coat near her chest and fetched a small, folded picture from under her clothes. "I keep this close to my heart because this picture is very important to me. It is all I have left of my son."

She unfolded the crumbled picture and pressed it against the side of Noreen's container. It was a picture of a newborn wrapped inside a blue blanket. He lay in a freshly painted yellow and white crib and had a few black hairs sticking straight out the top of his head. He had dark brown eyes and puffy cheeks. He was the most adorable newborn Noreen had ever seen. "He was declared a Left Hander when he was two, so he was sent to the other side, to your side." Mrs. Jackson's voice was quiet, "I need to know what happened to him."

"I don't know how I could tell if I know him from…"

"I know it's not much," she cut Noreen off, "but the only Left Handers I have seen besides you and your husband were lepers who were all incapable of comprehension and understanding. But you, you are different, and this is my only chance to know if my son is alright."

"I'm sorry I don't know."

"His name would be John Doe there, in the Town of West, like your husband. He was sent to an orphanage because we have no other family there. He is about your age, just three years younger. I imagine he looks like his father who has black, thick hair, um, is about five foot eleven in height and is much thicker than I in build. You must have seen him somewhere! Maybe in school?"

"We do not have schools in the Town of West, I'm sorry again." Noreen truly felt sorry for the woman regardless of the circumstances.

Mrs. Jackson bowed her head in defeat. "He is my only son. I had him when I was thirty-nine. All my life, doctors told me I was unable to have children until I became pregnant with him," she paused. Although she believed the woman to be out of line, Noreen figured she was revealing so much personal information because Noreen was someone the woman would never see again. "I was so happy when I was pregnant. I painted an entire room yellow, because I did not care one bit what the sex of my child was going to be. I was just happy I was going to have one! But he was taken from me and was never given back. I have worried about him every day for the past fifteen years!"

Noreen watched as the woman kissed the picture before folding and tucking it back under her clothes in its original place close to her heart. "He was a very beautiful baby. I'm sure he's doing just fine." Noreen tried to reassure the Right Hander. "The Town of West may not be the best place to live, but it is likely that your son is alive and well." Despite that the woman was of the other kind, Noreen felt she should say something more about her son, something to relieve the tension, but she could not tell if the mother had even heard her previous comment.

Not responding to Noreen right away, Mrs. Jackson straightened her shoulders and closed her eyes for several moments. "I have never been on the other side, in the Town of West, but I have heard many, many stories of the worst. I imagine that is why you are trying to escape from there."

"What you don't understand is that I work in Government headquarters as an epidemiologist, which means I am privy to a majority of our Government's secrets. Secrets no one in the Towns of East or West knows about for their own protection. My people," Mrs. Jackson paused, "not one Right Hander knows anything about your town unless they work for the Government. Of course they know of the Infection and its consequences, but they are given very little information about the other side, other than that, when their children are taken for being Left Handers, the Town of West is where they end up.

I cannot warn my people, even my husband, because I am under constant supervision. I must take a lie-detector test weekly, and if I do anything out of the ordinary, I am interrogated by our Government agents. I know what it feels like to be trapped, because I am emotionally trapped for the rest of my life. But my son, Darrell, he will be trapped physically in the Town of West for the rest of his life because no one ever gets the chance you have now.

Mrs. Foster, I know you are not a leper. I could tell Dr. Conroy knew that you are not a leper, and I could tell that everyone else here knows you are not one either. You are too responsive, too pleasant. That is why the decision to send you to the forest was such a difficult one, one that even Dr. Conroy could not make himself. But I am sending you there with hopes that you make it out of there alive with your loved one, because you both would not survive here for very long. If you stayed, you would become trapped here just like I am. I am giving you this chance because I do not believe it possible for you to cause harm to my people. We have done many, many experiments, all of which led me to believe that natural born Right Handers could never obtain the Infection, although I have yet to find a reason that explains why. I am also giving you a chance because a chance was exactly what my son, Darrell, never had and probably never will have."

A buzz sounded just outside the room, and Mrs. Jackson flinched. She used her hands to brush her face before she rushed back toward her desk. Noreen's mouth hung open from shock as she watched the woman hurry across the room. She could not believe what she had just heard. She had always thought Right Handers hated her people, but they in fact knew nothing of them at all!

Her head felt as though it were spinning as she tried to grasp what Mrs. Jackson had told her. Despite their differences, Noreen knew she needed to do something for the woman in return, and quickly, before the cameras were turned back on. She lunged forward, not even needing time to think. "Wait!" Noreen shouted. The woman paused to look up at her. "There are three orphanages in the Town of West. E-my husband, he is a John Doe, which means he grew up in one of the orphanages there. He may know your son!" Mrs. Jackson said nothing. "Visit our cell later tonight, and you can ask him of your son then!"

Mrs. Jackson stared from across the room with a face that was expressionless. Noreen waited for her response. "My sincerest good luck to you, Noreen."

Before Noreen could react, the woman clicked once and the lights in the room brightened and the doors to the room opened. "We are here for Subject B9996-5162," a strong looking man announced as he came to a halt merely a step within the entranceway. His feet aligned with his hips and his hands were clamped behind his back. Seven other men marched into the silver room and mimicked the first man's movements.

Mrs. Jackson nodded toward Noreen, and the eight men marched in unison toward her crate. "Subject B9996-5162 is to be taken to cell number 1225," she said mechanically. "Once inside the cell, she is to be released from her container and allowed to move about the chamber. There is a… Doe inside the chamber as well." Noreen recognized that she was the only one in the room to notice the woman's struggle as she spoke the derogatory word. "But the Doe is immobile for the time being, so it will not be a problem for any of you. Both the subject and the Doe are to be well cared for until their departure, understood?"

"Yes ma'am," the men shouted back in unison, and lifted Noreen's crate off the floor. Noreen looked around the men until she could see Mrs. Jackson. Staring into the silver box, the woman was expressionless and other than the rising and falling of her chest, she was completely still. Noreen wanted to thank the Right Hander again but knew it was not the time or place to do so. As the doors closed behind her, Mrs. Jackson peeked a glance at Noreen and acknowledged her by slowly closing and opening her eyes just once before staring back into the silver box in front of her.

Chapter 19

Noreen ran her hand lightly over the tight bandage, its once pure white color now dulled and darkened around the center of Eli's wound. Surprisingly, the wound itself had been well cared for, so Noreen left it alone and moved her fingertips over the dried blood that covered his back. She hesitated with her fingertips on his bare skin before touching the bloody slash closest to his neck. She spread her palms above the slit and inhaled a deep breath to calm herself. Several moments later, Noreen removed her hands from the Doe's skin and grabbed the cloth in her lap. After dipping it into the bowl of water on the floor beside her, she twisted the fabric until all of the excess water dripped back into the bowl.

    She placed her right hand gently on his back, just above the bloody slit nearest his neck, and pressed down on it for support before she raised the damp cloth with her left hand to his skin. She slowly eased the cloth onto one of his wounds causing the muscles in the Doe's back to tighten. She paused again before lifting the cloth and dabbing it cautiously to each lesion.

    Eli winced at her touch and each time the cloth would initially touch his back after it had been dunked in the icy water, but Noreen persisted to remove the dried blood from around his wounds, working from the bottom up. The cloth, along with the water in the bowl, was now tainted dark red, but its color did not bother Noreen. She dipped her hands into the water to dampen the rag without any fear of soaking her hands in the Doe's blood.

Eventually, she reached the deep gash just below his neckline. She scooted closer to him and moved her right hand further up his neck. His entire body felt so warm, despite having been trapped inside such an abnormally cold room for so long. She lifted the rag to his last wound, squinting her eyes to rid them of any tears that could fall down her cheeks. She could only imagine the pain he went through, but Noreen knew it would do no good to think such a horrible thought.

As she dabbed at the last wound, she saw Eli, out of the corner of her eye, reaching across his body with his left arm until he touched her hand as it rested on his neck. "I'm almost done," Noreen tried to sound indifferent. Eli squeezed her hand harder. Cleaning his wounds felt like déjà vu, as she remembered caring for his burned wrist long ago in a similar fashion.

After wiping away the dried blood from the last gash, she reached for the ointment one of the government workers had sent through the small, airtight drawer that reached through the wall of their cell to the inside of their chamber. Along with the ointment, the same worker surprisingly kept his word to Mrs. Jackson and gave them a bowl of water, cloth, two cups of water, and two sandwiches made from the same ingredients as the one Noreen had eaten for her last meal inside her glass container. This time, though, their sandwiches had been cold and the bread was not heated, but that had not stopped them from devouring the food like their starving neighbors on Day 19. Without Eli noticing, Noreen had stuffed the top slice of bread into her jacket pocket to store away with the other.

Removing her hand from under Eli's, Noreen twisted the rag over the bowl to squeeze out the remaining excess water from the damp cloth. She squirted the ointment onto the rag and dabbed at each of his wounds. "You know, that lady you told me about, Mrs. Jackson, she never came," Eli mumbled while Noreen spread the ointment.

"She will come," Noreen responded forcefully.

"Noreen, it's already morning."

"How can you tell?" she asked, knowing they had no way of telling time.

"They turned out the lights when we laid down to sleep," he paused and Noreen grimaced at the memory of sleeping across from him, too far to even touch, "and we woke up to the lights being on which means they'll probably be getting us soon."

Noreen ignored him and continued to spread the ointment onto his back. She knew he was right but did not want to admit it. She could not understand why the woman had not come. "Do you think you'll be ready to leave? I mean with your injuries and all."

"Cuts heal and my shoulder is only a flesh wound. I'll be fine."

Noreen sighed. She hoped he was right, but she couldn't count on it. She knew she would need to watch out for him more than he would be able to for her. Eli would hold her back, she was sure of it, but Noreen could never leave him behind nor did she mind taking care of him; she wanted him to get better, and she knew he would do the same for her.

After she finished spreading the ointment, she crawled beside him and hugged her knees to her chest while she rested her chin on her legs. To her surprise, Eli lifted his good arm over her shoulders and brought her close to him. "Thank you," he whispered.

Noreen lifted her chin and turned to face him, now resting her left cheek on her knees. She half smiled, "of course."

Eli kept his arm around her, but Noreen did not mind in the slightest. She did not care that the shoulder of her jacket touched the black, thick hairs of his underarm or that they both smelled of dried sweat. The warmth of his arm over her shoulders seeped through the thick material of her jacket and comforted her. It had been so long since they last saw one another, so long since they last held each other in their arms. Noreen had gone her whole life without truly knowing the man beside her, without ever feeling his touch, but now, after nearly a month apart, she knew she could not afford to lose him.

Noreen closed her eyes at the touch of Eli's lips on her temple. She smiled inevitably, feeling her face blush, so she quickly turned her head back until her chin rested on her knees. They were not strangers anymore, and at that moment Noreen realized they never had been. It had taken three years of unspoken acts of kindness for them to get where they were now, and Noreen wouldn't have it any other way. Eli tightened his grasp around her, but Noreen kept her eyes closed with her face still expressing its subtle grin.

After some time, the door to their cell opened and the air seemed to be sucked out of their chamber. Two men wearing dark green gas masks walked in with guns in their hands. A woman in a mask followed close behind them, her hair pulled back tightly into a bun. Her gloved hands were clamped behind her as she waited for the two guards to exit the room. Noreen lifted her chin off her knees and watched the men as they backed away slowly and shut the door. The air from the outside refreshed the musky smelling room but did not relieve the stench of their unwashed bodies altogether. The woman removed her mask. It was Mrs. Jackson.

Before Noreen could speak, she introduced herself to Eli. Unlike Noreen's conversation with her in the laboratory, she was no longer calm and composed but appeared rather apprehensive in her movements. Mrs. Jackson waited for Eli to acknowledge her before she removed the picture buried beneath her clothes. She held the photo of her son out to the Doe and asked him the same question she had asked Noreen.

Eli barely looked at it. Instead, he removed his arm from around Noreen and looked into her eyes as though trying to tell her something without moving his lips. Noreen did not understand his message. He turned back to Mrs. Jackson but hesitated, taking a breath. During the pause, the Right Hander took a step back to distance her from the Doe. "I am 6 foot 4," Eli began, "do you think your son would be shorter than me and slightly stockier in build?"

Mrs. Jackson tilted her head to the right as she examined the Doe whereas Eli simply stared back at her without expressing any particular emotion. "Yes," Mrs. Jackson answered, "that describes his father. When he was born, my son, Darrell, looked just like him."

"Well," Eli cleared his throat, "there was a young man a few years younger than me who fits that description. He lived in the bunk above me at the orphanage."

"So, you knew my son?"

"I believe so," he nodded. Noreen tried to match Eli's expression as she finally comprehended what he had been trying to tell her. The night before, she had told him the details understood about Darrell that she was given by Mrs. Jackson. Eli told her he had never heard of the boy based on the description alone which meant he was lying to the Right Hander, though she did not understand why.

Mrs. Jackson fell to her knees, causing both Noreen and Eli to flinch. "Is he alright? Is my baby alive and well?" She wept at the feet of the Left Handers.

Noreen was shocked that she accepted Eli's statement so quickly, just from a baby picture, but she believed the woman just wanted to hear everything was alright, just like how she needed her mother to tell her the same nearly a month ago. "Yes, he is doing well," Eli built on his lie. "He is one of the nicest young men I have ever met. You should be proud to have such a wonderful son." He furrowed his brows but kept his face remarkably unreadable; he was a much better liar than Noreen expected.

Mrs. Jackson cried even harder as she thanked Noreen and Eli repeatedly without coming close to them. Noreen felt a sudden pain in her chest as she thought about her mother again and how she must be wondering the same fate for her at that very moment. "Bless you, God bless you both," Mrs. Jackson dropped her protective mask to the ground and clasped her hands together in prayer.

After an uncomfortably long period of silence, the Right Hander finally picked up the dark green mask and slowly gathered herself onto her feet. "I am so very sorry your fates have led you on a path to the forest. And I am especially sorry that I am the one responsible for you ending up there," she wiped the tears from her cheeks, "but you see I have already submitted my decision to Dr. Conroy, and I do not have the authority to change it. I do have the authority, though, to visit you both before you leave like I am doing at this very moment." Mrs. Jackson reached into her coat pocket and removed a small, shiny object. She placed it on the floor and stepped away from it. "I will always be grateful for the information about my son. You have no idea how relieved I feel to finally know my boy is all right."

She placed the gas mask over her face and laid her palm on the colorless wall beside the doorway. Within the same instant, the wall lit up around the outline of her fingertips and a red line moved vertically down her hand to scan it. By the time the red line disappeared, the door opened and the same two guards appeared through the doorway. Noreen quickly lunged for the silver object and concealed the canteen inside her jacket before the guards could see it.

Once Mrs. Jackson was out of sight, the guards motioned for the Left Handers to come toward them. Noreen stood and turned to help Eli. With his injured back, she knew he would need her assistance so that he would not bend too far and open his wounds. One of the guards had his gun slung by a strap over his shoulder but the man behind him kept his weapon aimed toward them.

The man closest to them held his arm out and away from his body, using tongs to carry a clear bag with Eli's sweatshirt and flannel clumped inside. When the tongs were within reach, Eli grabbed the bag with his good arm, holding only one of the bag's straps so that Noreen could retrieve the items inside. Reading his mind, she kept one hand on her jacket and reached the other into the bag. "Dress him!" the guard furthest from them gestured with his gun toward Noreen. "You have exactly five minutes. Don't waste it."

The Right Handers exited the room and shut the door behind them, leaving Noreen and Eli alone with only minutes until their departure. The moment the door was sealed, Noreen placed the canteen on the floor and quickly used both hands to clothe the man beside her. "Is there any water in there?" Eli nodded toward the canteen as he pushed his arm through the left sleeve of his flannel.

Noreen stretched his shirt around his back as far as she could without ripping it. "Yeah, I think so," she responded. Eli shuddered at the pain the fabric produced against his skin but did not fight against it. He bent the elbow below his injured shoulder enough so Noreen could slide his arm through the second sleeve. Once both of Eli's arms were in the shirt, Noreen began fastening it from the bottom up, although the shakiness of her hands forced her to redo many of the buttons because she had fastened them in the wrong holes.

Eli was oblivious to her struggle but instead focused on the sweatshirt Noreen clasped between her thighs. "I don't need to put that on right now. We don't have time."

"If you don't put it on, they might take it!" Noreen took the sweatshirt into her hands and scrunched its sleeves. Eli obeyed and bent his knees enough so she could ease the sweatshirt over his head and pull his good arm through the first sleeve. "If we do this quickly, it'll be less painful."

"I don't know about that," Eli grunted as he bent the elbow of his injured arm to fit it through the second sleeve.

"Well, then the pain will be over sooner, how 'bout that?"

Eli did not respond but rather pursed his lips to hold back a scream as he attempted to force his arm through the fabric. "Stop, stop!" he cried out in pain. "I can't put that thing on- it's impossible!"

"But you almost have it!" Noreen tried to persuade him, but they both knew he was right and their efforts were destined for failure.

All of the sudden, the cell door pushed open and the malodorous air around them began vacuuming out as waves of fresh, unnatural smelling air took its place. Noreen quickly pulled Eli's sweatshirt off and threw it on the floor. Once again she lunged for the canteen, but before she could hide it in her jacket, Eli grabbed it from her hands and tucked it away in the back of his jeans beneath his flannel. The two guards marched inside with both of their guns raised.

"This way." the guard closest to them commanded. By the deepness of his voice, Noreen knew he was the same guard who originally set their countdown, and she followed him in silence with Eli and the second guard at her rear. They exited the cell and were guided into a distorted tube whose end seemed as though it did not exist. Eli was forced to duck inside the pipe whereas Noreen and the guards walked forward without difficulty.

In a blink of an eye, the walls of the tube blurred, though the Right Hander in front of Noreen remained clear in her path. She blinked again, thinking her eyes were playing tricks on her, but the walls ahead were still a haze. Turning back to see if Eli shared her difficulty, she froze mid-step with her head cocked to one side. The walls were clear when she looked at them dead on, and through them, they revealed the number of Right Handers watching her and Eli on their final march from the facility.

Eli bumped into Noreen, not realizing she had stopped, and the guard behind him instantly readied his gun to fire. "Ey! Keep moving!" the man yelled from beneath his mask.

Noreen followed the command in silence, but she kept her head turned to the side, in search of the man whose initials were engraved on her father's compass. While looking through the crowd, she found Mrs. Jackson standing by a set of double doors, far away from her colleagues. Her face reflected the same composure as when Noreen first saw her in the laboratory. She stared at Noreen without any alteration in her stance or expression while Noreen too matched her gaze. Neither woman gestured to the other, but as Noreen was about to look away from her, Mrs. Jackson reached below the neckline of her collar to scratch the skin closest to her heart. She lowered her arm to her side moments later as she turned to the exit.

She was gone before Noreen could acknowledge the unspoken gratitude the woman conveyed by touching the picture folded against her heart, but Noreen understood that the woman's discreetness was exactly how she wanted it, quick and undetectable. Noreen continued her search through the crowd, but of all the Right Handers watching them, Dr. Conroy was not one of them…

Abruptly, the guard a few paces ahead of her spun around and pulled down the hammer of his gun to ready it for fire. Eli stepped between Noreen and the gun, though the guard behind them also had his weapon aimed. "Go." The guard in front motioned with his gun toward the opening in the wall at their side where the glass container of Noreen's long entrapment rested.

"We both can't fit in there," Noreen shook her head, her words barely audible.

"Shut up!" the guard screamed at her. He did not lower his weapon, as he motioned for a second time toward the crate. He reduced his pitch even further. "Get in the crate, now."

Eli stayed between Noreen and the aggressive guard's weapon as they walked slowly toward the container. She crawled inside first, followed by Eli who was forced to use his good arm to push himself forward after lowering himself onto his knees. They both knew he could not lean his wounded back on the sides of the crate, and with the limited space, he was forced to remain kneeling, partially on top of her.

The guards bolted the crate behind them, and cool air began flowing in through the illuminated holes as it was lifted off the ground. The walls were no longer clear unlike before, so neither Noreen nor Eli could see or hear anything on the outside. Neither spoke to break the silence, not even when their crate was tipped and they were forced to hold on to each other to keep their balance.

With Eli gazing at a point on the bottom of the container, Noreen was able to study him without his knowledge. While his face did not reveal any particular emotion, she could see the fear that lingered in his eyes. She could only imagine how scared she appeared to him since she, too, was afraid of the next step of their journey. She wondered if her fear was the reason he refused to look at her, but that was, of course, something she would probably never know.

The thought of having to fight for her life against creatures hungry for her flesh absolutely terrified her, as did the thought of not having enough food or water or a safe place to sleep. She was afraid of the forest itself and getting lost in it forever, despite having a compass to guide her; she was afraid Eli would not make it in his condition, and she was also afraid of losing him, or even losing herself.

Noreen's hands began to shake; she had to stop thinking of the worst possible scenarios or her fear would take over. She closed her eyes and whispered to her deceased father, hoping he was watching over her and listening to her prayers. "Please guide me in the right direction, dad," Noreen whispered with each of her exhaling breaths, "please let us make it to the other side, alive and uninfected."

She opened her eyes to find Eli staring at her, but she ignored him and focused on the movement of their container. Every dip or tilt of the crate, Noreen felt was another step closer to finding her twin sister.

For a few seconds, the crate was motionless before it started rattling in short, quick movements in every direction. *We are on one of their vehicles*, Noreen thought, *another step closer*. She refocused when she was forced to press against Eli's chest so he wouldn't lose his balance and crush her beneath him. His teeth were clenched and his hand against the wall was turning white around its knuckles and fingertips. He was trying very hard to keep his balance. The crate jerked forward again and came to a halt.

They were lifted and lowered, until the bottom of their container was placed on still surface. Someone from the outside began tampering with the lock above them and a side of glass was lifted. Noreen crawled out first and looked behind the crate as she helped Eli to his feet. A barbed wire fence separated them from the armed guards standing beside the large truck that transported them to the forest. Among the guards, one was out of uniform and completely dressed in white. Noreen squinted her eyes, recognizing the man as Dr. Conroy; he was smiling at her. A rush of anger consumed her and she stepped toward the fence line but stopped herself at the sound of the same zap she remembered hearing on the day she entered Government headquarters.

Glancing directly behind the crate, Noreen found the source of the zap. Their glass box had been pushed through a hole in the barbed wire, large enough for only the box to slide through. Flashes of lightening were bouncing between the fence and the container's sides, preventing anything from going through the hole. Noreen glanced back up and scanned her eyes across the Right Handers watching them. The old man had moved back toward the truck, but despite the distance, she could still see his grin.

Without thinking, Noreen spit in his direction out of pure hatred for the man who destroyed her father, but her projected saliva sparked a streak of lightning at the fence line and caused her to leap back in fear. She could hear Dr. Conroy laughing at her. When she looked back up at him, he simply waved a final goodbye, entered into the passenger side of the truck and was driven away. They left Noreen and Eli alone in the Forest of Lepers.

Noreen clenched her fists as she turned back toward the forest behind her. At the sight of the massive trees in the near distance, her fists loosened. While some of the hemlocks reached familiar heights, most had roots much taller and larger than she could ever imagine. As a whole, the forest was nothing like she had ever seen. In contrast to the pure white crate or the silver rooms in the Government building, the forest was dark with countless shades of greens and browns in every direction. Even with all of its different complexities, though, everything at the same time appeared identical. Noreen swallowed as she pulled her father's compass from her pocket. She thought about what the deceased man had told her on the morning preceding his death, that she would not make it through the forest alive without his compass to guide her. As she stared at the rows of foliage before her, Noreen believed her father had been correct.

Despite her fears of becoming immersed inside the forest, Noreen did not want to waste any time, so she went to Eli and laid the compass flat in her palms; east was diagonally left from their position. Eli looked down at the compass, but neither of them moved in the direction of the pointing arrow. "Well," Eli broke the silence, "I guess there's no turning back now."

"Hah," Noreen barely moved her lips. She took a step forward, but Eli touched her arm to stop her.

"We should stay close," he started. His expression was firm, "it'll be safer that way."

Noreen nodded, but was distracted by another thought. "Do you think they can smell us?" she asked, changing the subject.

Eli looked around and rolled up his sleeves. There was no wind in the blistering heat, so the forest lingered with a stale, hot, and humid air. "I don't know," he lowered his voice. Noreen regretted asking him the question once she noticed the fear return to his eyes. "But we should start moving."

Noreen held the compass tightly in her hand as she started forward with Eli mimicking her steps from close behind. She was glad to be in front since the thought of someone or something grabbing her absolutely terrified her. Peering in each direction, she studied the forest around her. Almost all the trees had budded blankets of green, while the green itself covered the branches to their very tips and formed umbrellas that shielded the ground from the direct rays of the sun. Despite the foliage's coverage, though, the heat hovered through the woods in a windless swell that caused the pungent, earthy odor of moss and tree bark to linger in the air.

On the ground, roots and grassy shrubs covered the uneven surface as did their heavy footprints as they walked. Noreen was thankful she wore her brother's thick soled shoes, though her feet were sweating profusely in her double layer of socks. Her feet were not the only part of her body drenched in sweat; perspiration soaked her bra and dripped down the center of her spine. Every crease on her body was completely saturated, but she refused to remove any of her clothes. She needed her jacket to protect her upper body like her mother had insisted, but she also wanted to keep the only food she had as close as possible.

Hours passed, and while Noreen and Eli moved in silence, the eerie stillness of the forest seemed to be screaming at them. Other than the vibrating songs coming from the loud insects in the trees, the forest was generally quiet, and Noreen could not take it any longer. Her thoughts raced through her brain as question after question burst forth and begged for an answer. After some time, she could not help but ask her troubling inquiries out loud. "How many of them do you think are there?" she blurted out.

In reaction to the loudness of her own voice, Noreen covered her mouth with her hand, but despite her mistake, she felt as though her brain began running more smoothly. When Eli did not respond, she glanced back at him and realized he had not heard her. While she was observing the nature of the forest, Eli appeared as though he were searching for its predators. He looked almost paranoid, his eyes shifting constantly; he was more like the hunter himself rather than its prey. Noreen faced forward and took a deep breath. *We are gonna be fine. Nothing is going to happen to us.* Noreen repeated the two lines under her breath to calm her nerves. She had never seen Eli so afraid, and it absolutely terrified her.

A twig snapped and Noreen did not even have time to react before Eli jerked his injured arm out in front of her for her protection. Immediately, he pulled his arm back to his side from the shooting pain it caused his shoulder. Noreen touched his arm gently in gratitude but kept her focus on the area where the twig broke roughly ten meters away from them. She waited for another sound but nothing happened. The forest was motionless and utterly silent around them, with the exception of the vibrating songs from the insects. Noreen glanced at Eli. "You alright?" she whispered.

"Yeah, I'll be fine," he assured her.

Noreen nodded, but the fear building inside her sent shivers down her arms and to her fingertips. She felt cold despite the scorching heat that hovered across the forest floor. She was dehydrated and needed water, but even after hours of walking, there was none to be found. Feeling lightheaded, Noreen placed her hand on the Doe's lower back where the canteen was hidden and snatched it from its spot against his skin. She quickly twisted off its cap and chugged several gulps of the fresh water.

At that point, she did not care how angry Eli would be for drinking their water supply; she could barely stand, and the thought of collapsing in such a Hell was, in her mind, deemed unacceptable. Her stability returned, for the most part, as she consumed the pure tasting water down her throat. After taking a few more sips, she handed the canteen to Eli who grabbed it from her hands and tilted it against his lips.

Noreen stared at him in awe as he chugged the remainder of their water. By the time he finished, he stared into the empty container with a single slanted eye and looked over to Noreen apologetically after realizing what he had done. Noreen shrugged her shoulders in response. She could not be angry with him since she had been the first to grab the bottle from its hiding place. "We're gonna need to find more water," Eli mumbled reluctantly, tucking the canteen back into his jeans.

"We will, don't worry," Noreen said, more to reassure herself than for the Doe's sake.

Her words encouraged Eli enough for him to step forward and take her hand, along with the lead. His boldness comforted her, but it was not enough to rid the fear that shook her hand's nerves. She wondered, like the many times before, what Eli thought of her trembles or the frequency of their occurrence, but he never once mentioned it.

She looked around them with even more caution than when they first entered the forest. Something was out there, she could feel it. Unexpectedly, Eli spun around and ripped his hand away from her's. In the same instant, he placed the same hand over Noreen's mouth with a force that sent them both crashing to the ground. Twigs and branches snapped beneath them, but Noreen could not feel them since Eli had broken her fall. She sat in his lap with his hand covering practically the entire lower half of her face and the memory of Lawrence on her last night at The Cove returned to her.

Out of panic, Noreen ripped Eli's hand off her and she began to crawl away from him. She could not erase Lawrence's face from her mind nor his sickening grin. He was laughing at her and pitying her at the same time for being so vulnerable. As she heard more branches cracking behind her, she could only see Lawrence chasing after her. She winced at the touch of a hand on her shoulder and she turned onto her back with her arms crossed over her face to protect herself. It took her a moment to comprehend that Eli was the one hovering over her, not Lawrence. She took a breath to calm herself, but the fear in Eli's expression was worse than she could have imagined. "Stay down," he whispered to her with panting gasps.

In a blink, he was gone. Noreen sat up, unsure what had just happened, but scanning her eyes around the woods, she saw nothing. She raised one knee off the ground and waited with her hands by her sides; she was ready to make a run it if she needed to or if Eli signaled her to go. She pushed her hands into the dirt in an attempt to keep them from trembling, but they shook despite her efforts.

The sound of a hiss came from behind her, and Noreen shot herself around. Out of nowhere, a creature thrust itself on top of her and pinned her arms to the dirt. Noreen tried desperately to resist the leper's strength, but the female's tight hold on her was unbreakable. She could feel its long, jagged fingernails digging into her palms and breaking through her skin, but the pain it caused was of the least of Noreen's fears. It was not until the infected creature's drool trickled down its chin and landed on her cheek did she scream out in horror.

Her fate was inevitable, as it was clearly indicated by the vicious chomping of the leper's black teeth in the air above her. She was taunting Noreen and tormenting her before taking her first bite. Noreen wanted to close her eyes. The leper was going to consume her, and without any other way of escaping, closing her eyes seemed to be the only way to liberate her from the leper.

Something in the distance kept Noreen's eyes open. An image was rising up slowly from behind the leper's wild mane. It was Eli, and he was gripping a thick piece of bark in his hand. Just as the leper's hot breath was inches from her skin, Eli slammed the bark down on the female, again and again, until the leper released its hold on her.

Noreen scrambled backward, using her hand to quickly wipe the drool off her cheek before it seeped between her lips. She did not know if a leper's saliva could mutate her genes faster than its touch alone, but she refused to take any chances. She watched the creature tumble to its side and leap back onto its feet into a crouching position. The female touched its bleeding ear and hissed at Eli with fury, but Eli remained steady and grasped the bark tightly in his left hand, his right arm hanging close to his side. She chomped its rotting teeth again before lunging toward him, but Eli swung the wood and hit the creature's side, knocking it to the ground before it could reach him. The leper lay motionless in the dirt, and Eli slowly backed away from it until he fell to his knees.

Noreen crawled to his side but refrained from touching him. He dropped the bark and turned toward her. "Are you okay? Did she hurt you?" Eli panted, using his sleeve to wipe the drool off Noreen's cheek that she had missed.

"No, I'm alright. She didn't get me," Noreen replied.

Eli glanced down to her hands. "What about your hands, did any of her open sores touch you?"

"I don't-" Noreen stopped and stared behind him.

The leper was on its feet again, in a position ready to attack. Noreen screamed to warn Eli, but it was too late. The creature attacked him and clawed at his flannel. With only one of his arms capable to fight, Eli struggled to keep her off him. Her nails ripped through the cotton, and he cried out in pain. Without time to think, Noreen dove for the bark by Eli's side and grabbed it with both hands. She raised the wood above her, mimicking Madeline's actions on Day 19, and brought it down hard on the leper's skull. Dark red blood gushed out of the leper's ear as the female fell forward on Eli's back. Immediately, Noreen removed her right hand from the bark and reached out to Eli, still holding the wood in her opposite hand. He grabbed hold of her, and she pulled him away from the creature.

A pool of blood formed around the corpse's head in the dirt, but Noreen was not satisfied. She hovered over the creature to be sure it was dead, still holding the bark in front of her. She poked it with her weapon to roll the leper onto its back but lept back when she saw that the creature had died with its eyes open.

Noreen took a deep breath before examining the rest of its body. The female wore a dirty plaid dress that covered its shoulders and reached just below its knees. Its green and yellow patterns had faded and what Noreen assumed were once white socks were now stained brown. The socks were pulled up to the bottom hem of the dress, probably to protect the countless lumps that formed large tumors on its legs. The yellow tainted skin of its face was covered with red, oozing sores that left the female exceptionally disfigured. "It's dead," Noreen confirmed.

Eli sat up without responding. He gently touched his injured shoulder and winced. "You alright?" Noreen stepped away from the leper and toward Eli but refused to let go of the bark in her grasp.

"Yeah, she didn't bite me, but she scratched my back and shoulder pretty bad." Eli nodded toward his shoulder to show Noreen the torn threads of his flannel over the visible, ripped bandages covering his wound. "I tried to stop her, but-"

Noreen laid her free hand over Eli's as it covered the wound. Eli stared back at her but removed his hand from under her's to place it on the small of her back. In response, Noreen lowered the bark to her side to ease Eli's tension, and she placed her arm around his neck. She knew not to touch his back in their embrace, so she lowered her hand to his unwounded shoulder. She hugged him gently with his head resting on her stomach, as she gazed into the eyes of the dead creature beside them.

Chapter 20

*T*here was no way of knowing how long they walked, but the sun was setting which meant the day was coming to an end. It was raining lightly, and the air had already cooled down to what Noreen considered typical spring weather. The tune of the insects had changed melodies from their vibrating songs to what sounded like chirping harps, though their pleasant chorus was gradually getting quieter as the light rain transformed into a harsh downpour. It became hard to see the arrow on her compass, but Noreen felt it would be best for them to keep moving forward as long as they had light, and from Eli's fast paced strides, she knew he felt the same way. They decided to bring the bark with them, as it was their only weapon. They also decided to share the burden, switching bearers whenever ones arm became tired. It was now Eli's turn, and he carried it defensively as they hiked together side by side.

Noreen glanced over at Eli as he used his forearm to brush his wet, black hair out of his eyes. She did not have to gaze down to know that his clothes were just as drenched as hers. She could only imagine how terrible she looked at that moment but honestly did not care in the slightest. Her biggest worry was the soggy bread in her pocket, the bread she had no way of shielding from the rain. She hoped it was still intact and had not crumbled into tiny pieces. She would not know until it was time for them to rest. Luckily, though, the rain provided them with water from the numerous puddles that formed on the earth's surface. They stopped frequently at the deepest ones to cup the murky liquid into their hands and bring it to their lips for a drink. Although the mud turned the clear rain water brown, it refreshed their dehydrated bodies and tricked their stomachs into that of false satisfaction.

After some time marching through the rain, the compass's arrow was no longer the only blur; the downpour also caused a foggy haze that prevented them from seeing items in the distance. Eli was forced to yell to Noreen, though she walked close to his side. "The clouds are even darker now. We need to find shelter!"

Noreen agreed in another shout back to him, but she had no idea where they could go to find one. For a moment, she debated just sitting down in the mud and falling asleep in the rain, but when lightning struck a nearby branch, she decided against it. "Where are we gonna find one?" she shouted over to the Doe.

"WHAT?" Eli yelled, not hearing her question. Noreen shook her head at him and Eli turned away to continue his search.

They moved quickly, but with the rain hammering against their eyeballs, their search for a place to rest was becoming increasingly more difficult. Noreen tilted her head to the side and lifted a hand over her eyes to shield them from the beating pellets of rainwater. She peered to her right, and a large, dark shape caught her attention. She could not tell what she was looking at, but she started toward the dark figure despite any second thoughts that raced through her.

Eli yelled after her, but Noreen quickened her pace. The figure was getting larger and larger as she moved closer to it. Eli ran after Noreen and nearly bumped into her when she came to an abrupt stop before a hollow. They both squinted at the figure in disbelief. The tree was massive with roots reaching up to Eli's thighs. In its trunk, a hole sculpted out a tree hollow that was large enough for the two of them to fit inside. Eli placed his hand on Noreen's head and kissed it. Noreen smiled and they sprinted the last few meters toward the trunk.

Eli ducked inside first to make sure the hollow was empty. He brushed away a majority of the spider webs and gently lowered himself onto his back, in an attempt to lie comfortably without pain from his injuries to trouble him. Not all of his body fit inside the trunk, leaving his lower half out of the tree and in the rain from his feet to just above his knees. Noreen crawled in beside him and tried to make more room for him in the cramped space, but he refused to move in any further. While she was unsure if his refusal was due to the amount of pain it would cause him to resituate or if he just did not want to cause her any trouble, she did not argue with him and rather curled up in a ball by his side.

She had no choice in the cramped space but to rest her head on his chest and lean her body toward him, but while their intimate position pleased her, she could hear his stomach grumbling from beneath her ear. *The bread!* Noreen remembered the food in her pocket and jolted her hands toward her jacket. She took out the bread after ensuring that the compass was still tucked safely in her other pocket. The bread was soggy but still intact. She handed a slice to Eli.

"Where did you get this?" Eli stared at the bread as if it were an illusion.

"I didn't eat all of the sandwiches I was given." Noreen placed one of the slices in the hand of his arm wrapped around her. When Eli hesitated, Noreen shoved the food into his palm. "What's the problem?" she asked while nibbling on her slice.

"I want you to have it." He laid the bread on her side and lowered his hand back around her.

"No, I saved one for each of us. Don't you want it?" She lifted the bread and, leaning on her forearm, she turned enough so she could press it to his lips. "I can hear your stomach growling. I know you're hungry."

Eli's jaw tightened. "Stop. Just eat it, okay! It's not mine. I ate my share back at Government headquarters. I won't eat yours too."

"Fine," Noreen accepted, "if you won't have it, no one will." She tossed the bread onto his chest and squirmed around to devour her slice in privacy. She did not bother saving any of the food since she knew she needed it, and desperately craved it. She listened for Eli to take the bread but heard nothing. "Eli?" Noreen asked after finishing her slice. Eli grunted at her in acknowledgement of her question. "What else did they do to you?"

Eli understood who she was referring to and responded after a pause, "I'd rather not talk about it."

Noreen was quiet in respect of his privacy, only hearing the rain pounding against the base of their shelter. Then she asked him an entirely different question. "Can you tell me something about yourself?"

Eli huffed. "What's there to tell?"

"Everything. I mean, you know all of my secrets-"

"So you want me to tell you some of my own to make us even?"

"No, it's not like that," Noreen contested, "you don't have to tell me anything you don't want to. It's just that you know everything about me, even my darkest secrets, but I don't even know your middle name."

"It's just a name."

"You know what I mean," Noreen scrunched her eyebrows in frustration.

"Well, I don't know it," he responded. Noreen noticed his feet fidgeting out in the rain as he spoke, "I don't know my middle name."

"That's alright," she assured him while killing a spider that crawled on her jeans, "I don't even have one."

"See, I don't know everything about you," Eli squeezed her arm playfully. Noreen half-smiled, though she knew he could not see her since her body faced away from him. "I thought you told the Government your middle name was Elizabeth?"

"Yeah and I also told them I was your wife," she laughed briefly, letting it fade into the sound of the rain hitting the tree trunk.

Eli did not respond and for several minutes Noreen only heard his stomach growling and felt the rise and fall of his breaths. He inhaled a deep breath finally and began to speak in a serious, yet distant, tone. "I am an only child, from what I know, and I shared the same bunk with my only friend growing up, up until I could no longer fit in the bed.

Like all the other orphans, he was a John Doe, but to me he was Timothy Jack, not because that was his real name, but for some reason he always wanted to be called TJ. Don't ask me why. He actually never knew his real name." Eli laughed briefly at the memory before becoming serious once again. "I can understand completely how close our fathers were because TJ was like a brother to me. He died six years ago on Day 19, and that's the real reason why I never participated in the ritual." Noreen twisted her body to face him. She placed a hand on his stomach but remained silent while he took a break in his confession. He started on a new subject without further elaboration on the first. "I wonder often what life would have been like if the Infection never happened or what my mother and father would have been like as parents.

I've always pictured my dad as the kind of man who was good at everything and liked by everyone, someone who was a hard worker and a best friend, my best friend. My mom, now she's the one I would go to for advice and only she would know the right answer or know exactly what to do to help me or anyone else if they needed it," he paused again, his mind lost in thought. "If I had gotten the chance to be with my parents, I would've wanted to spend every minute with them. But I never got that chance. Kids with parents have no idea what it's like to grow up without them." His voice got quieter and quieter as he spoke, though he did not sound upset. To Noreen, he sounded lost in his own thoughts. She thought of her own parents then and the relationship she once had with the two. She wished she had spent more time with them than she had, since she would never have that chance again in the future.

"Your mother will be where we are headed; you will have that chance, it's not too late!" Noreen reassured him in a sympathetic tone.

"And my father?" Eli questioned. He took another deep breath. "Do you think he's still alive and somewhere out here?"

"It's possible," Noreen answered though she highly doubted it, "but I don't think it would be a good idea to look for him."

"Why not?" he asked confused.

She hesitated. "He probably isn't the same man he used to be, Eli. If he is alive, that means he has had to adjust to the life as a leper. I think it would be best to just picture him like you do and forever keep a positive image of him." She tried to sound as considerate as she could, but Eli simply answered with a single word of acknowledgement. She could tell she hurt him, but he needed to hear those words spoken out loud.

They remained silent for a long time, the rain clouds forming a thick blanket in the night sky and producing absolute darkness throughout the forest. Between listening to the rhythmic beat of Eli's heart thumping in his chest and the sound of rain trickling on the tree above them, Noreen felt herself falling to sleep. She closed her eyes but spoke to keep herself awake. "I have been meaning to ask you something."

"Yeah?" Eli answered after a pause. Noreen smiled, hearing him finally chewing the bread she had given him.

"Back when we were, well, when Mrs. Jackson came to our cell," Noreen yawned. She was able to whisper now since the rain had lightened, and it was much easier to hear one another inside the hollow. "Why did you lie to her and tell her that you knew her son?"

Eli finished chewing before he responded. "So she doesn't keep wondering what happened to him."

"But you don't really know what happened to him."

"Doesn't matter," he concluded. Noreen felt him aimlessly tracing his fingertips on her sleeve. "Now she has hope."

Noreen understood but was distracted by his touch. "Do you?" she finally asked after a loud roar of thunder shook the ground beneath them.

"For her son? I honestly don't know," he answered, ignoring the rumble, "but do I have hope for us? Absolutely."

"What makes you so sure?"

The tracing of Eli's fingertips stopped as he answered her. "Cause neither one of us would ever let anything bad happen to the other." Noreen smiled and they were silent again until Eli cleared his throat. "Well, I'm not all that tired, so I guess I'll take the first watch."

Noreen wished she had said something in their silence to make their conversation last, but it was too late. "Alright, thanks," she replied. She wondered if he could hear the disappointment in her voice, but he did not respond. A lightening strike hit the ground only a few meters away from their shelter, and his hold on Noreen tightened, bringing her even closer. "Eli?" Noreen forced his name out of her throat. He immediately loosened his grip, afraid he had hurt or displaced her. "No, no," she felt dumb for calling his name immediately after he moved her closer, "I just wanted you to know that I'm really glad you came with me."

She felt his hold on her tighten once again. "Me too, Noreen, me too."

Chapter 21

"Eli, wake up, Eli!" Noreen shook his unwounded shoulder until his eyes fluttered open. He shot up instantly, but Noreen pressed down on his chest to keep him from hitting his head. "You fell asleep and didn't wake me!"

"What are you talking about?" he yawned and slowly eased himself onto his side to face her.

"You were supposed to keep watch and wake me so I could take a turn, but you fell asleep!" she pushed on his chest again for emphasis, "something could have happened to us!"

Eli cursed and squinted at the bright sunlight shining outside their shelter. The ground was still soaking wet, but the storm had thankfully ended during the night. The temperature was much cooler as well, making Noreen shiver in her damp clothes; rainwater had leaked into their shelter during the storm, and they slept in a puddle of mud. "Aw man, I'm so sorry, Noreen. It was just so dark, and I couldn't see anything. I closed my eyes for one second; I don't know what happened!"

"You fell asleep, that's what happened." Noreen crawled out of the tree hollow and shook her arms to fling mud off her.

"I said I was sorry, why are you making this into such a big deal? Nothing happened to us!" he asserted.

Noreen helped him out of the hollow, pulling on his arms as his backside dragged in the mud until he was out. Eli held his back as he stood to his feet and brushed mud off him. "I know," Noreen calmed down and folded her arms across her chest, "but something could have and that scares me."

"Noreen? Scared? Since when?" he joked with her.

"Very funny," Noreen responded sarcastically. She stepped away from him and started toward a bush where the ground started to slope downward. "Just look away for a sec, okay?"

"Yep," Eli obeyed and turned his back to her, giving her the space she requested in order to relieve herself.

She looked around subconsciously, before unbuttoning her jeans and pulling down her underwear. She placed one hand on the mud below her and the other on her thigh as she squatted. A fly buzzed past her and Noreen swatted at it, almost losing her balance. It came around again, and Noreen swung her hand, barely touching it with her fingertips. The fly was unharmed, but it flew away.

She sighed and glanced back toward Eli to make sure he still faced the opposite direction, realizing that he too was relieving himself. She looked away to give him privacy and directed her focus to the ground as she pulled up her jeans. She gasped in horror at the sight below her. Thousands of worms squirmed in the wet mud all around her. Immediately, Noreen finished pulling up her jeans and ran up the hill, falling on her backside in the process. Even more earthworms curled and twisted on the ground beneath her, causing her to jump up and run on her toes back toward the shelter. Eli raced over to her when he noticed her look of disgust. "What's wrong?" he asked once he reached her side.

"It's nothing. There were just a lot of worms and it, well, it surprised me." she refrained from adding that she urinated on a bunch of them as well.

"What kind of worms?" Eli pressed.

Noreen did not understand why it mattered but answered regardless. "Earthworms I think." Eli smiled and rushed past her to the area she had fled. "What are you doing?" she called after him.

Eli hovered over the space where she had just urinated. "I'm getting us breakfast!"

"You're kidding right?" Noreen followed him back toward the mass of worms.

Eli ignored her and rolled up his sleeves. He knelt down, and just as he was about to cup his hands into the wet mud, Noreen stopped him. "Wait!" she insisted, not wanting him to grab the worms covered in urine. "Get the ones over there, not here."

He tilted his head in confusion but obeyed. Noreen exhaled in relief as he dug into the mud she indicated but leaned away when he held out his arm with a handful of worms squirming in his palm. "You can have the first bite," she contended.

The Doe shrugged and bent his good arm toward him. He closed his eyes as he threw the entire handful into his open mouth. Eli gagged the moment his teeth crunched together. He held the same hand over his mouth as he continued to gag and chew. Noreen stepped toward him but refrained from patting his back to help with the choking. She waited by his side until he swallowed. "Ugh!" he exclaimed with a face expressing more disgust than Noreen's. He wiped his eyes with his forearm before digging his hand back into the dirt and raising his arm toward her. Noreen stared at the dirty, curving creatures in his hand and paused, but her stomach screamed at her to take them. Sluggishly, she picked one up between her thumb and index finger and held it above her mouth. The worm's body extended before she dropped it between her lips.

Noreen chewed fully before swallowing. She hesitated, assessing its flavor. "They aren't that bad," she concluded and grabbed another from the Doe's palm. She tossed the second worm into her mouth, and Eli's jaw dropped in disbelief. Noreen swallowed before grabbing a third. "Try one without so much dirt on it this time, it's not so bad!"

Eli curled his upper lip and poured the handful of earthworms into his right hand. He wiped the mud from his left palm onto his jeans before lifting a single worm. He mimicked Noreen's continuous motion and tossed the worm into his mouth. She waited for his reaction before eating the three worms squirming about her palm. Eli nodded after swallowing. "You're right, but let's just hope that in the next day or two their taste won't get any worse."

"What do you mean?" Noreen asked as they continued to eat their breakfast.

"We'll be hungrier then," he answered her. Noreen could not imagine being any hungrier than she was at that very moment, but she nodded nonetheless. She continued filling her stomach with the worms while Eli paused to retrieve the empty canteen from its hiding spot against his lower back. He opened the mouthpiece of the canister and held the cap out to her. "Can you hold that for me?"

Noreen looked down at the worms covering the ground and then back to Eli. She raised an eyebrow, but he ignored her questioning glare and continued to hold the cap out to her. Noreen maintained her expression, and Eli raised both of his eyebrows back at her. Losing the stare down, she took the cap and watched him with uncertainty as he shoved his hand into the mud and scooped up a pile of the worms. Resting the canteen between his thighs, he picked out an earthworm and dropped it into the bottle. "What the hell are you doing?" Noreen shouted at him. "Water is supposed to go in there!"

"What water?" Eli shouted back. He pursed his lips as he picked up one of the worms between his fingers. The worm extended its length as it dangled in Eli's grasp, and he dropped it into the canister. "These earthworms only surfaced because of the storm. I'm saving them for later, because once the ground dries up, they'll be back in the ground and harder to get out. If we take a bunch now, we can eat them later when we're hungry."

Noreen parted her lips. She was surprised he had thought of such an idea but was happy, once he finished his explanation, to help him fill the canister. Once filled, Eli used his finger to squish the worms down further to get as many of them as he could inside while Noreen ate the remaining worms around her boots. She continued to eat until she reached the point where she felt no more could fit in her stomach. She stood and began walking around to digest them faster and relieve her sudden cramps.

She paused in a patch of sunlight that filtered through the tree's foliage. The ground was drier there, and the earthworms had already submerged back under the surface in that particular spot. The sun's heat intensified with its rays beaming down on her, but the warmth, with the cool post storm breeze, was satisfying. She turned back to face Eli and noted, for the first time, the flies that surrounded him. His back faced her; his focus on the worms.

Noreen studied the V-shape of his back and noted how his wet flannel clung to his skin. The edge of his hairline was wet and water dripped onto his collar. He bent forward to scoop his hand into the mud causing his shirt to rise up and reveal his lower back. A black belt held up his jeans, but his lifted shirt revealed the two dimples indented into the skin of his lower back. Noreen blushed, not understanding why, and looked away from him.

She stepped out of the sunlight, thinking the heat must have flustered her, and waited for Eli to finish eating and approach her. Instead of moving toward her, he tucked the canteen back into his jeans and jogged back toward the tree hollow. After fetching the piece of bark, they had used to fight the leper the day before, he walked over to Noreen with concern in his expression. "You feel sick or something?" he asked. Noreen shook her head, but Eli motioned toward her, "but your face, it's all red!"

Noreen brought her hands to her cheeks. "I probably just ate too fast, no big deal," she lied. She had not realized her face had become so flushed from watching him. He asked again if she was absolutely sure she was alright, but Noreen ignored him, removing the compass from her pocket and taking the lead.

They hiked east for days, only stopping to rest in the bases of large trees, to eat the earthworms they found, and to drink from the puddles that remained. Other than mud and puddles, the ground was mostly covered in leaves and broken tree limbs that had fallen during the storm that occurred just nights before. It was their third day in the forest and the chirping melody of the nocturnal insects was replaced by a vibrating chorus as time fast forwarded into early afternoon. The noise coming from the insects combined with the thick gusts of wind off in the distance created an almost peaceful tune in the air. When they passed a leper during its mealtime, the pleasant tune changed into repetitive, trilling sounds of tragedy.

They had passed several other lepers in the forest. Fortunately for Noreen and Eli, this creature, like the others, had already found its prey and was too preoccupied devouring it to notice them creeping past. As they moved with caution, Eli clutched the bark and held it out in front of him. He walked between Noreen and the leper for her protection, but Noreen knew that with his injury, he could do little to defend her. By the time they were far enough from the leper, Eli lowered the bark and they continued their march in the eastern direction. Every so often, they were forced to hide behind the thickness of the nearby trees or duck into bushes if they heard the hisses and trills of lepers screeching above the sounds of the insects and the distant winds.

Noreen thought of her twin sister often on their journey. She wondered what Nicole was like and what her favorite things were. She marveled at the idea of having someone who would be able to finish her sentences for her and having someone who could understand her with a single expression. Having someone look exactly like her, Noreen thought, would be absolutely fascinating, but she knew it was too good to be true.

Rolling up her sleeves, Noreen evaluated her bony arms, and the memory of her reflection in the mirror on her last day at home clouded her vision. Her skin had been covered by her mother's oversized, jean jacket, but underneath it and her brown top, her ribs formed bumps and dips along the fitted material. She was very thin, so thin that she no longer had a monthly menstrual cycle. From that realization alone, Noreen figured her twin would never look exactly like her.

Nicole would look normal, she thought, *and act normal.* She pictured Nicole to have the same light blue eyes as her's, but her sister's full cheeks would make them seem much smaller in comparison. Nicole would have dimples in her cheeks and white curls covering her pale scalp, but unlike Noreen, her bones would be well hidden beneath her skin and her ribs would only show when she was laying down with her arms raised overhead. She would have a loud, contagious type of laughter, and most of all, she would be happy.

Noreen rolled her sleeves down as she experienced an overwhelmingly hopeful feeling inside her. She whispered to her father's spirit under her breath and asked him once more to watch over her and Eli and to keep them safe. She glanced over her shoulder when she finished, hoping Eli had not heard her prayer. Looking back at him, she knew he had not. His eyes were lost again in fear, and the hand not clenching the bark was strained tightly into a fist. Noreen took a deep breath, and turned away from him.

Gazing ahead, she narrowed her eyes suspiciously. She slowed to a stop, causing Eli to bump into her. The collision made Noreen drop the compass into the dirt, but she immediately stepped away from the Doe and bent down to retrieve it. "Why'd you stop?" Eli whispered to her as he raised the bark.

Noreen pulled down her brown tank from under her jacket and used it to wipe the dirt off the face of the compass. "Can you see over that?" she nodded ahead of them at a massive tree that had fallen and split into two separate halves. She raised her chin to see over it but saw nothing.

Eli stared off in same direction as he stepped beside her. He stood on the tip of his toes, making Noreen feel even shorter beside him. He shook his head. "No, but let's go around it, just in case."

Eli took the lead this time, forcing Noreen to follow. He held back the large branches for them with his elbow, so neither he nor Noreen would be grazed by them as they stared off in the direction of the fallen wood. "Watch your step," Eli distracted her.

She followed his command and avoided tripping over a large root in their path, but her focus returned to the fallen tree in an instant. "You think that was from the storm last night?"

"Probably," Eli concluded. He did not elaborate on his one word answer. Looking back again, Noreen noted their distance from the fallen tree. She could not help feeling the immense sensation of paranoia, similar to Eli's. *What if something was behind it? And what if that something was following them right now? What if-*

"We still going east?" Eli's voice distracted her again, this time from her own uncertainties.

She glanced down at her compass to notice its arrow trembling in her shaking palms. She lifted her hands to her face to read it more closely. "Uh, sort of," she mumbled, "we're heading more toward the Southeast rather than east, but when we get far enough away from the fallen tree, we should be back on course."

"Good," Eli responded with another one word answer. He brushed a cob web from their path.

"Uh," Noreen started. Eli acknowledged her with a grunt to encourage her to continue. "Can you pick it up a little?"

"You see something?" Eli cocked his head back toward the fallen wood, his eyes filled with fear.

"No," Noreen paused, "but, I have this feeling that something is watching us."

"So then it'd be a bad time to stop for water," he pointed down at a deep puddle near their path and started toward it.

Noreen bit her lip and scanned the forest. "Yeah, I think we should keep moving."

Eli disregarded her concerns and lowered himself to his knees before the pool of water. "It'll only take a minute," he said, shifting his eyes in either direction. Noreen hesitated, feeling utterly drawn by her instinct to run and by her throat as it pleaded for her to pause. That was the only puddle they had seen in a long time that was not already dried up by the sunlight shining through the trees' umbrella, yet she could not get over the feeling of being watched.

Eli looked around cautiously a final time before he leaned down to cup water into his palm. He kept his back as straight as possible to avoid pulling or tearing the wounds across his skin, but Noreen could tell he was very uncomfortable. After drinking several gulps, he leaned back on his heels and gestured for her to come toward him.

Noreen hesitated and slowly looked in each direction. Nothing out of the ordinary moved or even made a sound, so she stepped beside him and gazed down to the water at her feet. She watched small waves ripple across the water's surface each time Eli lowered his hand into the miniature pool. With his torso leaning forward and his hands on his knees, he swallowed the refreshing liquid.

Noreen continued to stare at the little ripples that quickly ceased to exist. She saw her reflection staring back at her each time the water stilled. White ringlets zinged out of her frizzing ponytail, but that was not what disturbed her; it was her face that worried her, as it appeared even thinner than she expected. She rotated her jaw in different directions and touched her face to confirm that her mind was not playing tricks on her through a distorted lens, but to her dismay, it was not. Her cheeks had hollowed deeper and her dimples seemed to have disappeared. She was turning into a skeleton just like her father.

Noreen released her gaze from the puddle in disgust and instead looked directly ahead of her. To her disbelief she saw a figure watching her through the trees. She could not tell if what she saw was a hallucination until she blinked, and the figure was even closer by the time her eyes reopened. A leper was now in clear view, and Noreen was his target.

She could feel her hands shaking violently at her sides, but she refused to release herself from the leper's stare. They both remained grounded, but the creature was in a hunched position and ready to attack. His ripped jeans came to his calves, and his feet were shoeless. As for his upper half, his yellow, tainted chest was bare, revealing a horribly bony and blistered skin. The male had nothing covering his sores, but his open and infected lumps did not appear to concern him. A dark brown beard concealed the majority of the narrow curvatures of his face except for his eyes, and while Noreen could not make out their exact color, she could see the darkness within them.

With their eyes locked and neither moving toward the other, Noreen was afraid to make any sudden movements, but she needed to get the Doe's attention. Eli drank from the puddle, oblivious to her distress, even when she muttered his name between unmoving lips. She muttered his name again even louder while slowly tucking the compass into her jacket pocket. Rather than being acknowledged by Eli, the leper saw her lips move, and he took a single step forward. Panicking, Noreen grabbed the back of Eli's shirt and forcefully yanked him back. He stumbled but twisted his body in time to land on his hip rather than his shoulder. The leper started to race toward them, and Noreen grabbed Eli even harder as she screamed. "GET UP! WE HAVE TO RUN!" She pulled again on his collar, not caring how much it hurt him.

    Eli scrambled desperately to his feet, but the leper was gaining on them. Noreen knew she had to react quickly or the leper would attack them in seconds. With the leper closing the distance, she lunged for the bark Eli had set on the ground and waited for the creature to reach them before she swung the weapon hard against its stomach. The leper plowed through the bark, ripping it out of Noreen's hands and breaking it with his momentum, but he toppled forward into the dirt. Eli grabbed her hand and yanked her forward until she was running in front of him, so this time she could not fall behind.

    They let go of each other's hands to pump their arms faster. Refusing to look back, Noreen kept her eyes on the ground to focus on not stumbling over the roots and broken tree limbs beneath her. "FASTER! HE'S GAINING ON US!" She barely heard Eli's voice screaming from behind nor could she hear anything at all over her gasping breaths. As they sprinted down a hill, Noreen raised her arms to block the low branches from scratching her face. "GO NOREEN GO! WE HAVE TO MOVE FASTER!" Eli's commands distantly echoed through her ears, but she felt herself slowing down. Her vision was blurring, and black masked the corners of her eyes as her sight funneled inward.

    Noreen fought against it by blinking her eyes rapidly, but this only caused her sight to worsen. With her vision weakening, she could no longer avoid the obstacles at her feet; her foot caught a root as a result and she toppled forward onto the ground. In an attempt to avoid slamming into her, Eli tried slowing himself down, but the steepness of the hill made him somersault forward and into the mud behind her. They both rolled down the hill with the leper chasing after them. Branches whipped at them as they picked up speed, but by no longer needing the stamina to run, Noreen found it easier to control her breaths. As a result, her vision began improving with her range of sight returning to normal.

  Her blurred vision was the last of her dysfunctions to disappear, but by the time her eyes recovered, she was forced to close them. Her abrupt exit from under the tree's shadows was a thin opening to the bright and radiating lights of the sun's magnificent rays. Noreen and Eli shot out from under the tree's umbrellas one after the other, noting the mud they slid on became hard, dry dirt beneath them. Noreen stretched her arms above her, attempting to block the light, but Eli grabbed her wrist instead. He screamed from behind her, but Noreen could barely hear him. The blaring sound of what she had thought to be distant winds echoed louder and louder in her ears. She realized the sound was not wind but water.

  Suddenly, her feet felt like they were flying, followed by her knees, thighs and stomach, until her entire body dangled over an edge with only Eli's hand holding on to her. She looked down to find a fast paced river surging wildly beneath her. She screamed as loud as she could while Eli struggled to keep her from plummeting into the water. Not only was she unable to swim, but the fall alone was enough to kill her. She could not see the leper from her dangling position, but she knew he was getting closer.

  Eli's repetitive shouts hushed her screams as she finally heard them. "I got chu! I got chu!" His confident desperation, though, would not save her. He did not have the strength to pull her up, using only his left arm, and he certainly could not lean on his wounded shoulder to brace himself. He lay on his stomach, and Noreen could see his knuckles turning white on his right hand as he tried using his wounded arm to pull himself back. His face creased in pain and Noreen understood she would have to let go to save him.

She began scratching at Eli's hold on her to free herself, but his grip only tightened. "What are you doing?" Eli shouted down to her. His expression revealed a combination of confusion, distress, and panic.

Noreen felt a tear flow down her cheek as she continued pulling at his grasp. "Let me go!" she screamed at him. Eli stared at her in shock.

"NO! I'm not letting you go!" he yanked his arm back forcefully, but Noreen merely swayed in the air alongside the cliff. She knew he would never let her go, and she had to do something before the leper reached them. With all her strength she reached her neck up enough until her face nearly touched his. "Meet me at the end of the river!" she panted before laying her lips on his. His lips were still wet from his frantic consumption of the puddle water, and felt chilled and soothing against her's. She watched Eli until he closed his eyes as she kissed him, and she felt his grasp on her lighten. Taking hold of her opportunity, she ripped her wrist out of his hand and broke their lips apart.

Noreen closed her eyes, not wanting to see his face as she heard him scream painfully after her. She opened her mouth, but with the force of gravity upon her, she was unable to yell back to him or even yell at all. Her chest and stomach felt like they were ripping through her skin as her body plummeted through the air. Her back broke her fall and crashed through the water's surface. She forced her eyes open, no longer able to hear Eli's screams.

Chapter 22

Above the surface, the river flowed without disruption. No ripples were caused by Noreen's splash, nor did the current break around her. Her body became the river's puppet as the rapids tugged and pulled her limbs in every direction. Noreen fought against it by flailing her arms and legs in desperation but the river overpowered her, and the current flipped and rotated her forcefully beneath the water's surface. Water gushed into her mouth as her head bobbed up and down. She choked on it and gagged pitifully until it drained out of her throat. She was forced to squint as more and more water sprayed into her eyes when her head broke the surface, but the current flipped her again, ripping the breath from her lungs.

She was able to gasp a final breath before the current pulled her completely under. Noreen jerked her arms and legs frantically, but her movements were too sporadic. She had no idea what she was doing and the rapids took advantage of her struggle. Gravity pulled her down as her breath escaped her lungs.

Her body rotated again and again until it was low enough that the white, foamy current could no longer flip or turn her. Her back faced the surface, but she did not try to turn herself. Endless shades of blue veiled the river's bottom until images flashed over her eyes with spurts of her past clouding her vision. Noreen squinted at the sight of her mother's mirage sinking below her. She was wearing a black, long dress that extended far past her toes in a dark, lacy train. She reached out for Noreen and Noreen stretched her arms out for her mother in return, but she could not reach her. Her mother's image faded into the blue and was replaced by Charlie's, then Louise's, and finally her father's. All four of the figments wore black and through the blurriness that hovered over their faces, Noreen could make out their terrified, miserable expressions.

The air in Noreen's throat bubbled to the surface as the last figment appeared beneath her. It was her own face staring back at her, but her image was faintly different from her appearance in a mirror. The figment smiled and wore white, unlike the others. Her body was more filled out around her waistline, chest, and cheeks and she had short curls that fanned out above her shoulders. It was not Noreen's image, but the image she had dreamed of her twin sister.

She reached out for Nicole, like she had with her parents and other siblings, but Nicole did not reach back. Instead, she pointed past Noreen while continuing to wear a faint smile across her puffy cheeks. Noreen turned her head in the direction of her pointed finger as her image vanished into the darkness. To Noreen's surprise, as she turned to face the water's surface, a clothed hand swung at her arm and grabbed her into its palm. The hand yanked Noreen and her head pushed through the surface.

Noreen wheezed, sucking air into her lungs, but coughed hysterically between each her breaths. As her body was pulled with the current, she wondered how Eli could have gotten to her so quickly unless he had jumped from the cliff to save her. The hand pulled her toward the edge of the river like a guardian angel and laid her on the ground. She rested her cheek on the warmth of the damp rocks beneath her and waited for her breathing to return to normal as she listened to the sound of the second wave of breaths wheezing beside her.

She lifted her cheek to meet the face of her rescuer but covered her mouth in horror as she realized that the man beside her was not Eli. Long black and gray hairs covered the stranger's face as he scrambled from his knees to his feet. He grasped Noreen's arm again as he stood and yanked her downstream by dragging her alongside the river. Noreen pleaded with the man to let her go, reaching her free arm toward his grasp. She felt the wet cloth between her fingers and pulled at it desperately until it ripped apart. The leper's yellow tainted skin was revealed, causing her to throw back her arm and scream out in horror.

    The leper dragged her over the lumpy ground, not once glancing back to acknowledge her frantic cries. He stepped lightly over the rocks beneath him despite having such a large frame. "Let me go!" Noreen cried, but the leper ignored her.

    A sharp rock ripped through her jeans and scratched against the back of her thigh, so she lifted both legs off the ground to prevent further damage. The weight of her body on her back, though, placed too much pressure on her spine as it scraped against the rocks, so she lowered her legs in defeat. But as she watched the sharp rock get further and further away, an idea struck her.

    The leper kept his head forward, so Noreen grabbed one of the larger stones she passed and gripped it firmly in her hand. With a grunt, she threw it at the back of the man's skull but just missed him. The leper spun around to face her. His movements forced Noreen's arm to smack against the ground and caused her to tumble across the rocks. She landed on her stomach and began to crawl on all fours away from him, but the leper simply stepped over her and blocked her path. Noreen gasped and scrambled onto her back. She retreated until her hands sank into the edge of the river. She gasped again at the water's icy touch and reluctantly lifted her face to her captor.

    The leper standing before her was much older than she expected. His gray and black hair no longer covered his eyes and therefore revealed the tough wrinkles of a masculine, once handsome, face of an elder. The wrinkles on his forehead and around his mouth made him appear angry or annoyed, but Noreen, surprisingly, did not believe the man to be expressing either of those emotions.

Severe indentations warped the lines of his forehead down to his cheeks, marking him with horrible, infectious scars. Dozens of small, red lumps clustered across the baggy skin around his eyes and neck and appeared as though they were on a trail that was spreading down beneath the coverage of his hospital gown. Noreen assumed by his apparel that he was one of the souls to survive Dr. Conroy's experiments. He cleared his throat. "I'm not going to hurt you!"

Noreen ignored him and glanced around for some sort of an escape, but she was trapped. "I can help you!" The leper regained her attention. He touched his throat before continuing to speak in his hoarse tone. "I know you don't belong here." He took a step forward, and Noreen flinched, causing him to come to another halt.

Noreen took another rock in her hand and threw it at the creature, this time hitting the leper's chest. She went to grab another, but the hand supporting her sank into the wet ground and she fell back into the river. She gasped and wailed her arms in the air. The leper grabbed one of her arms even though the level of the water was too low to drown her. He tossed her back onto the rocks. Noreen breathed heavy, and looked from the river back to the leper. He touched his hand to his throat again. "I can get you out of here, but only if we make an agreement."

Noreen tensed. She did not know what to do and whether or not to believe the creature that had rescued her. He was not like the other lepers she had encountered in the forest, and it frightened her, yet at the same time, relieved her. The leper took another step forward, and Noreen instinctively covered her head with her arms. She squeezed her eyes closed and waited for him to grab her but nothing happened, so she stole a peek at him. To her bewilderment, he was holding his hands alongside his ears as though admitting his surrender.

Noreen swallowed, but before she could think of what to say, she blurted out, "What kind of agreement?"

The leper cleared his throat, but his voice was still rough, "I know of a way out, but you must come with me. I will explain when we get to our destination. It's not far."

"Where is it?" Noreen's voice quivered.

The leper looked away suspiciously and adjusted the weathered, old duster that hung over his shin length hospital gown. "I can't explain here," he said, leaning toward her. "It is not safe for either of us, you must come with me right away!"

Noreen hesitated. "Why should I trust you?"

The creature touched his throat and leaned forward as he struggled to speak. "Because if you don't let me lead you away from here and pretend that you are my kill, then that leper behind the large hemlock to our Northwest angle will eat you alive."

Noreen swallowed and glanced in the direction the man described. She hoped he had been bluffing, but she saw a female leper eying her as she clawed at the bark of the tree she hid behind. Noreen inhaled and looked back at the leper leaning toward her. She nodded in defeat, and he immediately jerked forward to grab her. Noreen screamed at his unexpected movements but understood that his actions were mostly an act for the female leper, or so she hoped.

The man's covered hand was wrapped around her arm once again, but after yanking her off the ground, his grip loosened. Noreen unwillingly walked close to him, her head just above the height of his shoulder. Their close proximity forced her to inhale the dreadful odor he emitted, though she realized she also reeked with a similar, unpleasant stench. She glanced at the stranger briefly before turning her direction to the uneven path ahead. His hair fell over his eyes, and she wondered how he could see where they were going, but she feared questioning him.

The river was getting wider and its current slowed as they moved downstream. She assumed the female was still following them but refused to look back and check. The leper guiding her quickened his pace, forcing Noreen to almost jog beside him to keep up. Abruptly, he turned toward the river and walked into its current. Noreen halted at the river's edge, but his grip tightened. She lurched forward from his pull but caught her balance by placing her shoes on two rocks submerged beneath the water's surface. She pushed her heels against the rocks and leaned back, resisting the creature that tugged her forward.

The leper turned back sharply, tossing the hair that draped over his eyes, only to have it fall back down into the same position. He used his free hand to quickly remove it from his sight. "You won't drown, the water here is shallow." He tugged Noreen's arm and she fell forward, but he caught her before her body hit the water.

"I-I can't swim!" Noreen stuttered, shaking her head from side to side.

"It would take days to reach the other entrance from here, and the leper following us will not wait that long to attack. This is the only way."

"How do I know this isn't a trap or that you two aren't working together?" Noreen glanced back toward their stalker.

The disfigured man clenched his jaw without responding and wrapped his free hand around her waist, bending his knees to scoop Noreen over his shoulder. Noreen screamed as blood rushed to her head and everything around her was reversed. She used one of her fists to beat against the leper's back, using the other to grab the back of his coat and push against it so she could lean away from him. She had never been so close to a leper, but unlike the others she had seen, his skin was thankfully covered everywhere they touched. Her head dipped under the water and back out again, so she grabbed onto the back of the leper's coat, using both hands to hold on. She gasped for air, but he disregarded her wheezing breaths.

The river came up to the creature's waist, but he pressed forward. He moved through the water cautiously to keep his balance while Noreen was forced to arch her back to keep from dunking her face into the water; her blood, simultaneously, was sent back toward the remaining parts of her body as she glanced back across the river. Behind them, the female leper stepped into the water until it reached just above her ankles. She paused, choosing not to go any further, but she continued to watch Noreen, fully exposed in the sunlight.

Her dark skin remarkably manifested a yellowish tint around her inflamed sores. Her black, coarse hair was braided tightly against her skull. Even from across the river, Noreen could see the leper's chest rise and fall dramatically, her hands clenched into fists at her sides. Noreen dropped her gaze to avoid the leper's eyes, but its hissing continued to buzz in her eardrums.

She returned her head upside down to see past the man's waistline. The current, that once flowed downstream, changed direction and now blasted them from every angle. She closed her eyes to rid them of the spraying water, but her head plunged into the river. She worked hard to keep it out of the water and spare her overworking lungs. Looking around the leper's side again, his elbow jerked back as he used his arms to paddle. He almost hit her, but Noreen dodged his arm by arching her back once again. She held herself in the arched position until her back began twitching in agony. She lowered her head into the water to relieve her pain.

She was forced to hold her breath for nearly a minute until the water level lowered enough for her nose and mouth to break the surface. As she panted heavily, the leper came to a stop and reached back to grab Noreen's jacket. Swiftly, he bent his knees and lowered her into the river with the water now reaching just above her thighs. She held her head with her hand to steady herself, and stretched out her other arm to obtain balance.

She blinked slowly and opened her eyes wide as she felt her blood flowing back down to her toes. "This way," the leper directed her.

Noreen lowered her arms. She responded with a silent nod and clasped her hand tightly around the seams of the man's trench coat. She had no choice but to follow him from close behind, since she was unsure if she could keep her balance through the fast paced current.

Gradually, the water level lowered down under her knees, and remained level about halfway down her shins. Such a low current gave Noreen enough confidence to remove her hand from the leper's coat, though she stayed close to him. Peering around his frame, she saw a projecting natural arch that connected to a mountainous rock wall towering overhead. As they entered, the same rocky structure appeared to block their path, but this did not stop the leper from guiding her to their destination.

He led her alongside the wall, picking up speed until they reached a narrow crevice that contained an entryway through the rock's barrier. With the turn of his hip, he squeezed through the crack and motioned Noreen to follow. Noreen paused and looked around her, in search of an escape from her captor, but the water level rose in every direction. Because she could not swim, she was forced to follow. She faced the crevice between the rocks and brushed through the wall easily without even having to turn to fit inside.

The leper waited on the opposite side and told her to crawl slowly down the rocky mound and wait for him at the bottom. Noreen gave no verbal acknowledgement of his command but obeyed him as she slumped down to the ground. Twisting only her right palm inward, she lifted her backside and began crawling down the slope, in awe of the sights around her. Numerous small holes projected light down from the rocky ceiling, and Noreen saw the enormous cave she was enclosed in.

Other than the small mounds of rocks piled sporadically throughout the cave, the floor was far smoother than the craggy ceiling. A thin layer of light, brown dirt covered the ground to the edge of a large, still pool alongside the cave's right side. Its clear water reached an unknown depth, and its color faded away to black. She continued examining the cave and without even seeing the western half, she was hypnotized by the most incredible sight directly ahead of her.

At the far end of the cave, a row of headless dead fish hung upside down by pinkish roots that wrapped around their tails. The roots were tied around a long tree limb balanced over four other branches whose ends were imbedded in the dirt. Noreen's stomach growled, and she began crawling down the mound at twice her original speed. "Slow!" the male leper commanded, but Noreen ignored him and accelerated down the slope.

Suddenly, the rocks beneath her began to tumble as her quickened pace disrupted the peace of the mound. Before she knew it, her body was being carried down the moving slope. She opened her mouth to scream, and a high pitched cry echoed throughout the cave. The cry, however, did not belong to Noreen's throat.

The daggers dripping from the ceiling began to shake and, one after another, several of the sharp rocks crashed to the floor. Noreen covered her head to protect herself but was forced to remove her hands when the moving rocks tossed her onto the dirt. She tumbled across the ground until her body smacked against a small mound near the cave's center. Twisting to the side, Noreen looked back, and almost immediately, she crawled around the small mound to escape the wrath of the avalanche crashing toward her. She stopped on the opposite side of the pile and leaned back to brace herself. With her palms pressed into the dirt for support, Noreen closed her eyes and prayed for the flood of rocks to stop or to merely tumble around her.

As though answering her prayers, the leper's harsh voice thundered across the cave, and the piercing trill transformed into a distant echo that bounced off the surrounding walls. The sound of the tumbling rocks began to lessen seconds later, and Noreen opened her eyes to look around.

The landslide had slowed to a stop with the male leper carefully easing his way down the remainder of the slope. Noreen looked up at the ceiling above her and saw the tip of a single dagger swinging from its base. Immediately, she dove to the side just as the tip broke off and darted to the area where she had just been seated. She stared at the blade, now in pieces at her feet and exhaled an uneven breath.

Along with her exhale, a second breath came from close behind her. Slowly, Noreen turned around and found a small child staring at her, holding one of the headless fish within his tiny hands. His mouth was closed and his bottom lip pouted out. He scrunched his eyebrows together and brought the fish closer to his chest as he stepped away from her. Noreen blinked. The mysterious child standing before her had no sores or scars, not even a hint of yellow on his ghostly white skin.

She reached a hand out to the child, but before she could touch the boy's dark hair, the leper came between them. Noreen jerked her hand back. "What do you think you were doing?" the leper's voice was low. "When I tell you something, you listen! You almost ruined our main entranceway!"

Noreen disregarded his command and pointed at the child standing behind him. "What is he doing here? Why is he here?" her voice was barely above a whisper.

The leper glanced at the young child. He hesitated to prepare himself for Noreen's reaction. "My son," he replied.

Noreen shook her head as she repeated the word 'no' over and over. She finally stopped when the leper nodded his head toward something behind her. Noreen followed his gaze to another crevice cutting through the wall but saw nothing. She turned back to the leper, but the man's gaze lingered in the same direction. "It's okay, she's harmless!" his voice strained.

Noreen knew he was not speaking to her, so she looked back for a second time. Unlike before, a shadow stretched onto the wall on the opposite side of the crevice. She swallowed before fully turning her head to face the shadow's owner to find another leper leaning out of its hiding place.

The female wore a dirty, olive green kerchief that covered her hair and forehead, revealing only a few strands of gray that framed her cheeks. A scarf wrapped around the lower half of her face, just beneath her eyes, and covered the skin down to her neck. She was small, so small that had it not been for the few strands of gray, Noreen would have thought she were a child.

Covering the leper's chest was a long blouse whose color, like her trousers, was unrecognizable. The worn material was too large for her petite frame and the sleeves extended past her arms, hiding her hands in return. In fact, other than the yellow, blistered skin surrounding her eyes, no other part of the leper's flesh was revealed.

Noreen turned back to the male leper, feeling cornered between them. She lifted her knee off the ground, having to step back to keep balance but nearly stumbled onto the mound at her heels. Her heart pounded in her chest. She no longer thought about the fish dangling in the boy's hands but how his existence was conceivable. *Two lepers cannot bare a normal child free of the Infection.* She flexed her hands. "How is this possible?" she asked.

The female leper remained in the corner, still half hidden behind the hollow crack, while the man cleared his throat to prepare his voice for speech. "Lydia conceived him six years ago. He is ours." The boy peered around his father, still clinging the fish to his chest. Like the color of his skin, the whites in his eyes were mesmerizing.

"But he should be, he should be a-" Noreen could not finish her sentence, but the male leper understood its meaning.

He stuck out his neck and touched his throat, like the many times he had done before. "He is right handed, and therefore, he cannot have the Infection."

"We were shocked, too," the small woman said, holding her hand over her scarf to keep her face covered. She spoke in an abnormally soft tone, but it somehow echoed off the cave's walls and bounced into Noreen's eardrums. She turned from the male and back to the female as each of them spoke. "We did not plan for this to happen," the female continued, "I am fifty-four years old. I had Oliver when I was forty-eight."

Noreen felt as though her head was spinning. "Why are you telling me all of this?"

The veiled woman came out of her hiding place and moved along the far wall. The boy ran to her, swinging the fish in his hand. The moment he reached his mother, the child buried his face into her stomach. Noreen's eyes widened, though she could not understand why this shocked her so much. *The boy was hugging his mother, but his mother was also a leper.* Noreen shook her head.

The woman bent down to her son, and uncovering her lips, she whispered something into the boy's ear. He nodded and glanced back at Noreen before turning back to his mother. Swiftly, the leper kissed her son on the cheek, and the boy started toward his mother's hiding place to disappear into the darkness. Noreen could not believe what she had just witnessed. "He-he has no fear!" she breathed.

"No, not of us, but of you," the female leper corrected Noreen, staring off in the direction her son had gone.

"Me?" Noreen gasped. "Why would he be afraid of me? I'm not-"

"Like us," the woman held her scarf over her face to cover it again and she turned back to face Noreen. "That is why he is so frightened. He has never seen anyone like himself before, someone without the Infection."

"We are the only people he has ever known or talked to," the male leper cleared his throat.

"When he talks," the female added.

Noreen tilted her head in confusion, waiting for one of them to continue. Finally, the man stepped forward. "He is not like a normal child. His problems go far deeper than what is seen on the surface... He does not laugh or play. He has seen more death, more suffering than you ever will in your entire lifetime. But my boy, he does not deserve this life. I do not want him to grow up like this, not knowing what else is out there. He deserves to be with people of his kind." His voice picked up speed from his excitement.

"I still don't understand."

"We are old, child." The female leper inched closer, though she remained several meters away from her. "We will not live long enough to hide him and protect him against the other lepers. He will die here if he stays. We have been waiting for someone like you to come and take him away from here, because we cannot."

"That is why I brought you here," the male cut in. "We watched you and the man you were with being chased by that leper. We could tell that neither you nor your partner were one of us, so we followed you. When you fell from the cliff, we lost sight of your partner, but with the leper no longer chasing you, I was able to go after you and bring you here." He paused and cleared his throat. "I know of an exit to the Town of East, I created it years ago before I met Lydia." He glanced over to the other leper as he spoke. "We will take you there but only if Oliver goes with you."

He turned back to Noreen and found her leaning as far from him as possible with her back pressed against the mound. She parted her lips to speak, but no words could escape her throat. *An exit, it was exactly what she needed, and this- this man was willing to take her, but what about Eli? She promised to meet him at the end of the river, so they could reunite and leave the forest together. But what if she waited for him, and he never came?*

"You don't have to take care of him for long," the male leper interrupted her thoughts. "Just guide him to the other side and drop him off at my wife's home. It's been almost fifteen years since I last saw her, so I don't know where she lives or what she looks like anymore, but I can give you all the information I know of her."

Noreen shook her head. "How do you even know she would take him in?"

"I know my wife. She would raise Oliver, I know it!"

"And the Government? You don't think they'll be suspicious when a six year old child becomes part of your wife's family?"

"Well, what do you think you'll do when you get there?" The leper raised his voice enough to shake the daggers on the ceiling above them. He waited for their vibrations to end before he continued in a softer tone. "The Government will find you too, and question you if necessary, but you are here and determined to make it to the other side. Lydia and I have discussed this many times, and we have a plan, do you?"

"Y-yes," Noreen stuttered, "yes, I have a plan." The leper waited for her to elaborate. "My sister- I have a sister-a twin!" She shut her mouth as soon as she finished her explanation. The pressure the stranger placed on her forced her to reveal information she had not wished to expose.

The leper paused after her response. He squinted his eyes, as though evaluating her more closely, but after a few moments, he shook his head. "Your plan may work," he lowered his voice further, "but that is if I show you the exit, my exit. It is the only way out!" Noreen parted her lips to speak, but the leper took another step forward. She closed her lips and leaned back further until her head buried halfway into the mound. "I have showed Oliver where to go. When I take you both to the other side, I will let the two of you lead the way. Once you make it through, I will destroy the exit so neither of you can return to the forest. You will probably have to restrain him, for he will be very upset, but you can handle him."

"How do you know–"

"There is no other way!" The leper cut her off. "You will take him to my wife's cottage. Like I said, I do not know where it is, but you will have to find it. You will tell her that Oliver is a Right Hander, and she will accept him. If she needs further explanation on what to do, tell Charlotte to tell her neighbors that she adopted him from the orphanage as a John Doe."

Noreen's eyes widened. "What did you just say?" She suddenly felt her legs go numb beneath her as her backside slid down the mound and landed on the floor.

"A John Doe," the leper repeated.

"No, not that," Noreen stared back at the leper, seeing Eli's face as the man took a step away from her. The dark hair and tall, masculine build, she was ashamed of herself for not realizing it sooner. The leper was Eli's father. As soon as he turned away from her to call the other leper, a single word escaped her lips. "Will."

The man turned at the sound of his name with a puzzled expression that caused Noreen to smile. "You!" she gasped. The man took another step away from her. "You knew my father! You are him, you were my father's best friend. You are William Foster!"

It took him a moment to comprehend, but after several seconds, he lifted his hand over his mouth in shock. He mumbled to Noreen, but his voice was too gruff to fathom, so he cleared his throat. "Noreen? Little Noreen Satchell?"

Noreen nodded and her eyes watered. After everything, the man her father had befriended was still alive. The man Eli had always wondered about was, in fact, worthy of his admiration. He never turned to cannibalism; he found a shelter and a source of food and water. He even had a child, a child with the same green eyes and dark hair as Eli's. It was the brother Eli never had, the half-brother he would get to meet and spend the rest of his life with. Noreen felt a pain in her chest, and her optimistic visions ended abruptly. *What if Eli was already dead?*

"Why would the Government send you here?" Mr. Foster interrupted her thoughts. His face reflected his worry and concern. "Has something happened to your family?"

"No, but, um," Noreen paused, afraid to tell the man of her father's fate. "I was taken on Day 19, because my father thought it would be my best opportunity to reach the other side, so I could reunite with Nicole."

"Your father made it? The Government let him go?"

Noreen took a deep breath; she had forgotten that the man did not know the Government had sent her father into the forest. She began to explain to Will exactly what her father had told her before he died, leaving out the part that concerned Eli. The leper nodded to express his understanding. "He told me everything about my sister and you, right before he died," she finished.

The man's face became grim, and he turned away from her. He stared into the water to his left and released an unsteady breath from his lungs. A tear leaked out of the corner of his eye causing him to wince and hiss terribly. Noreen tensed until she realized that his hisses were not meant for her but were the product of the irritation his tear produced against the sores framing his lid. He muttered unrecognizable words to himself beneath his breath while Noreen pulsed her hands by her sides, in an attempt to keep them from trembling.

By the time Will looked back at her, she no longer was watching him but was staring off in the direction of the female crouched in the corner. Mr. Foster followed her gaze to the woman, but before either leper could speak, the female bowed her head and excused herself silently, disappearing through the crack between the walls. Mr. Foster caught Noreen's eyes again, and she knew it was time he learned of his first born.

"As you know, I am not here alone," Noreen started, "and I am not leaving the forest with-" she hesitated before speaking his other son's name, "with Oliver, until I find the man I came here with." Mr. Foster nodded in silence. "I told this man that I would meet him at the end of the river, and I know he will be there." Her voice and her hands trembled uncontrollably. "I know this because he has never given me any reason to doubt him before. He has always been there for me and, oh God, he is just such a good man and is so good to me. And I think if you met him, you would love him just as much as I do." Will cocked his head to the side, waiting for her next words. "But you would love him differently than from how I do, because he is your son. Eli is your first born son."

Mr. Foster fell to his knees. He gasped for air, ducking his head toward his chest and covering it with his palms. He whipped it back just as fast, tears running down his cheeks. He shouted out in pain, causing the daggers on the ceiling to vibrate above them. Between his screams, a cough would erupt from the leper's throat along with repeated hisses and cries. Noreen crawled back, fearing he would harm her, but her crawl was unstable, as her hands shook wildly beneath her.

The man continued to cry and yell and cough and hiss until he cradled his knees toward his chest like he was a child again. He took deep breaths and stared at a small rock poking out of the dirt. His fingers combed through his graying hair until they reached his earlobes. He pulled at his hair and screamed.

Daggers fell from the ceiling down to the floor as Noreen moved up the small mound until losing her balance at the top and tumbling down the other side. "No-Nor-Nor." She could hear Mr. Foster desperately trying to shout her name, but he was unable to voice the entire word from his throat. Noreen ignored his calls and stared at the ceiling above her. Resting her back against the dirt, she watched the daggers crash around her.

After what felt like hours, Mr. Foster's cries faded to silence and the echoes ceased. The last dagger crashed to the floor beside Noreen's elbow and broke into thousands of tiny pieces across the dirt. Noreen turned away from it, refusing to think about its shattered pieces by her side. Eli's father stood before her, and though he was more in control than before, his heart and lungs pounded aggressively in his chest. "He must never see me," the leper gritted through his teeth, "he must not know I am alive!"

Noreen nodded in agreement, not only to calm the leper, but because she knew he was right. If Eli knew his father was alive, if Eli was even alive, he would never want to leave his father, which meant that he would live amongst the lepers forever. "And the child?" Noreen's voice rose to just above a whisper. "Will Eli go the rest of his life never knowing that Oliver is his half-brother?"

"It would be for the best," Mr. Foster grumbled. Noreen could not tell if his expression was disguising some underlying emotion or if the man truly felt strongly against her inquiry.

"But that's not fair, for either of them!" she disagreed, her voice full of confidence. The leper no longer terrified her as he did before. "I spent practically my entire life not knowing I had a twin sister. I would do anything to change that! Eli has no one right now except for me. Yes, he will get the chance to meet his mother after so many years, but that is if she is still alive and if we can find her. At least, give Eli a piece of his family he can hold on to, give him a piece he won't have to let go!"

Mr. Foster buttoned his trench coat, considering Noreen's argument. He looked at her finally and held out his cloth covered hand. Noreen accepted his gesture and allowed the leper to help her to her feet. "I am going to look for my son," he started. "If I find him, I will guide him to the end of the river and that is where you will be waiting for him." Noreen's lips quivered, but Mr. Foster seemed to compose himself. "I will not let him see me at any point, and you are not to tell him anything about Oliver until after you leave the forest. The exit will be destroyed by the time you reach the other side, so Eli will never be able to return here or try to find me. I am dead to him, is that clear?"

"Yes." Noreen could barely speak the single word without trembling. She wanted to do or say something to thank the man, but he did not give her the chance. Before she knew it, her father's old friend was running toward the exit hidden among the walls where Lydia and Oliver had just gone. He disappeared within its cracks, leaving Noreen overwhelmed yet hopeful that he would find Eli and lead him to her.

Chapter 23

A thick layer of leaves was in the far corner with green branches lined horizontally beneath them. Over top laid an unzipped jacket that stretched across the bottom half of what Noreen assumed to be William and Lydia's bed. Beside the bed, several pairs of shoes lined up against the wall, reaching a pile of wood stocked neatly in a pyramid. At the other end of the cave, several shirts were tied together and held up by numerous sticks dug efficiently into the dirt. The shirts created a corner of privacy, something like a small dressing room, with a number of undergarments and outerwear draped across the rack. Noreen wondered where the two lepers and the boy found all of the extra clothes but decided it would be best not to ask.

Lydia entered the room with the boy clinging to the back of her blouse, his head buried once again in her clothes. She did not approach Noreen but instead walked straight toward the pyramid of wood while holding the boy's fish in her hands. Before picking up the bark, she turned around and laid the carcass across the boy's forearms and reached her covered fingers onto her scarf to adjust it tighter around her. While the woman prepared a fire and circled numerous rocks around the base of its flame, Noreen remained silent and stared off in the direction of the second entranceway between the cracks of the cave's walls.

At the scent of burning wood, Noreen turned her attention to the small fire whose smoke rose up and through a large hole directly above it in the ceiling. The leper carried a large, wooden contraption over to the fire and placed the four legged rack over the flame. Once she adjusted the rack into place, she gently took the fish from the boy's arms and laid it across the apparatus. The boy ran back toward the other hanging fish and untied three more, bringing them to his mother. Noreen's stomach growled from its appetizing scent, but she remained far from the flames.

Minutes ticked by on some nonexistent clock as the woman flipped all four of the fish to grill each of their sides to perfection. When the fish were done, the boy ran back toward the pyramid of wood and retrieved three flat pieces of bark from behind the pile. He held two of the pieces between his legs just below his oversized, ripped jeans. He held the first out as a plate for their meal.

His mother leaned toward him and uncovered her lips. She whispered words into his ear too low for Noreen to discern. The boy shook his head in disagreement, but Lydia ignored him and placed the fish onto the bark. Oliver looked over to Noreen but instantly dropped his gaze. He took the remaining two pieces of bark from between his legs and handed them to his mother before he walked toward Noreen ever so slowly.

With each step, Noreen saw more and more of the boy's resemblance to Eli. She lifted her back foot and shifted it forward, unintentionally causing the boy to jump and toss the fish into the dirt. He raced back to his mother and buried his face into the back of her blouse. Noreen stared at the leper, using all her willpower to wait for the woman's approval before she lunged for the lifeless meat. Lydia bowed her head, and Noreen dove for the fish. She used her hands to hold its sides as she bit into the meat. She devoured the fish to the point of licking its bones clean, and as she did so, she heard a soft giggle.

She looked up to find the young boy laughing at her from behind his mother's blouse. In response, Noreen wiped her jaw with her forearm and forced her lips to curl upward in an attempt to please the child, though she was still hungry. Miraculously, as though reading her thoughts, the boy came forward with the same plate in his hands. This time, he lifted the fish by its tail and laid it gently onto the floor a few feet away from her, but he still ran from it just as fast as before. Noreen ate the second, larger fish more slowly to savior its flavor and with only a few bites left, Lydia walked over to Noreen silently and knelt down in front of her. Noreen looked up and flinched, not realizing that the leper had come so close to her.

    Holding her scarf with a single hand, the leper spoke to her in a calm tone, but Noreen did not hear her. In the background, the young boy picked up a small glob of some mushy substance and tossed it between his lips. Once he swallowed, he forked his fingers and scooped up some more. Before Noreen could watch his next move, the leper stood to block her stare.

    She allowed her scarf to drift just below her upper lip to reveal the red sores covering her yellowed skin. With her eyes narrowed, they nearly disappeared behind her swollen cheeks. Noreen held her breath, unable to disguise her shock. The leper had captured her undivided attention and spoke to Noreen louder than before. "The pool behind you is fresh water," her voice echoed. "We all drink from it and have never gotten sick. I am sure it is safe for you to drink as well." She covered her face with her scarf again, and Noreen looked away from her, ashamed for staring at the leper's deformities.

    Recognizing her embarrassment, Lydia reached out her arm and turned it palm up. Like William, her hand was loosely wound by thick pieces of ripped cloth, but she quickly unraveled it to reveal layers upon layers of damaged skin. "I do not get offended by your stares," Lydia began, "I was also frightened when I first saw myself like this. Granted, I am much older now, and I probably have more sores covering my skin than I could imagine, but over time, I have accepted my fate, and I am no longer afraid."

Not knowing how to respond, Noreen simply nodded. She glanced at the leper's hand for an instant but quickly returned her gaze to the ground to keep from staring like she had before. She could not understand whether the woman wanted her to grab hold of her hand or if she was just gesturing to her. Lydia remained quiet and unhelpful to Noreen's predicament.

Both fear and indigestion burned inside her throat as the leper continued to hold her bare arm out to her. Noreen swallowed down her unpleasant sensations as she raised her hand slowly toward the leper's. Her fingertips reached for it and came just inches from the diseased palm, but before any contact could occur, Lydia lowered her hand and began to wrap the cloth back over her sores. Noreen hesitated in confusion, her stilled hand lingering in the air for several moments, until she finally comprehended what was happening. She mimicked Lydia's movements and brought her hand back down to her side.

"Though *I* am not afraid anymore," Lydia emphasized the word 'I', "You have every right to be. I am contagious, Noreen. That means with one touch, I can give my disease to you. I do not know how the Infection spreads, but what I do know is that a Left Hander can catch it at any time. It can lie dormant in your veins until one day it decides to take over just like that!" She pretended to snap her fingers but barely brushed her thumb and middle finger together to avoid breaking open her sores. "One day you wake up with an awful, horrible pain and do not understand what is happening until you rip off your bed sheets and see blood running down your arms and legs from the oozing sores on your skin. I will never forget the look on my late husband's face when he saw me that morning." She paused and Noreen looked up at her. She could tell the leper was speaking from the memory of her own experience as a leper.

"What happened after you found out?" Noreen asked quietly, though she was afraid to hear the woman's response. "If you don't mind me asking…"

Lydia hesitated and glanced behind her at Oliver. "Not here," she said as she turned and started for the crevice in the far wall. She yelled over to Oliver before she slipped between its cracks. "Wait here, honey, mama will be back soon."

Noreen followed her, keeping a distance between herself and the child as she passed him. Once at the exit, she slid easily through its cracks and continued to follow the hunched leper as she bent down to move under the path's low ceiling. A bright light illuminated the path from a small opening several paces ahead, forcing Noreen to use her arm to shield her eyes as she moved forward. She bumped her head on one of the gray and brown crystals that hung down from the ceiling and was forced to hunch over like the petite woman who guided her.

"Don't touch anything around you!" Lydia's voiced echoed. Her figure almost seemed to glow from the light that shined past her.

Noreen obeyed her directions and moved cautiously, but without warning, the woman's figure disappeared into the sunlight, leaving Noreen to follow blindly after her. "Lydia?" she called, unsure where the woman escaped to.

"Just follow the light, you're almost here." the leper answered Noreen in her calming tone.

Noreen followed the woman's voice, shielding her eyes from the light's intensity. Within seconds, she exited the dimness of the cave and stood on the outskirts of the dark hideaway. The blinding light of the sun instantly warmed the skin underneath her dampened clothes and dried the straggly hairs that dangled along her jawline. Noreen straightened her back while her eyes adjusted to the sunlight, having to blink many times before she was able to see anything at all.

Once her vision adjusted, her eyes were drawn to a grand willow tree whose limbs drooped into a massive lake around her. The lake enclosed the small patch of land where she stood, trapping Noreen on the small peninsula. To her right, Noreen noticed how a river widened and spilled out into the lake, the same river, she supposed, that had nearly drowned her. She smiled as she observed her surroundings, not realizing until then how close she was to the end of the river.

Starting from her right, Noreen scanned her eyes across the edges of the lake. She found that, each part of the forest surrounding the water looked identical, all except a single field of grass that split the enormous trees into two halves. *That is where I will go to reunite with Eli, that is where he will find me.*

Abruptly, the wind carried a voice that whispered through the leaves of the willow tree and blew into the gaps of Noreen's earlobes. She glanced back to the drooping tree where the voice beckoned her name and she remembered Lydia. She followed the leper's voice hypnotically, brushing aside the strands of long, thin leaves that drooped far past the length of the ground. Moments later, she was engulfed inside its walls and stood with Lydia inside the tree's coverage.

"No one can see us in here," Lydia said as she rested a single hand onto the base of the tree. Noreen squinted her eyes through the branches that circled them, but the lack of visibility to the outside world confirmed the leper's statement. The tree's branches reached far down and dipped into the surface of the lake. She glanced back at Lydia who now used the tree as a wall to carefully lean against. Lydia stared at the thin leaves of the tree, mesmerized by their beauty. She drifted into thought, into what seemed to be distant memories, and Noreen waited patiently for her to voice them.

"My husband was exposed to the Infection, but leprosy never took over him; it took over me instead. I was forty years old at the time. I had no children or living relatives. My husband gave the Infection to me without even knowing it, but I will never hate him for something he could not control.

After many years of caring for me and hiding me in the attic of our cottage, our neighbors betrayed us. They told the Government where I was hiding, and in return they received a three day supply of rotted meat. That was the value of our worth to them." Lydia looked back at Noreen. Even though her face was covered, Noreen could tell how hurt she still was simply from the look reflected in the leper's eyes. "They took my husband and me away from our home, and they experimented on us for months. It was not long before the scientists found that my husband was a carrier of the disease and that he had unknowingly infected me." she paused at the thought of the painful memory. "The night he found out, he killed himself, leaving me to face the Forest of Lepers alone. I will not get into the details of how I found him or how I felt when he abandoned me, but just know, like anyone would have felt, I was absolutely terrified.

I was a forty-three year old woman by the time I was left in the forest. I did not have the strength to kill or stamina to run, but I did have something I consider to be far more desirable: knowledge. From my early years as a botanist before the Infection first broke out, I knew when I entered these woods which plants I could eat and which were poisonous. I would hide for days, eating edible leaves and berries, in the holes of the massive trees until I eventually found this cave. It was a couple of years later when I found William nearly dead from starvation. I took him in and nursed him back to health, aside from the leprosy, of course."

"Why would you take him in?" Noreen interrupted her. "He could have torn you apart if he had turned to cannibalism. How did you know he would not turn on you?"

"When I first came across William, he was kneeling beside a deceased leper, praying. Though he was never a reverend, he was giving the creature his last rites. When he finished, he stood and kept moving. He could have eaten the creature but he had chosen not to. He was not, is not, like the other lepers I have seen."

She paused, and Noreen's mind wandered. She thought of Eli, and she imagined how proud he would be if he knew of his father's nobility. He would be honored to call William his dad, but, of course, Noreen recognized that Will was not the only noble member of his family. Eli too reflected kindness and humility, traits not often found in a Left Hander's world. He resembled his father more than he could ever imagine, and Noreen hoped that someday she would be able to tell him that.

Lydia observed Noreen's distant expression and slowly walked toward her, stopping about an arm's length away from her. "William told me of his family. He told me that he had a wife and a son in one of the first conversations we had together. He is not the type of man to betray his family by any means, but you see, the two of us make a good team. I, being barely over five foot three, needed protection and William, well, he is more than large enough to protect me. He, on the other hand, needed me to tell him what foods are safe to eat and which are not. We protect each other because we enjoy each other's company, and know that we would never be able to make it in the forest alone.

After depending on one another for so long and being so close, I got pregnant with Oliver. I did not think it was possible. I do not regret having him, he is my only child and I love him, but I am getting old. Every day we fight death, every day we risk our lives for each other, and one of these days I will not see tomorrow. One of these days, William will not either. I know it is too much to ask of you, and I know William has already practically demanded it, but will you please take our son? Will you take Oliver with you and save his life?"

Noreen looked at the leper standing before her and smiled with sympathy. "I will." she accepted.

Lydia bowed her head to Noreen and thanked her. "You have no idea how much this means to me!"

Tears formed at the corners of her eyes, but Noreen remained silent. Her smile, like her spirit, faded as the memory of her mother waving her final goodbye flooded through her. She had waved through the parted shutters, the same parted shutters through which Noreen had witnessed her weep each day in solitude, but not once did Noreen run back inside to comfort her. She wished she had.

With Lydia's head still bowing down, Noreen wiped her eyes with her sleeve to remove the tears that dripped down her cheeks. Lydia lifted her head shortly after and spoke. "I do not know why you are here or how you know William's first born, but I do know that he is here with you, William told me that much before leaving us. I just want you to know, I consider any son of William's a son of my own, so I will do anything to help you find him." Noreen smiled with her lips closed to express her gratitude, but Lydia changed the subject before she could thank her. "There is a cascade behind this willow. It flows into the lake just like the river does. This water will be safest for you to drink and bathe in."

The leper stepped away from Noreen and pulled aside a group of branches that covered the cascade. Noreen moved toward the stream and bent down on her knees before it. She looked up at Lydia who bowed her head once again to gesture for her to drink. Noreen peered back toward the stream and cupped her hands into the flowing water. The refreshing touch of the liquid on her lips reminded her of Eli's moist pair kissing her's after he drank the puddle water. Sudden nausea came over her.

She wondered if the leper that chased them toward the cliff had attacked or if William would ever find Eli and lead him to her. She wondered how long the canteen of worms would last and where Eli would find fresh water to drink. As she continued to think of the man she had grown to love, a rush of guilt churned in the pit of her stomach. She was ashamed of herself for eating the fish and drinking the fresh water when she knew Eli was out in the forest somewhere on the brink of starvation.

With most of the puddles probably dried, Noreen feared he would not last long without water, if he was not already dead. Thinking those last six words, she exhaled the air she accumulated inside her chest. She had to keep telling herself that he was alive, she had to believe he would be okay because she was not going anywhere without him.

"What's wrong?" Lydia asked with concern as she watched Noreen holding her stomach. "Do you feel sick?"

"I'm fine," Noreen lied, swallowing the regurgitated fish back down her throat. She could feel Lydia staring down at her. "I am still full from the fish," she lied again.

Noreen leaned away from the stream, her eyes filling with tears again. In an attempt to block them from gushing down her cheeks, she shut her eyes as tight as she could. She could not stop hearing Eli's voice replaying over and over in her head. He was calling her name, exactly as he had when she dropped into the river. She could see his face as she kissed him and remembered how confused and terrified, yet pleased, he looked the moment her lips pressed against his.

She wanted to go back in time and warn him about the leper sooner or run faster than she had. She wished he was with her at that very moment, drinking from the stream and having a stomach utterly satisfied after a full meal. If he was still alive, he was probably still nibbling on the same earthworms they had packed into their canteen. He probably did not have any idea where he was or where he was heading since he did not have the compass to guide him.

Noreen slipped her hand into her pocket then as she thought of her father's compass for the first time since before falling into the river. Expecting it to be there, she reached her fingertips far enough for them to barely disappear into the pocket of her jacket. It was empty. In a panic, she shoved her hand in further but still felt nothing. The compass was gone. Now Noreen would have to fully rely on Eli's father to lead them out of the forest, but he was not there and she did not know when he would return.

Unexpectedly, Noreen felt the branches touch her shoulders as Lydia released them and stepped back toward the tree's base. "I cannot force you to drink, but if you don't, you will die," she said strongly, "and if you die, you will be deserting the man depending on you to meet him at the end of the river. You will desert him, just like my husband deserted me. Don't let my husband's fate become yours and please, please do not let my fate become Eli's."

Noreen whipped her head back to face the leper, but she was already gone, leaving the thin, draping branches of the willow tree swaying in her place. She turned back to the stream and watched the water trickling over and between the wet stones. Without pause, she cupped her hands in the water and took a drink.

Chapter 24

The weeds were limitless into the sky. They broke through the hovering clouds and continued upward until their tips reached far past a visible distance. Noreen walked through the tall grass, brushing each golden strand apart like she was combing her fingers through the thick locks of her of lightly tinted hair. She was lost in the maze of grass, but fear never struck her consciousness. She was searching for something. She could feel its presence upon her. Each step she took, she was getting closer and closer to it until a gunshot sounded, sending hundreds of black swans showering dark flames across the sky. They cut between the strands of grass, forming a thick blanket that covered the few wispy clouds and darkened the sky within seconds.

Breaking through the smoky film, five bursts of white dove in and out of the dark blanket until the five pure, noiseless seagulls formed a defined arrow pointing in the opposite direction. Using the seagulls as her guide, Noreen sprinted through the field, chasing after the flying arrow. The weeds seemed to magically comb aside and bend away from her before she even reached them. Her body felt weightless as her feet almost flew over the ground in a fluid motion.

She followed the birds until their wings pushed back through the black swans' blanket and disappeared from her vision. Her running eased to an effortless jog and eventually stopped. A bright light shined through the weeds, and she curiously leaned toward it, brushing aside the final golden strands of grass from blocking her view. Before she could decipher the source of the light, Noreen's eyes fluttered open and she woke up from her dream in a daze.

    She sat up to relieve her back of the uneven rocks that spread across the ground beneath her and stared into the fire by her feet. Daylight had not yet pierced through the holes of the rocky ceiling, therefore limiting the amount of light to just inside the fire's realm. She watched as its smoke drifted up and out through the cracks of the ceiling. It had been two weeks and four nights that Noreen had slept on the lepers' floor, yet there was still no sign of Mr. Foster or Eli. Lydia slept on the opposite side of the cave with Oliver on their cloth covered bed, and Noreen slept far from them on the dirt covered rocks. Never was she offered any of their extra clothes for a cushion, but once Noreen was told of their origin, she had not wanted anything to do with them. The jackets and shirts piled sporadically throughout the cave had been stolen off the bodies of the deceased lepers of the forest.

    Noreen shivered at the thought, and lifted her backside off the ground to grab hold of a sharp rock poking through her jeans. She tossed the rock away from her, only to hear a faint shriek echo immediately after the rock was thrown. Noreen jerked her head in the direction of the sound and squinted her eyes into the darkness. "Who's there?" she whispered loudly. "Lydia? Is that you?" She waited for a response but received only silence. "Show yourself!" Noreen demanded as she gathered herself on her knees. Moments later a small, dark figure stepped forward until it stood just outside the fire's realm. "Oliver?"

    The shadow fidgeted half a step forward into the light. It was the Right Hander, as Noreen had guessed. The child clamped his hands behind his back and leaned his head away from her, aligning his chin to the bare skin of his chest. In the light, the color of the boy's dark hair matched Eli's precisely, though Oliver's reached much further down, until leveling off unevenly just above his underarms. He wore the same dark blue, loose fitting pants that he wore each day, with the same leather belt that looped twice around his small waistline. His pants were ripped off just above his ankles, revealing two tall socks that partially covered his ghostly white appendages.

Noreen swallowed. She did not know how to act toward the child. He had never approached her without his mother hovering close by. Noreen scratched her scalp before leaning her arm over her head and grabbing her ponytail. She used the time to think of something to say to the child. Eventually, she lowered her arm and placed her hands on her thighs. "I'm sorry," she began, "did the rock hit you? I did not mean for it to." She paused and the boy's lips moved. "What did you say?" She strained to hear him.

Oliver closed his lips bashfully, and stepped back out of the light, though his shadow remained. "Please don't be afraid!" Noreen begged. She felt as if she were talking to herself rather than a timid, young child, but she continued nonetheless. "I just didn't hear you, that's all! It's hard to hear in this place, with all the echoes, but if you say it one more time a little louder, I promise I will stop talking so much and leave you be." The momentum in her voice died down progressively, as she felt even more awkward for rambling on with her attempt to persuade him. She looked away from the boy's shadow and glanced back into the fire.

"No," the boy stated. Noreen jerked her head in the child's direction; she was hearing him speak for the first time. Oliver continued to talk loud enough for her to hear, but his words were indecipherable. Noreen remained silent, afraid to interrupt and potentially scare him away from her. After a few moments, Oliver stepped back into the light and paused mid-sentence.

Unsure what to do, Noreen simply nodded, prompting Oliver to lift his cheeks and curl his lips in the shape of a smile. Noreen smiled back and the boy grinned even wider, enough to reveal his merely toothless mouth. Noreen controlled her shock by tightening her grasp on her thighs, though her muscles tensed at her shoulders. Most of his baby teeth had rotted away, leaving only a few brown, stained pieces left in his entire mouth. She now realized why the child would only whisper what he needed to his mother and why he only ate globs of mush. The lack of care for the child's baby teeth took a severe toll on his speech by modifying his words with practically indecipherable mutters and mumbles.

"So, you are alright?" Noreen overemphasized each word. She nodded as she asked the question, hoping he would also respond with a nod back to her. Thankfully, he did. "Okay, good, well, it's still not light out, so I think it would be a good idea if we both went back to sleep."

"My moder," Oliver became serious. He looked down at his feet as he fidgeted, with his ankles moving outward and back.

Noreen leaned toward him and stared blankly at the floor as she attempted to decode his speech. "Your mother?" she recited his words back to him.

"Cee shaysh yur hure to t-takh meh a-awayh." Oliver talked slowly, but his words were still altered significantly.

Despite his lack of clarity, Noreen comprehended what he was trying to tell her, and she repeated his words in her head. *She says you're here to take me away.* A pain struck her heart, and she felt as though it were breaking. She scolded herself under her breath. She should have known her presence in the cave had been questioned. She should have expected Lydia to explain the situation to her son. Noreen continued to clutch her thighs as she replied to Oliver, but her words stumbled in spite of her attempts to control them. "Well, your 'uh' mother and father, well, they feel that it would be best if-"

"I down wahnah gowah!" Oliver raised his voice at her. His bottom lip trembled, leaving Noreen speechless.

I don't wanna go. His words rang in her ears, and she wished she had not understood them. She had no idea how to respond to the child; she did not know how to tell him that he had no choice in the decision and that he would have to accept it. It was a decision that he would someday have to understand, but he was too young now to comprehend what was happening to him. He did not deserve to lose his parents but neither did any Doe in the orphanages back home or in the Town of East. No one deserved his fate, but he had no choice. He would not last in the forest, he *will* die here if he stays, but how can someone tell a six year old something like that?

Noreen took a deep breath; her thoughts were running faster than her brain could grasp them. She opened her mouth to speak but no words came out. The boy stared at her, his lip still trembling, when suddenly another figure came up behind him. A clothed hand lightly rested on the child's shoulder causing him to flinch before he turned around and threw his arms around the enormous figure.

The hand on the child's shoulder wrapped around the boy and lifted him into the air. Noreen clenched her teeth. William Foster stepped into the light, holding Oliver in his arms. "You won't have to worry about leaving, my son," his voice echoed through the cave. Noreen saw another shadow stretch across the floor beside the leper's, but it was far too small to belong to Eli. It belonged to a very petite figure whose eyes illuminated from the fire and seemed to watch her in the darkness. "What I was looking for was nowhere to be found," Mr. Foster faced Noreen with a grim expression, "and I looked everywhere!"

Noreen shook her head repeatedly as tears swelled at the corners of her lids. Lydia rushed forward into the light from her position beside her mate and ripped Oliver from Mr. Foster's arms. She carried the child away from them and into the darkness. Mr. Foster stepped forward when Lydia was out of sight, but Noreen raised her hand in front of her to stop him. She pressed her opposing palm into the ground to help herself to her feet as she pointed a single finger at the leper. "You must look harder!" she demanded.

The man mimicked Noreen by also shaking his head as he clenched his jaw together. She could tell he was trying to choke back the tears wanting to escape his lids. "I looked everywhere I could think of, but I could not find him."

"No-no-no-no you couldn't have! He is still out there! He needs our help!"

"He is DEAD, Noreen!" The leper struggled to scream at her through his damaged throat. "I searched everywhere! There is no body to be found, no clothes left behind. When that happens, it means he was eaten!"

"YOU LIAR!" Noreen screamed back at him with tears flooding down her cheeks. Her face reflected the color of crimson as she panted rapid breaths.

"Do you not think I want to find my own son as much as you want to find your 'friend'? He is the son I have wondered about all his life; the son I have loved all his life! I want more than anything to find him alive and safe! You will never understand how much he- "

"-means to me!" Noreen finished his sentence for him, "I love him! I love him more than anything! He is all I've got, and I am NOT leaving here without him. You can give up on him if you want, but Eli has NEVER given up on me, and I won't give up on him. I have waited for him every day since you left, and I will wait every day until he finds me. And he will find me!"

Noreen whipped her head to the side and grabbed one of the pieces of bark sticking halfway out of the fire. She thought of Eli burning his wrist with the embers in her fireplace as she snatched it out of the flames. She ran from Eli's father with the flaming torch in her hand, using its light to guide her up the rocky mound, the same mound she had nearly destroyed when she first arrived at the leper's shelter. When she reached the top, she slipped through the crack of the entranceway and threw the burning wood into the river. She used the moonlight now, not wanting to be seen by the predators of the forest. Balancing on the rocks, she climbed up the side of the wall and followed the unmarked path Lydia had, more than once, shown her. It was the path to her escape, the one that avoided crossing the river, and the one she climbed each morning before the sun rose above the tree tops.

Chapter 25

*T*he water was calm with only a few small ripples flowing over the rocky edges and fading back toward the lake's center. A light fog hovered over the surface of the water, creating an unclear and blurred vision of the opposing side. The morning dew wet the surface of the ground alongside the freshwater while the sun slowly rose over the horizon. It was the start of the nineteenth day that Noreen had waited for Eli diagonally across from the river's end and in the middle of the large, open pasture. Any other location surrounding the lake would hide her beneath the trees, so she stood alone in the midst of the tall field of grass that reached just below her hips. Unlike the days before, when she kneeled beneath the tips of the weeds and waited, today Noreen stood tall and invited fate to approach her.

The grassy field reminded her of the pasture outside her home, having the same golden brown grass blowing gently in the wind. She would pass by the field, carrying heavy buckets of sloshing water in her hands. Louise would rush toward her from the house, pestering her with words of sarcasm and harassment, while her mother would be calling to her from inside. The woman would be in the kitchen, and Charlie would just be coming home from a long day at the harbor. A flask of liquor would be jingling in her pocket, waiting to be given to her dying father in their nightly transaction that occurred beneath the kitchen table.

The field behind her home witnessed every walk Noreen had taken on each ordinary day and every secret that would be unraveled on each atypical night. The field she stood in now never heard any of her family's secrets. It rested in a place with no windows to peak in and no doors to send a howling breeze through its cracks. It lay in a dangerous world, and Noreen stood in the heart of it.

Each day she came to the field, Eli's face seemed to get more and more distant when she tried to visualize him. His features became less distinct, and his expressions progressively blurred. She was losing him with time, along with her sanity, but she refused to give up on him, she refused to let him go.

A strong breeze lifted the straggly curls that covered her temples and Noreen used three of her fingers to brush the strands back to their sides. Her hair was no longer in a long, knotted ponytail but tied in a loose bun on the back of her skull. She wore the same clothes as any other day with the same jean jacket of her mother's down to the same number of socks she layered inside her brother's old boots. She had only soaked her clothes twice since she arrived in the forest, in the same freshwater she drank from outside the willow tree's branches on the miniature sized peninsula. It was the only place hidden entirely from outside wanderers and the only place Noreen felt safe to wait naked until her clothes dried. She supposed now that a repulsive odor undoubtedly emitted off her, but her nose remained oblivious to her scent.

Although she had not slept most of the night, she had more energy than she normally had after a full night's rest. The bruises Lawrence gave her, from what seemed like years ago, were almost completely gone, and her open wounds had transformed into scars. The largest area of scaring stretched across the inside of her left wrist. It covered her tattoo forever, over the only place where she was linked to the people of her kind. Noreen touched her wrist using the fingers of her right hand and felt the heat radiating off her skin. She closed her eyes and whispered her father's rhyme under her breath.

From past to present,
From pride of a peasant,
The Right may slither,
But the Left will not wither.

When Noreen first heard his rhyme, she could not agree more with her father, but now her heart somewhat disagreed with him. The birthplace of all this slithering evil indeed came from the scientists who leaked the Infection and tore her country apart, but the pure wickedness did not come from one's label as a Left or Right Hander, it came from the beholder within that person's character. Circumstances like Day 19 changed her people or rather exposed their innermost evil to control their actions. The spread of the Infection changed people, and changed the lepers themselves, to work against their own kind for survival. But some stayed true to their values, even lepers like Lydia and William, while others let desperation and hunger control them, like Charlie's ex-fiancé Madeline.

Eli was always someone who showed true character, someone that held on to his values even when times got rough. He was someone who considered Noreen his equal, who Noreen could argue with but never get angry at. He was the man she loved, and the man she refused to live without.

Noreen opened her eyes just as the sun appeared to sit atop the edge of the lake. She blinked at the bright light glistening through the breaking fog. Opening her eyes a second time, she could barely glimpse the outline of the distant trees whose images reflected on the surface of the water. She turned her head, hoping see the grand willow tree through the lightening haze, but it was still hidden in the mist. A chilly breeze gusted against her back sending cold shivers up her spine. She crossed her arms and followed the breeze with her eyes as it blew through the grass.

A small, lone butterfly caught her attention and stole her eyes away from the breeze that drifted toward the water. The butterfly's heavenly white wings flapped effortlessly as it sat perched on the tip of a golden weed. Noreen cocked her head, mystified by the resting creature, and took a step toward it. The butterfly remained on the weed, flapping its wings to keep from being carried away by the gusting wind. Noreen continued to walk toward the harmless beauty until she stood less than a meter away from it. She reached out her left arm, and faced her palm up, as though disoriented by the insect. In an instant, it fluttered into the air and flew past Noreen's waiting arm, flapping just inches away from her eyelashes.

Focusing on the insect, the surrounding area was blurred around her. Noreen drew back her arm slowly as she watched it gliding past. She turned her body with her moving pupils until her back faced the water. In the corner of her eye, a dark, blurred figure disrupted the field of weeds and stood motionless in the distance. Noreen removed her eyes from the distracting butterfly and glanced in the direction of the figure.

A man stood just on the outskirts of the forest where the trees met the tall grass. His clothes were torn, revealing bloody slashes on his bare chest. His denim pants were almost completely brown from the massive amounts of dried dirt packed onto them. He had dark hair that reached to just above his shoulders while a black scruffy beard covered the lower half of his face, down to his neck. A blood red cloth wrapped around his right shoulder and across his chest, tying just beneath his left underarm. It was Eli.

Noreen felt as though she had swallowed the white butterfly whole and it was now fluttering around in the pit of her stomach. Her heart raced more violently than it ever had before, and she was unsure whether she would be able to remain conscious. She started to run toward him, using all her strength to rip her arms back and lift her knees through the tall grass. He moved toward her as well, using only one of his arms to push himself forward.

As the gap between them diminished, Noreen drew her arms out in front of her and threw them around Eli's neck. They kissed passionately near the edge of the field, making up for lost time, when they were forced to live apart. Eli cupped his hands around Noreen's cheeks and tilted his head faintly as Noreen twisted her fingers through the strands of his long, disheveled hair. When their lips parted, Eli kissed the remaining parts of her face with gentle pecks, from her cheeks up to her forehead.

"How?" Only the single word escaped Noreen's lips. Tears flowed down her cheeks and ran over Eli's fingertips.

Eli used his thumbs to wipe away her tears before leaning his forehead against hers. He smiled as his own tears welled up in his eyes and rolled down through the dark hairs of his jawline. He breathed heavily, licking his lips before he spoke. "Do you remember what I said to you before we left? When you were so angry at me for protecting you? Do you remember?" Eli paused as he stared into her blue irises. "I told you that I would risk everything to be with you, and I will, Noreen, I always will!"

The moment Eli's lips closed, Noreen wrapped her arms tighter around him, bringing them closer together and prompting Eli to bend forward and wrap his arms around her waist. Tears continued to flow as they embraced. Noreen leaned her head against his and she rested her chin on his uninjured shoulder. She stared into the woods behind him, lost in thought.

As she stared into the forest, she saw another figure emerge from its hiding place, but rather than erupting into a state of panic, Noreen waited until the figure's face revealed itself. When it did, she recognized the face of Eli's father, watching them yet keeping his distance. Noreen smiled at Will as she embraced his son, but he did not smile back. Instead, his eyes narrowed and he clenched his hands into fists.

Noreen could not understand what was upsetting him, but before she could comprehend, the leper was racing toward her. He expressed enough anger and rage in his attack to transform Noreen's joyous tears into helpless cries of terror. She pulled away from Eli to warn him, but another leper lunged at him from its hidden stance beneath the tall grass, and the Doe was sent crashing onto his side. Noreen screamed, but it was too late; the leper bit into Eli's wounded shoulder causing jolts of excruciating pain into the depths of his skin. He cried out in horror while Noreen desperately pulled at the leper's matted hair with hopes to rip the creature off him. Within seconds, Eli's father lunged for the leper attacking Eli, and both creatures tumbled on top of one another into the grass.

    Noreen tore off her jacket and pressed it hard against Eli's bleeding wound, demanding he hold it in place with his other hand. She reached around his side and helped him to his feet. Keeping her arm around him, she helped him walk quickly out of the field and into the forest. "This way!" She heard Lydia calling to them, and Noreen followed her voice instinctively. Eli moved with her, too preoccupied with his pain to comprehend what was happening.

    Noreen looked back toward the field when she heard Mr. Foster's raspy voice scream out in pain, but she pressed further into the forest. She needed to get Eli out of there. "Hurry!" Noreen turned to her left as Lydia's voice sounded closer. A light fog hovered over the moss covered dirt, making the roots in the ground hardly visible, but Noreen urged Eli with her arm to move faster through the forest. Eli cursed from his pain, but Noreen barely heard him; instead she listened for the voice guiding them to safety.

    Unexpectedly, Lydia appeared through the blurriness of the fog, holding Oliver's hand as she approached them. Her pace was fast, almost too fast, as it seemed as though she were practically dragging her son behind. The moment she reached Noreen, the leper ripped her hand from Oliver's and pushed the child toward her. "Take him and don't let him go!" Lydia commanded. Eli stumbled backward at the sight of the leper coming toward them until his back smacked against a massive hemlock tree behind him. He cursed at the pain from the initial impact but continued to moan from the stinging of the aftershock. He looked up finally and stared at the leper with narrowed eyes.

Lydia's deformed and sore covered face was fully revealed, but her attention was not focused on the Doe. Instead, she was instructing Noreen to run in the opposite direction. "We are close to the Town of East's border. You must run to it as fast as you can before anything else attacks! And please, keep Oliver safe," she paused as she glanced down at her child. The boy lifted his arms to reach her, but the leper reluctantly stepped even further away from her son. "As you get closer you will begin to see clouds of smoke," though her words were directed toward Noreen, her eyes were locked with Oliver's. "Follow those clouds until the end. Oliver, he will know what to do from there!"

Noreen struggled to hold on to the leper's son as she spoke. "I will, but what about-"

"I will take care of him," Lydia peeked a quick glance at Eli before turning her attention back to Noreen. "Oliver's father is a strong man, he will be fine, but you must go! NOW!" At her final word, she sprinted away from them and disappeared into the fog in a matter of seconds. Oliver screamed the indecipherable words of his language to call after his mother.

"Eli, come, quickly! There is no time to explain!" Noreen picked up the child and rested his bottom on her hip. Eli remained hesitant, as he bent forward from the pain shooting through his back and shoulder. "Trust me, Eli, we must go, now!" Noreen held out her hand to him. Eli hesitated for another moment before grabbing hold of it. The two of them ran, hand in hand, in the direction Lydia indicated with Oliver bouncing on Noreen's side. He pounded his fists on her back over and over as he cried out desperately for his mother. "Do you see any smoke?" Noreen panted, ignoring the child's cries.

Eli removed his hand from Noreen's to keep her jacket pressed tightly against his bleeding shoulder. "No- nothing!"

They surged forward, but Noreen became fearful that they were lost running in the wrong direction. The trees all looked identical, with their heights towering above them, and masking over the sky. Noreen wondered how she would be able to see the smoke through the thick veiling treetops.

Constantly looking around them, she gazed up at the sky each time a patch of fog would lighten in her path. After a few more strides, she gazed up once more and, through the veil of the trees' canopy, she saw puffs of grayish white drifting with the wind in the opposite direction. Noreen began running faster with adrenaline pumping through her veins. She chased the low clouds, the child's screams now pitiful whimpers sobbing into her jacket.

"Look!" Eli shouted from beside her. He used his elbow to point forward. Following his gesture, Noreen noticed the trees thinning out in front of them, as did the hovering fog. A brown film, created by unnatural smog, covered the distant background as they reached the point where the trees ended. Noreen squinted but was barely able to make out the uneven land before them. The two slowed their pace, stopping at a tall barbed wire fence that blocked their path. "What now?" Eli gazed over to Noreen standing beside him.

Noreen remembered Lydia's words echo through her brain as she tried to find the answer to Eli's question. *Follow those clouds. Oliver will know what to do!* Lydia's words struck a nerve, and she immediately set the child on the ground. Holding his arms at his sides, she kept Oliver in place, though he squirmed defiantly beneath her grasp.

"Oliver? You must listen to me, okay?" She tried to keep her voice calm, but she knew it could never sound as soothing as Lydia's. "It is very important that you tell us where the exit is. The exit out of the forest. Your mother said you know where it is!" The boy refused to answer her. Instead, he shook his head and continued to cry. He mouthed the word 'moder' with his lips.

"Your mother is gone! She is not here to help you right now!" Noreen raised her voice impatiently. "This is not a game. There are things in this forest that will kill us!"

The child's whimpers stopped, and he stared at her. A wave of guilt pinched her heart as she stared back at the child's petrified expression. She lightened her grip on him and felt Eli's touch on her shoulder. He kneeled in front of Oliver, while smiling sympathetically to Noreen as though waiting for her approval. Noreen nodded back to him and lowered her arms to set the child free in front of her.

"Hey there," Noreen could hear the pain in Eli's voice as he held her blood stained jacket to his shoulder, but somehow, he sounded almost more calming than Lydia. "My name is Eli. And you are…?"

"Oliver," the boy choked out.

"You know, I was once told by a very brave man," he caught Noreen's eyes for a moment before he continued, "that my father wanted to name me Oliver before I was born. But my mother really wanted Elijah and so that's my name. But between you and me, I think I like Oliver better." Eli smirked and the boy's lip twitched, though he did not smile back. Noreen felt as though her heart stopped. She could not believe how well Eli was talking to Oliver, without even knowing the child was his half-brother. "I bet you that your mother is perfectly fine, and your father is, too!" Eli continued, "but they won't be if they find out that you aren't safe. Now, Noreen made a promise to your mother, and her promise was that she would keep you safe, and I want to keep you safe, too, so that means you're gonna have to show us the way out. If you do, I promise that you will be safe, and your parents will not have to worry."

Oliver glanced from Eli to Noreen. His expression was serious, though a hint of confusion and uncertainty was revealed by the presence of a small crease that formed between his brows. He turned away from them then and searched the perimeter. In an instant, Oliver started to run. Noreen drew a glance at Eli, but he was already on the move after the child, so she too raced after him. She followed the brothers as they ran along the fence line, wondering why Oliver had chosen not to run back into the forest. She watched him stick his neck out and lean forward as he ran, revealing the bones that protruded from his arched back. Noreen could have very easily caught up to Oliver and stopped him, but she had the feeling he was leading them to their exit.

Eli's broad frame suddenly blocked her view of the child, forcing Noreen's attention to focus on the torn slashes of material that were once his blue and black checkered flannel. The bleeding wounds that she had once cared for were now thick, menacing scars stretching across his reddened skin. Traveling her eyes further up his back, she came to his shoulder where she noticed blood seeping quickly through her jacket. Without Eli even realizing it, he was pumping his blood faster and faster with each step, causing it to flow more quickly out of the open wound. Noreen opened her mouth to yell after him, but Eli had already stopped and lowered himself to his knees. She looked ahead of him and saw the child crawling into the bushes that edged the bottom of the fence line.

Without hesitation, Noreen mimicked Eli's movements and followed the boy into the thickly leaved underbrush. While she used her hands and knees to crawl beneath the branches, Eli laid flat on his stomach, using his elbow, forearm, and knees to push himself forward. With Eli's body so close to the ground, Noreen was able to see the child ahead of them until the sunlight dimmed and his figure became merely an outline.

The dirt beneath her began to slope downward and she felt gravity's tug pulling her into the underground tube. The air thinned as she lowered herself into the confined space, so she tried to calm her breathing. Eli's pace slowed down, causing Noreen to pause and wait for him to squeeze his broad shoulders through the manmade cavity beneath the bushes. Out of nowhere, she felt hands clamp around her ankles and begin to drag her back into the forest. The memory of Lawrence dragging her toward him returned and her breathing accelerated. Each time she blinked she saw Lawrence's face smirking at her and his drooping eye winking malevolently over and over again.

Noreen dug her fingers into the dirt, attempting to slow herself, but pain overwhelmed her as the tip of one of her fingernails snapped off in the dirt. She screamed for Eli's help, though she knew he could not save her; Eli was stuck inside the tunnel with no way of turning back. She could hear him calling after her, but despite his cries, his image slowly faded behind the branches of the underbrush.

The foul words Lawrence had more than once used to harass her and unnerve her with echoed in her ears and drowned out all sounds around her. Like her last night at The Cove, the fingers wrapped around her were dragging her back toward the Hell she was so close to escaping from. With each tug, they hauled her away from the man she loved, taking Lydia and William's secrets with her. With every yank, she felt further and further away from her twin sister, the sole motivation for her entrance into Hell and her battles within it. Whatever sickening and horrifying creature who had its hands around her ankles, though, was not going to stop her now, not when she had traveled so far and suffered so much.

She reached for the base of the final shrub using the determination that erupted inside her. Her hands grasped around its branches as the leaves whispered the menacing words of Hell's nightmarish demands. Lawrence's face no longer hovered in her mind, and she could now hear the desperate calls of her lover deep inside the tunnel and the wheezing pants of her abductor at her back, pants that revealed the creature was weakening. Knowing what to do, Noreen pulled on the base of the shrub, making grumbling noises as she held on for her life. The creature's gasps grew increasingly shallower as Noreen resisted its strength, until the opportune moment arrived and she let go of the base.

In a flash, Noreen's body whipped backward and crashed into the startled leper whose yank finally jolted Noreen out of the underbrush. Before the creature realized what was happening, Noreen jumped to her feet and dove on top of her, pinning the female to the ground. Clenching her left hand into a fist, Noreen punched the creature directly between its eyes.

The creature's face went blank, but Noreen continued to attack it, letting out all of her anger on the leper's living corpse. Strength she never knew she possessed expelled out of her, as the bones of her wrist ripped through her scars and re-broke through her skin. Her pain seemed to be numbed, though, as more and more anger erupted out of her.

After all the pain and misery she had gone through, after losing her father and leaving her family behind, after being experimented on and deserted in the forest of Hell with nothing but a canteen and a compass, with no chance of survival, *with no chance of survival.* The words lingered in Noreen's brain, and she paused with her fist midair. She was ready to strike again until a hand touched her shoulder. Noreen whipped around, holding out two fists that were prepared to fight, but unlike what she expected, she found Oliver standing before her with fear in his eyes and a pounding chest. Noreen looked down at her blood covered fists that now shook uncontrollably by her sides. Without warning, the child's arms wrapped around her neck. Noreen gasped at his unexpected embrace, and she wrapped her arms around the boy, careful not to touch her bloody hands to his back. With her weight on her knees, she became the child as she cried helplessly onto the boy's shoulder.

After some time, their arms parted, and the boy tugged on her shirt as if silently telling her it was time to go. Instead of following after the child, Noreen glanced back to the motionless leper. She stared at the dark blood that covered its unprotected flesh and how it made the leper's facial features practically unrecognizable. An observing leper sensed the creature's immobility and emerged through the thickness of the fog. It glared at Noreen but was hesitant to attack the immobile creature until Noreen wiped her blood stained hands onto her clothes and turned back into the bushes. As she descended into the underground tunnel, the horrifying sounds of tearing flesh steadily faded until the haunting noises of the forest were silenced altogether.

Chapter 26

A bright, yellow light beamed around Oliver's figure, creating dark silhouettes on either side of the tunnel. What had started out as an endless hole of complete darkness had evolved into a tunnel with an alluring light that illuminated Noreen to her exit. She closed her eyes as she moved forward, believing the light to be heaven's rays guiding her to her destiny. Her right palm still remained gently wrapped around Oliver's ankles, since he had led her blindly through the previous darkness, until it was suddenly ripped out of her loose hold.

Noreen's eyes flew open to a hand that reached out to her but whose arm disappeared into the blinding light ahead. She grabbed hold of Eli's hand without hesitation and allowed him to help her out of the constricted tube by use of only a single of his arms. Once her feet hit the ground, he wrapped the same arm around her. "I'm so sorry!" he cried. He blurted the words out quickly, "I could not turn around, I could not fit, so-so I pulled myself to the end of the tunnel. Before I could go back in, Oliver had already gone after you and I-"

Noreen could hear the guilt in his voice and see the concern reflected in his troubled expression, but she did not find fault with him. "It's alright, I'm alright," she reassured him.

Eli simply nodded, not able to think of the right words to respond to her, and Noreen turned away from him before he could apologize any further. She studied the illuminated, circular tunnel and dropped her arms from around the Doe's neck. She put pressure on her bleeding wrist as she walked to the center. Her feet stood on a wooden plank that connected to two silver tubes at each of its ends. Peering at the floor, Noreen noticed how the tubes continued to connect to an endless number of planks in both directions. "Where are we?"

Oliver mumbled something back to Noreen, but neither she nor Eli could understand him. Noreen stepped toward the child. "What did you say?"

Again his words were indecipherable. She glanced over to Eli who simply shrugged his uninjured shoulder. "Okay, well, do you know a way out?" she asked Oliver. The boy shook his head and Noreen sighed.

"I heard something that sounded like explosions earlier. It came from that way," Eli chimed in as he pointed to the right, "but I think it would be safer if we went in the opposite-" He stopped mid-sentence at the sound of another explosion and his jaw tightened. He stared off in the direction the noise came from, as though he were anticipating the cloud of smoke that began racing toward them.

Without even the chance to run, they were submerged in a thick black cloud. Noreen shut her eyes to protect them from the debris that stung her corneas, and she coughed from the smoke in her lungs. Releasing her wrist, she held her arms out in front of her and slid her feet across the wooden planks in search of the brothers. She could hear their coughs somewhere close to her.

Remarkably, four pinkish red dots developed beneath her eyelids, influencing her to open them. To her surprise, patches of yellow emerged through the smoke and formed four cones of light gleaming from their centers. One of the lights came closer and closer until it shined directly on Noreen's face. She blinked her eyes rapidly from the light's brightness. "What the-?" The voice of a stranger rang in her ears, and she felt herself lifted off the ground and carried through the cloud of darkness.

She did not resist the man who carried her and instead waited until the stranger led her to safety. Before she knew it, the sun was shining down on her and the smoke from the tunnel dissipated into the atmosphere. The stranger that carried her wore a yellow helmet with a bright light that shined outward. No hair was visible outside his helmet, but it appeared to be waxed around its edges, giving Noreen the impression that it was shaved regularly. He had brown eyebrows and a cleft chin with short, trimmed hairs that nearly disguised it. As he lowered Noreen to the ground, she scanned her eyes across the crowd of large, strong men surrounding her.

Her coughing eased as another man with a yellow helmet carried Oliver in her direction and another walked beside Eli to guide him out of the tunnel. They were both covered in black soot, and, gazing down, Noreen realized that she too was the color of ebony. While the men led Oliver and Eli to her side, she noticed that Eli still clutched her jacket to his shoulder.

"You three!" A large man with a clipboard got her attention. He waddled toward them with his feet fanned outward as he walked through the crowd. "What in God's name were you all doing in there? This is not a silly playground, you hear me? Don't you know this is a mine shaft? You all could've gotten yourselves killed!" He screamed angrily at them, but they remained silent. "Someone hose these damn kids off now, or I will fire every one of your lazy butts!"

Almost instantly, the men dispersed in a random and rather chaotic manner, until one of the smaller men not wearing a helmet sloshed a bucket of water into Noreen's face. Noreen gasped at the icy touch of the water on her skin. She heard two more buckets splashing Oliver and Eli behind her, but she was too preoccupied with wiping the ash from her face to turn to see them. As she lowered her hand to her side, she saw the man who had carried her out of the tunnel take off his helmet and move toward her. He blinked as though he were witnessing a revelation. "Nicole?"

Noreen whipped her head in the man's direction and felt as though she were unable to breathe. No longer was she trapped in the Left Hander's world, nor was she tangled in its web. She was now one among the Right, and she never felt more at home. She glanced over to Eli without altering her expression before she took a single step in the man's direction and nodded.

ACKNOWLEDGEMENTS

Foremost, I would like to thank my parents, Robert and Linda Brendli, for their patience and support. My book would never have been completed without their encouragement. I wish to thank my sister, Kristen, for never letting me down when I needed her most and for being the greatest friend I could ever ask for.

Thank you to my dear friend and neighbor, Mrs. Pat Rose, for all of her advice and guidance regarding the publishing process for my first novel.

A very special thank you to my cover designer, Jayne Hushen, for her hard work and to Andrei and Sergiu Cosma at PhotoCosma.com for capturing such an intense and alluring image in the Surreal Forests of Romania.

I would like to thank Mrs. Linda Cauley and many of my other professors at James Madison University for providing me with information I have used in my novel. It was very beneficial during my research.

Last, but not least, I would like to thank my publisher, Wayne Dementi, and my editor, Dianne Dementi, for polishing my manuscript and making my dream of becoming an author reality.

ABOUT THE AUTHOR

As a current sophomore at James Madison University, my education continues to expand my knowledge and understanding of the world from a writer's perspective and as an individual. Even with schoolwork, running and friendships, I never ceased to write, I could not stop; it is a part of who I am. Friends would often ask how I could possibly have so many papers to write as I sat in my dorm room staring at my computer screen, but I would simply shrug my shoulders and continue working on my novel. Two years later, all my hard work has paid off, and my biggest dream has come true. I published my first book before I turned the age of twenty and yet there is still so much more to come.

Katherine (Katie) Brendli is a resident of Midlothian, Virginia, and is studying Special Education in hopes of becoming a high school teacher for students with autism. Her passion to write was inspired by her grandmother and author Arlene Carruthers and was encouraged by many of her family and teachers. The idea of Katie's first book, *Left*, came to her at the age of twelve and was further developed once she reached college. Katie is dedicated to a lifelong devotion of writing and hopes her actions can encourage other young writers to pursue their dreams of becoming authors.